FABERGÉ

A Becky White Thriller

Book 3

JO FENTON

To Ray, for your constant support and encouragement.

A thousand freezing needles hit my face.

Open my eyes. Close them again fast. Engage other senses.

The wind feels like it's from Siberia. Another Beast From The East. It's not winter though. I've been unconscious for a while, but I'm sure it's early April – unless I've been out of it for several months.

The violent rain and bone-seeping cold are killing me from the outside, but the spiked wheel inside my head and the pain in my aching shoulders are internal. They are not of natural origin. Full consciousness is returning though.

I want to reach up and touch my head, to locate the source of the pain, but my hands are tied tightly behind my back. That explains why my shoulders are so bloody sore. I try to stretch my legs out, but they also appear to be bound together. This has one minor – very minor – advantage. The fabric between my legs is about the only dry patch of clothing on my whole body. I suspect it won't remain that way for long. My jeans, jumper and jacket are already saturated.

The needles ease slightly as the rain softens. I dare to open my eyes again. It's dark, and I'm lying in a ditch. I lift my head a fraction. The spiked wheel spins faster, and I squeeze my eyes shut in an effort to stop it. A moment's deep breathing slows it to a manageable level. I allow my eyes to reopen and try to evaluate my surroundings. The ditch is full of grass, scratching my hands and neck. I can smell the distinctive aroma of gorse nearby. I'm on the moors somewhere. There's a lot of moorland in Lancashire. I may even have been taken further afield. Yorkshire and Derbyshire are filled with similar terrain.

The rain increases in intensity, and once again those needles spear my head and hands – the exposed parts of my body. I close my eyes and pray. I try not to calculate my chances of being found. Dying of exposure is not how I would have chosen to go, but it is beginning to look inevitable.

ONE

Becky

THREE WEEKS EARLIER - TUESDAY

The tall woman under surveillance leaves the town house through the front door. She's wearing a beige trench coat and knee-high boots. Her stylish appearance matches the confidence in her demeanour as she sashays to her expensive red SUV.

I raise my Kindle and pretend not to notice her. It's 2.45 on a drizzly March afternoon, and she needs to pick her kids up from the primary school down the road. I guessed she would leave early to get a decent parking spot, but I thought she might have had the decency to look more flustered. According to her husband, the house from which she's just emerged belongs to his business partner, and he's pretty sure they're having an affair.

My phone pings. I glance at it before answering.

"Hi Joanna. Everything okay?"

"Fine. How's it going?" She doesn't sound very enthusiastic.

"Nothing exciting. She's heading off now. I'd better follow. Speak later."

My enthusiasm levels match those of my friend. The

private detective dream has been mundane since we solved our first murder case. The bread and butter for the White Knight Detective Agency has revolved around infidelity and the occasional suspected fraud. I prefer the fraud, but none of the three cases we have at the moment are exciting enough to raise my pulse rate.

Starting the car, I follow my prey to the school. It makes sense to park further away; close enough to watch her, but far enough not to block a space for the other parents and grandparents on the school run. Seeing her get out and chat to another mum on the pavement, I set off again, and drive to HQ – aka Joanna and Will's house.

***

Settled on Joanna's couch with a mug of tea, I stretch my legs out. They're stiff from sitting in the car most of the day following Mrs Blackstone.

"I can't be doing with these cases for much longer. Is there anything more interesting in the pipeline?"

Joanna looks thoughtful, but before she can answer, there's the sound of a key in a lock, and the front door opens. Will walks in brandishing a newspaper.

"Hi Becks. Mum, is the kettle on?" He waits for her to nod, then slips into the kitchen. He returns a couple of minutes later with coffee and the newspaper, which he was mean enough to take with him. "Have you seen this?"

"Didn't get a chance." I grimace at him and he laughs. "What is it?"

"I've been visiting Chloë. She had an inset day from school, so I took her to Blackpool to the zoo, but when I dropped her off, I picked up the local paper, and it makes for interesting reading." He lays it on the coffee table, already opened at the key article. He reads aloud.

*"**BANK VAULT CRACKED IN EGG HEIST** – In the early hours of this morning, the oldest bank in Preston was raided in a daring robbery. An estimated three million pounds in cash was taken, but more significantly, a vault was accessed. It is believed that the unique Fabergé egg, known as Necessaire, was removed from its secure hiding place where it's thought to have resided for nearly seventy years. The man who placed it there is now deceased, but his family is offering a reward of twenty thousand pounds for its safe return.*

"So, what do you think? D'you fancy an egg hunt?" Will's eyes are alight with excitement.

"Yeah, why not? It's got to be more fun that what's going on at the moment." I pick up the paper and skim through the rest of the article, but it's mostly about the bank, confirming that no one was injured, and that there appear to be no clues.

"I know it looks fun, but don't forget, you two, we are under contract to do the boring jobs that are driving us all bloody crackers. We still need to do those too." Joanna's expression is grim as she reminds us of our bread and butter.

"I know, Mum, but there are three of us. I'm sure we can squeeze in a couple of hours a day to sort this out."

"Fine." Joanna holds her hands up in surrender. "But I think we need to plan this. And assign tasks. Becky, have you ever been involved with detecting a bank robbery before?"

"There have been a few over the years, but mostly idiots in balaclavas holding up the cashier staff in broad daylight. Nasty, and there have been a few injuries, but we've always caught the perpetrators. This is different. You're right. It will need planning." I read through the first paragraph again. "Will, can you find out about CCTV?"

"That'll be a police job, won't it? They won't give me access."

"Use your special skills to get the information. I'm sure you've hacked into police records in the past. And you're supposed to be teaching me and your mum how to do it."

"I'm not supposed to teach you how to hack the police. That's not what Roger said."

Actually, Will's protests are justified. Roger asked Will to train us in hacking, after he recruited us to his secret service team. Joanna has been working for him for a couple of years now, along with my husband, Matt.

"Okay, I added the bit about the police, but Roger would want us to learn how to hack the more difficult and sensitive institutions. It could prove useful."

"Let me see if I can do it before we get cocky. I've never tried."

"Well, if you can't do the police hack, maybe you can get into the bank's CCTV. That might be better actually. Go direct."

Will has a long swig of coffee before answering. "That could be an option. Either way, I need to work on it by myself before showing you or Mum how it's done. Maybe when you're writing up this plan to schedule all our time, you can slot in a couple of sessions for hacking lessons." He grins. "Otherwise, it's never going to happen."

"Sure." I need to knuckle down to my other lessons too – the ones Roger asked me to keep to myself – the Russian language. I've been finding it challenging because of the different alphabet and some strange pronunciations, but I'm getting to grips with the basics now. Perhaps focusing on Russian lessons during surveillance would be more sensible than reading steamy romances.

Joanna interrupts my train of thought. "What should I do to get started? I can think of a few ideas."

"Let's start with those then. What are they?" I smile at her. We've been working together for about two months now, and I'm getting used to her ways of working. She knows exactly what she wants to do, but wants my buy-in too.

"While Will is checking out CCTV from the bank, I

thought I'd have a little drive round the area and do an old-fashioned scout for clues. Do you fancy coming with me, Becks?"

"Yeah, why not? Tomorrow morning? Then I can stake out Mrs B again in the afternoon. She seems to spend all her mornings at the gym, so I should be safe to go to Preston for a while."

"Great. I think that's the best place to start."

"You said you had a few ideas. What were the others?"

"We should learn a bit more about this egg that's been stolen. I wouldn't know it if I fell over the bloody thing at the moment."

"That's a fair point. I'll leave you to research that one. I need to write up my report for Mr B this evening."

"Why the deadline?" asks Will.

"No idea, but he wanted an update by tomorrow, just to know if his suspicions have legs."

"Do they?" He grins at my wording, so I expand.

"Well, they're not quite sprinting down the street yet, but they're strolling round the block."

Joanna and Will both laugh at that. I finish my coffee and wish them a nice evening before heading home to write that report.

Waiting for me in my lounge is Roger, sitting casually on my sofa chatting to my husband, Matt. He stands up when I enter and greets me with a handshake.

"How are you, Becky? I haven't seen you since your successful completion of the Troy case."

"I'm fine, thanks. How are you?" I know he's going to ask me about my progress with the subjects he asked me to study. He doesn't disappoint.

"And the Russian? How's that coming along?"

"Okay. It's still early days though."

"Not really. I suppose I gave you six months to become

proficient. I'm condensing that to three. You're going to need it in your new case."

"What do you know about our new case?" I glance over at Matt, who's following the conversation with obvious interest and some concern. He beckons to me to sit down, and I take a seat on the chair opposite the sofa. Roger sits back down too and takes his phone from the inside pocket of his grey suit jacket. He touches the screen a few times before handing it to me.

The screen shows the same article that Will had shown us.

"I want you to take this on," says Roger.

"It sounds like more fun than shadowing unfaithful spouses. We were just discussing this earlier today." I skim through the article to see if there's any additional information in the online version, but it looks identical. I scrutinise Roger as I hand him back his phone. "Why do you want us to work on this?"

"I believe the blend of skills you and your friends provide may solve this case." His words are encouraging, but as usual his face is unreadable.

"Why would you get involved in something like this?" I ask, before glancing at Matt, hoping for reassurance that I'm not being unforgivably rude. He nods a fraction and winks, but just in case, I add, "I hope you don't mind me asking."

A hint of a smile crosses Roger's face. "How much do you know about the Necessaire?"

TWO

Joanna

TUESDAY

With Becky gone, Will and I sit down in front of our laptops at the kitchen table. We've always enjoyed each other's company, especially when my bastard ex-husband was out of the house. It was such a relief, and Will has always been such a sweet boy – now grown into a lovely young man.

I check the newspaper for the name of the stolen egg, and type 'Necessaire' into Google. To discard the stupid number of items about toiletries, I add the word 'egg'. This narrows it down to about three hundred thousand results. I get up and make another coffee. I have a feeling I'm going to need it.

It is difficult to discover much about the egg, as it's technically been lost since 1952, when it was sold in London to 'a stranger' for £1,250. There are suspicions it's been sitting in the bank vault since then, but no one knows for certain, even though the bank manager claims that it's true, and that the thieves took the egg in the raid.

I struggle to find a decent description of it. There's a single black-and-white photo of an egg sitting in a box. It appears to have patterns on it, and it's described as decorated with rubies, diamonds, sapphires and emeralds. Apparently it contains a 'surprise' of women's toilet articles, whatever the hell that means. After this description, I'm still not convinced I would know it if I fell over it, but it is supposedly unique, so maybe I'm being unfair.

The company of antique dealers who sold the egg in 1952 was named Wartski, and they followed the buyer's request for anonymity – very kind of them, but not helpful to us. We're going to have to assume for now that the news article was right, and the stolen egg is the Necessaire. It will be a shame if it isn't, but a bank robbery is a legitimate reason to work on a case.

My phone pings. Becky has sent me a WhatsApp.

'Roger is instructing us to work on the Preston bank heist. He wants us to find this egg.'

'*Why?*' I've not heard from Roger for a while. He seems to prefer going through Becky, and I don't think he's forgiven me for a stupid mistake I made last year. Although by rights, he shouldn't know it was my fault.

'He didn't provide that information, but he will pay us to work on it for a month. £1000 each!'

'*WTF!*' I've always suspected Roger's payment methods to be unconventional. Not that he'd do anything illegal, but I don't know how these payments are justified on his expense tab. When I've worked on projects for him in the past, money appeared in my bank account already taxed, and shows as payment from '*R Taylor, Local Government*'. He clearly has his channels that he can work through, but quite what he's expecting for a month's salary of one grand… I dread to think.

My past work for him was pretty straightforward. Technical analysis on samples that one of his minions would provide in test tubes, under cover of a chance meeting on a park bench at lunchtimes. I would hang on to the samples until after five, when the office was clear, then run them through the most appropriate machine to get an accurate result. I'd drop off the result, either via printout or a USB stick, on the way home, buying a newspaper from a contact at Edinburgh Waverley railway station. Payment was usually around £20-30 per sample, so the suggested salary for the egg hunt seems absurd by comparison.

The ring tone on my phone disturbs these thoughts.

"Hi, Becks. What do you think is going on?"

"I don't know, but it feels quite exciting. How's your research been going?"

I fill her in on my discoveries about the egg and its poorly-known history.

"How's Will getting on?" she asks.

I glance at him. He's deep in concentration, and appears oblivious to everything. He has headphones on and is staring at the screen of his laptop.

"Good question. He's miles away right now, even though he's sitting across the table from me." I stand up and go round to look at his screen. My computer knowledge is good enough to recognise a jumble of code, but beyond that I'm stuck. I debate whether to disturb him, but he glances round and up at me with a startled expression.

"What's up? Who are you on the phone to?" he mouths.

"He's awake, Becky. Do you want a word with him?" At her request, I hand over the phone.

"Is everything okay?" he asks. He doesn't put it on speakerphone, so I have to make do with his side of the conversation. "Wow. That should tide us over for a bit until the other idiots decide to pay us. Yeah, I'm just working on it now. The police system is complicated, but I've not given up yet. I'll keep going for tonight, otherwise I'll have a go at the bank's cameras. Yep. No problem. See you then." He disconnects the call. "Sorry, Mum, did you want another word with her?"

"Not desperately, I don't suppose. What did she say?"

"I assume she told you Roger's going to pay us?"

"Yes. Quite a hefty sum for a bit of poking around." I take the phone back.

"I think it's great. Anyway, she's coming here at nine tomorrow, so you can leave as soon as the traffic's clear. I'm going to stay here and crack on with this."

I plan to spend the evening watching TV. There's only so much investigating a person can do at this stage of a case, and with Will busy trying to break into the police network, I settle on the sofa to watch Colin Firth as Mr Darcy in *Pride and Prejudice*. I get as far as the second episode when my phone rings again. It's not a number I recognise, and I answer cautiously.

"Hello?"

"Joanna!"

My throat closes up. I know that voice.

"Lou, what do you want?" I wince. I know I sound hoarse, and far more anxious than I would want my ex-husband to know.

"It's no' a crime to want to speak to yer wife, is it?"

"It is when that ex-wife has an injunction against contacting her, so yes."

Will has wandered in with a glass of wine and grabs the phone.

"Dad, what the bloody hell are you doing? How did you get this number?" This time he puts the speakerphone on. He places the wine on the coffee table.

"I've got me contacts, laddie. And there's nae point in your ma changing her number again. They'll just find her."

"What do you want with her? Or with me? You've done enough damage for one lifetime."

The bastard laughs and disconnects. Will sits on the sofa

next to me and puts his arm round my shoulders. I'm shaking, and angry with myself for getting so affected.

"Is that wine for me, love?" I try to laugh, but it comes out more like a sob. Will hands me the glass silently, and I drain it in one.

It takes time for the alcohol to take effect, but gradually the shaking subsides, and I can speak. Will is still at my side.

"Do you think he knows where I am?" I twist round to look at him, and see concern and doubt on his face.

"I hope not, Mum, but I think we can add some security here without infringing the rental agreement. There's lots of easy-to-install equipment these days. We've already got the CCTV at the door. I'll head to B&Q in the morning and see what I can get."

I know I must settle for this solution, but it doesn't feel like enough. Memories of the bastard's violence towards me are never far from the surface, but after his phone call I can almost feel the sting on my skin from his beatings. They were rarely visible. He preferred to take out his anger on my back, arse or thighs, using whatever implements were to hand. He favoured his belt, but candlesticks, books and empty bottles were also fair game.

"Mum, snap out of it. Come on. Don't let him win. He's gone, and if he comes near you again, he'll be back inside before you can blink." Will's sharp tone helps me break through the recollections, and I shove them away from me.

"Can he not go back inside on the strength of threatening me, or even for contacting me? I was sure that was in the injunction."

Will hesitates, and something in his expression holds me back from further questioning. I'm not sure if it's pain or fear, but he's clearly conflicted.

"We'll sort it, Mum. Don't worry. I'm here, and I'm not a wee laddie any more. I won't let him harm you."

THREE

Becky

The journey to Preston is uneventful, with the traffic easing as soon as we get on to the M61. Joanna seems subdued, so I put the radio on to lift the mood. The rain holds off until we're walking from the car park into the town centre, but then it pelts down. There's no point going back to the car for umbrellas, so Joanna and I make do with the hoods on our jackets.

"This is bloody ridiculous." Joanna grabs my arm and points to a coffee shop. "Let's get inside and plan a strategy before we drown."

Settled with coffee and pastries in a corner next to a radiator, we begin to dry off. It has the added advantage of being quiet, as it's 10.15 on a workday.

"This was a brilliant idea, coming in here." I have a bite of my chocolate éclair while I check Google Maps on my phone. "The bank doesn't look far away. Actually, there are a few banks nearby. Did the article say which one it was?"

"That might have been helpful." Joanna rolls her eyes. "Why don't you message Roger and see if he knows?"

I type a quick text and hit *Send*. One of the staff comes over and starts clearing the table next to us. I smile at the woman as she glances at us, and she nods and smiles back. She appears to be in her sixties and a bit on the chubby side, and has a friendly face.

"Excuse me for asking, but do you know anything about the recent bank robbery?" I ask. It's a spur-of-the-moment question but feels right.

"Yes, I do as it happens." She checks her watch. "I'm due for a break in a few minutes, so if you like, I can come over and tell you all about it. I assume you've got a good reason for asking. Although many people round here have their eye on that reward. I suppose that's as good an excuse as any." Her voice is friendly, and she doesn't seem to mind being questioned.

I raise an eyebrow at Joanna, and she nods slightly.

"We're private detectives," I say in a low voice, and hand her a business card from my wallet.

"Ooh, fascinating! I'm Maggie. Let me take these crocks back, then I'll grab myself a cup of tea and come and chat. Would you like a top-up, ladies? On the house?"

I'm halfway through my coffee, so accept gratefully. Joanna looks as though she's about to decline, but correctly interpreting a glance from me, thanks the waitress and orders an Americano.

Maggie returns a few minutes later with a tray of drinks and some biscuits.

"I told my boss that you were needing information, and I'm well placed to help, because my hubby is manager of the bank that was robbed." She sits down and leans in towards us. Her breath smells faintly of cinnamon and apple. It could be a lot worse. "So, what do you want to know?"

"Everything you can tell us. Let's start with how your husband found out about the robbery." I smile encouragingly, and she beams back.

"We were in bed asleep, like decent citizens ought to be at

two in the morning, when Iain's phone went. Because of his job he needs to keep it on all the time. He's got the knack of waking in an instant, has my Iain, so he answered it straight off. There was this automated message telling him that there'd been a break-in at the bank, so he jumped out of bed and started getting dressed. I was properly awake by then, and I said to him, 'Don't you go rushing down there in the dead of night. The villains might still be there, and what if they've got guns, eh? It's not worth you getting shot over.' So he listened to me, but carried on getting dressed, and then he thought a bit, and rang the police to make sure they knew. The system is supposed to contact the police at the same time as letting him know, but it doesn't hurt to check."

"Were the police aware?" asks Joanna.

"Yes, and they said that on no account was he to go there. They had a Squat Team going out and would let him know when it's safe."

Joanna's brow furrows, and I feel mine doing the same for a moment.

"SWAT team – the specially-trained weapons guys." I smile as comprehension arrives.

"That's what I said," says Maggie, looking indignant. Then she grins. "Squat, swat, what's the difference?"

We all laugh.

"So what happened next?" I ask.

"It's six before we get another call, and my Iain's been pacing the floor for hours instead of going back to sleep like any sensible person would. Anyway, he put the call on speaker, given as he knew how interested I was, and it was the police, asking him to go in and check if anything was missing cos one of the vaults had been broken into. Honestly, ladies, I swear, I thought he was going to faint. Went white as a sheet, he did, but he hung up, and sat on the bed for a minute. He looked that frail. I said, 'Do you want me to drive you down there, love?' He refused at first, but when he stood up, he was all of a wobble, so I got dressed myself and ran him to the bank. Swarming with police it was, and he wouldn't let me get out of the car on account of the rain, but asked me to pick him up again later." She pauses for breath.

"Did you find out anything else when you picked him up?"

"I was just getting to that, lovey." Maggie wags a finger at Joanna. "I got a call about an hour later. We live about ten minutes' drive away, so I'd had time to get home and have a cup of tea. I wasn't due at work until twelve that day. So when I collected him, poor man, he was soaked through, but more than that he was distraught about this rare egg that had gone missing. 'What sort of egg?' I asked him. 'A Russian Imperial egg with jewels on. It's nigh-on priceless, and now it's been stolen. That's my head on the block,' he says. Well, thankfully, his boss at head office came up yesterday and said it's not his fault. They've looked at the footage on the security camera and decided there was nothing my Iain could have done to prevent it."

"Who has the footage now?" I think of Will trying to hack systems. It would be a lot easier if we could just get the data legally.

"I think there are a few copies about, lovey, but my Iain has the original, cos it comes straight through to his computer. Do you want a copy for your investigations? I could ask him if you want."

"That would be fantastic, thank you." I try to remain outwardly calm as she takes out her phone and makes a call, but my heart is doing excited flip-flops inside my chest. This could save us hours.

"Yes, love... All fine here... Yes, I'm talking to these detectives... Can they have a copy of that security camera stuff? Not the police; proper private detectives. More Hetty Wainthropp than Inspector Morse."

I stifle a giggle and carefully avoid catching Joanna's eye. I don't think I'm quite old enough yet to resemble Hetty Wainthropp. Maggie's conversation with her Iain drifts on to other topics for a minute or two, but then she disconnects and beams at us.

"If you're okay to wait here for a while longer, loveys, my Iain'll bring a memory stick over with the security video on it. I have to get back to work now, but I'll bring you over another drink if you like?"

Twenty minutes later, a tall skinny man with a moustache walks into the coffee shop. He goes over to Maggie, who's cleaning tables, and greets her with a kiss. She leaves her cloth on a nearby empty table and brings the man over to us.

"This is my Iain. I'm sorry, loveys, I'm rubbish with names. Can you introduce yourselves again?"

"I'm Becky. This is my business partner and friend, Joanna. To be fair, I don't think we introduced ourselves properly earlier."

Iain shakes hands with each of us, and extracts a small brown envelope from a man-bag.

"Maggie tells me you're detectives. Do you have any ID? I can't hand this over to any Clare, Jill or Sally, you know." He laughs a little nervously and wipes his hands on a handkerchief that he extracts from his trouser pocket.

I fish out my business card and hand it over. I can see he's dithering, so flash my driving licence at him so he can see that the name on the licence matches the card. When I changed my name after leaving the police force, I got all my other IDs changed too. It was expensive and messy, but it's much better to have everything tied up.

He glances at his wife, who nods and smiles. He appears to come to a decision. "Okay, I'll trust you're who you say you are. The USB stick is in here, ladies. It's password-protected. If you give me your mobile number, I will send you the security details via encrypted WhatsApp message."

While I'm scribbling down my phone number, Joanna invites him to sit and join us, but he declines.

"I'm sorry, dear. I only have a few minutes to spare. Is this the number? Is that a seven or a four?" He shows me the slip of paper I've given him.

"A seven, but what am I thinking? You've got my business card. The number's on there." I point at the card on the table, where he put it to inspect the driving licence. "That top number is mine."

"Whose is the third number on the card?" he asks, as Maggie waves a hand and returns to her cleaning duties.

"That's our other partner, Will. He's busy today, so couldn't join us. He's our tech expert, so he'll be the one looking at these."

"Should I send the details to him instead? I'm not comfortable spreading passwords far and wide."

We agree, and I text Will to warn him to expect a message from a strange number, with login details for a USB stick.

'*What's on the stick?*' comes back within a minute.

'*CCTV footage from the bank!!!!!*'

'*I've just bloody hacked it. I've been working on that for half the night!*'

'*Maybe there's a difference. Who knows? There could be another clue. We'll be back in time for lunch. See you soon.*'

"Will's expecting the login details, so please send them directly to him." I don't need to tell Iain that he's been pre-empted.

With the information sent to Will, Iain checks his phone a couple of minutes later. "He's received it. He's said thank you. Very polite. We don't always get that. Seems like a nice chap."

"He is," says Joanna. "He's my son. It's nice to have him working with us." Obviously she doesn't know the subtext yet, but Will is far too polite and professional to show his irritation to a client, suspect, or any other individual that we're called upon to liaise with.

After a brief chat with Iain and Maggie, during which he offers to help with any questions we might have, we thank them and prepare to leave. A sudden thought has me delving into my purse. I press a ten-pound note into Maggie's hand.

"Just in case your boss changes her mind about the coffees being free. And either way, thanks for all your help. We really appreciate it."

She looks almost ready to cry and gives me a huge hug, squeezing me until my ribs feel as though they'll crack.

"You're so kind. Thank you."

We leave and make our way to the bank, following directions from Iain, who found time to stay for a few more minutes to talk to his wife.

The bank is now open. Apart from a cordon around the back door, there's little evidence of the break-in.

"I was expecting a broken window at least," Joanna says. "There doesn't seem to be any sign of that. Do you think anyone would notice if we went inside that cordon of yellow tape?"

"Let me do it. I never told anyone, but I got a duplicate police badge once when I thought I'd lost mine. When I resigned, I forgot I had this one." I extract an authentic police badge from my handbag and grin. "If anyone asks, I've a right to be here. It might be tenuous though, so keep watch just in case. I'd rather this remained unknown until necessary. And there might be a few questions about a Manchester DI investigating a crime scene in Preston."

"Okay, DI White. I'll keep watch." She chuckles, and wanders casually along the alleyway leading back to the street.

I was DI Wiseman back then – in the days before I felt the need to hide my identity from the world – but there's no need to correct Joanna just now. I glance round. We're in a back yard. And there's a security camera trained on the back door I want to inspect. It would be far more sensible to get Will to enlarge the images, and I'm not keen to get spotted on today's feed. I stroll back to Joanna.

The drive back is much chattier than the outbound trip, as we review all the information we've received. The first thing I do when we get back to the car is tell Joanna that Will had just hacked into the bank's security videos when I'd messaged him.

"Oh shit! Was he really annoyed?"

"He wasn't overly chuffed, but at least now we can get him to play around a bit more than if he just had Iain's memory stick. It will also be interesting to see if Iain provided the whole picture."

"Why?" Joanna clutches at her armrest as I do an emergency stop. "Bloody taxis. He could have killed us. Git!"

"It's okay. I had my eye on him. I thought he was going to do that. It wasn't as bad as it could have been." Out of habit, I glance at the Uber that's just pulled out in front of us and check his number. GU15TYY. "Great reg plate though. It kind of says 'Guilty'. Anyway, what were you asking me?"

"Can't remember. Something about the memory stick. Probably wasn't important." She changes the subject and we move on to other topics. It's only when I'm pulling off the motorway that she says, "Oh yes, that was it. Why do you think Iain might not have provided the full CCTV footage?"

"No strong reason. He seemed a bit too eager to help us. It might not be him, but the lack of broken windows raises the possibility of an inside job. There are other signs in that direction too."

"Such as?"

"How did the burglars know to break into the vault where the egg was kept?"

FOUR

Will

WEDNESDAY

I go to the bathroom cupboard and grab a couple of paracetamol. I badly need time away from the computer. My head is pounding, although I don't know how much of that is down to fury at receiving the data in a bloody file after trying for half the night to hack it. My phone is on the table next to the laptop. I grimace at it, then put it in my pocket, grab my jacket, and go out for a walk. Fresh air might help.

A long walk around the streets of North Manchester calms me down a bit. Mum and Becky can't have known they could get their hands on this data, otherwise they'd have warned me. They knew what I've been working on. It's just the timing. Less than a minute before I got the message, I got the breakthrough. I'll need to look at those images soon, but I still feel stressed.

The residential streets are quiet, as expected on a weekday at eleven in the morning – just a few dog-walkers and the occasional jogger or mum with a pram. I turn a corner and spot an old man in pyjamas crossing the (fortunately empty) road. He's by himself. I speed up.

"Excuse me, Sir, are you alright?"

"Fine, Johnny m'boy. Just popping to the shops for some sweets for you. Mint humbugs – your favourite."

I take a deep breath. "I've got enough sweets, thanks. It's going to rain. Let's get you home." I glance up at the sky as the first raindrops fall, then scan the street, anxiously searching for someone who might know this old chap. To my intense relief, a man of about Mum's age pops his head out of the window of the house opposite.

"Sodding hell. Has Dad got out again? Can you keep him there for a minute, mate? I'll be with you in just a mo."

I gently coax the old gentleman towards the house, and after a couple of minutes his son appears, clad in a grey sweatshirt and jogging bottoms. He looks a bit grey himself.

"Are you okay?" I ask as he staggers towards us.

"Recovering from chemo, mate. I was just resting, but decided I hadn't heard Dad for a bit, so I got up and checked the house. I was starting to panic a bit, to be honest, but thought I'd look out of the window." He lowers his voice. "I think I'm going to have to look into getting him some care. I just can't look after him properly myself at the moment." He takes a deep breath as he reaches his dad's side and grips his arm in a firm hold. "Come on, Dad, it's raining. You can't stay out here, and neither can I."

"Are you all right with him, or do you want a hand?" I watch as he hesitates. He looks torn.

"If you're sure you've got time, mate. I wouldn't say no. I wish I could manage, but I'm so sodding weak at the moment, and can't face anything."

I nod, and go to his dad's other side, although I suspect the son needs almost as much support. "You get inside. I'll bring him in."

When we're indoors, the son takes his dad into a room at the back of the house, and returns a moment later, locks the front door, and puts the key on a high shelf.

"My fault he got out. I'd left the key in the front door. I've got no excuse for forgetting." He holds his hand out to me. "I'm Glen Thorpe. My dad's Harry Thorpe. Do you want to come through and sit down? I can get you a coffee or a beer or something?"

"I'm happy to sit down, but I'm not bothered about a drink thanks. Your dad called me Johnnie in the street. Have you got a brother?"

"I did have. He was killed in a road accident when he was sixteen. Bloody kids were joy-riding and mounted the pavement. My little brother was listening to his headphones and enjoying an evening walk. Died in hospital. There's only me left now to look after Dad, and if this chemo hasn't worked… Well, he'll be better off in a home."

"When will you know if it's worked?" I find it difficult to know what to say in such circumstances, but Glen seems quite matter-of-fact, which makes it easier.

"I had my scan yesterday. I'll see the doc next week. Bloody terrifying by yourself. The next-door neighbour pops in to look after Dad when I'm out. She's very good really. Kind woman. A bit batty, but her heart's in the right place."

I'm drawn to Glen. He looks to be about the same age as Mum, and he's struggling with this awful situation with a fair bit of courage.

"Did you work before you got ill, or have you always been a full-time carer for your dad?" I know it's none of my business, but he doesn't have to answer if he'd rather not.

"I'm an accountant. Working from home gives me a lot of flexibility, but it's been difficult through chemo. Some of my clients have been happy to wait for me, but it's depended a lot on when their accounts were due. Between being diagnosed and starting chemo, I worked my arse off to get everything done that had a deadline before April, but the clients that hadn't sent me stuff by then had to find someone else. Cancer's crap for business."

"I'm sorry to hear that. We've just started our business, and we'll be needing an accountant at some point, so if you're up for it we can give you a call and discuss terms when we're ready?"

"Sure. What business are you in?"

"Private detectives." I feel my cheeks getting pink. I don't know why, but it's embarrassing saying what I do. Although it would be more realistic, but not sensible, to say, 'Illegal computer-systems hacker'.

All the same, Glen looks impressed. I suppose not everyone has met a private detective. He glances at his watch.

"I'd better check on Dad. He's been very quiet. Are you okay to wait here?"

I check my own watch. It's nearly midday.

"It's time I was getting back. I've got a meeting shortly with the other partners, and one of them needs to get out on a job this afternoon." I fish my wallet out of my pocket and hand him a card. "Give me a shout if you need anything, or just fancy a drink one night. I've not been in Manchester long, and apart from work, I don't really know anyone. It'd be nice to get to the pub occasionally if you can get someone to look after your dad."

"Yeah. That sounds great. Why not? Once I've got this bloody scan out of the way and I know what's what, I'll give you a bell. Thanks for helping with Dad. He has some days that are better than others, but I think I might need to look into a care home for him."

I nod sympathetically and thank him for the chat. I feel a lot better than I did before.

Once back outside, I hurry towards home. My phone goes ballistic within a couple of minutes of leaving, and I glance at a sudden influx of WhatsApp messages.

Mum and Becky are clearly back and waiting for me. I tap quickly, '*On my way. Got delayed.*' I break into a slow jog. My jeans aren't ideal running gear, but I'm wearing decent trainers, and I'm home in just a few minutes.

Inside, Mum's making sandwiches and the kettle's on. We exchange stories over lunch, but I won't have any really useful information until I've waded through the camera footage.

Once fed, I settle myself down at the laptop. I dither for a moment. Hacked images, or files from Iain? I'll start with the hacked images, given I've worked so damn hard to get them. Iain's files will almost certainly show the same, but I prefer not to make assumptions. I'd downloaded the hacked files this morning, so I open up the first one, and start watching.

FIVE

Becky

WEDNESDAY

I leave my friends' house after lunch and drive to the house I was staking out yesterday. While I was writing my report for Mr Blackstone last night, I remembered the identity of the house owner. I had been told when we took on the case, but the egg heist had ejected it from my mind.

I dropped the report into the client this morning before picking Joanna up, but I have a copy with me. Noticing that Mrs B's car is parked a couple of doors from the house in question, I peruse the key paragraph.

'The house owner, who you have previously confirmed as your business partner, Eric Ulyanov, has not yet been seen with your wife, but her car has been parked near his house for the last three school days from 1:30 – 2:30 in the afternoon. Your wife has then been seen leaving that house, immaculately dressed, and returning to her car. She then drives to the school to pick up the children.'

I glance at my watch. 2:05. It's a bit early for her to be leaving just yet, and I open my language app on my phone, prepared to do twenty minutes of Russian. But as I look down, movement halts my gaze, and I focus instead on the woman running from the house in question. She doesn't look as well made-up now. Her long hair is loose and tousled. Lipstick is smeared across her mouth, and she's running in her stockinged feet, her expensive-looking shoes dangling from her hand. In her other hand is a neat black handbag. A bruise is forming around her left eye.

I hesitate for just a moment, then shoving my phone back in my bag, I jump out of the car.

"Excuse me. Are you okay?"

"What has it to do with you? And why have you been sitting in that car for the last couple of days? I saw you yesterday, and you are here again today."

"I was just waiting for someone. It doesn't matter now. You look like you could use some help." I wince slightly at the suspicion in her glance. It's justified, but I am trying to assist her now.

"Oh my god! I've just realised. My bastard husband has set you to watching me." The strange sentence structure confirms my suspicion that English isn't her first language.

"Why would you think that?" I'm careful not to deny it, but there's no harm in a little prevarication. She's very pale, and it's starting to rain. "Get in the car. You'll get wet." I get in the car myself and open the passenger door for her.

She considers for a moment, but as the weather goes from a few spots to torrential downpour in ten seconds, she gets in.

"I am Anastasia Blackstone, although I suppose you know that." Her laugh is bitter. She has a faintest hint of an Eastern European accent.

"I didn't, actually." Thinking back, her husband mostly called her "my wife". Although on the information form that we'd given him to complete, he'd named her as Ana. Notably with one n. "What's happened in there? I didn't see you go in, but I would lay a bet that you didn't have that bruise."

"You are right, of course. Why would a woman go into a house to see a man that beats her?"

"Why did you?" I keep my tone neutral, but I'm far more intrigued now than when I thought this was a straightforward affair.

"I need to get out of here, but I am not ready to go home." She touches her face tentatively.

"How about you come back to my office, and I'll get you a coffee and something for that bruise?" I know Joanna won't mind.

"Will you bring me back here to pick up my car and collect my children later?"

"Of course. Come on, you won't want your children to see you so distressed. We can find some make-up to help disguise that bruise as well."

She's obviously reassured, as she puts her seat belt on and rests her handbag on the floor by her feet. I put the radio on Classic FM as soon as the engine is on, and she smiles slightly. I want to wait until we're in a safer environment before I start on the questions.

We're at Joanna's less than ten minutes later. Will answers the door.

"Hi Becky. Mum's popped out. Are you okay?"

"This is Anastasia. She needs a bit of quiet and a cup of tea while I help her out. Can we come in?"

"Sure. Can't believe Mum's not given you a key yet." He retreats into the hall as we follow him inside, and glances over his shoulder. "Go into the lounge. I'll get the kettle on and bring the first aid kit."

"Thanks, Will." I turn to the damsel in distress as I precede her into the living room. "Come in and sit down. Let's have a look at that bruise."

She stays quiet while I tend to her injury, accepting a cup of tea and a chocolate biscuit from Will with a murmured 'Thank you.'

"Do you want to tell me about it?" I ask when Will's out of

the room. He showed me by a flick of his head that he'd be in the kitchen. Sometimes people will open up more on a one-to-one basis.

"I suppose so. Will it go in your report to my husband?"

"No. Unless you want us to tell him."

"Is it not a conflict of interest?" She brushes hair away from her face and tucks it behind her ear.

"He hasn't paid us yet. I can refuse payment if it's appropriate to do so. You look to be more in need of our help."

"I imagine you find it hard to make a living at this if you are so kind."

"We've just accepted a commission that will keep the wolf from the door for a while." I'm likely to get into all sorts of trouble about contracts with Anastasia's husband if I switch allegiances like this, but on the other hand, I suspect something else is going on here, and I might just be able to sort everything out.

I glance at the coffee table, where Will has left the plate of biscuits, and offer another one to our guest.

"I should not take this. I am a model. I cannot afford to put on weight."

"You've had a shock. I'm sure a couple of biscuits won't hurt, but it's up to you." I wait until she takes one, then put the plate back on the table. Even though I shouldn't, I help myself to a biscuit too. I probably weigh twice as much as Anastasia, and the middle-age spread is refusing to shrink. "So, are you able to tell me anything?" I keep my voice neutral, although I wish she'd get on with it. She's going to realise shortly that it's time to pick her kids up from school.

"I know Simon suspected me of carrying on with his partner. He has always been a jealous man, but lately he has been almost paranoid. It has not helped that I have had to keep secrets from him."

"What sort of secrets?"

She looks out of the window and then down at the carpet.

"I am being blackmailed. Not for money though. So in some ways, my husband is correct. I have been having sex with Eric, but only to stop him from… from acting on his information."

"I really want to help you, but it's difficult to do so unless you tell us the whole story."

She glances at her watch.

"I do not have time to now. It's a long history to tell, and I need to get to the school. I am too late to pick up my car first. Would you be able to take me to the school and then drive me and the children back to my car, and watch until we are safely away?"

"Of course, but can you just tell me one thing first?" I wait for her to nod. "Why did Eric hit you? I assume it was him that gave you that bruise?"

"I said I would not play his games any longer. He wanted to… increase the extent of our activities, and it ceased to be within the boundaries of acceptability. There is only so much I can stomach. I already feel like a damn prostitute. His tastes are becoming more perverted with each session. I cannot continue. When I told him so, he hit me and threatened exposure once again. I am beginning to think it may be preferable."

"How about I come and see you and your husband this evening when the children have gone to bed, and you can tell both of us the background to this at the same time? I can protect you if Simon takes it badly."

"Bring your friend Will. He looks strong. You are sweet, Becky, but you do not look as though you could take on a man of my husband's stature when he's in a rage."

"I'm a black belt in various martial arts, but I'm very happy to bring Will along."

I direct her to the bathroom so she can tidy her hair, and offer some foundation to cover the bruise. Five minutes later she's ready to leave, and at a quick glance no one would see there was a problem. I take her to the school, collect a sweet and chatty young lady of about seven or eight and her quieter younger brother, and take them to pick up their mum's car. It's a relief to get to our destination without incident. The kids are both young enough to need car seats, and are illegally sitting in the back strapped in with only with my adult seat belts. I decide to get a couple of booster seats to keep in the boot in case of future need.

"Thank you, Becky." Anastasia holds out her hand before getting out of the car, and I clasp it warmly in mine. "I assume you know my address?"

"Yes. See you later. I'll watch you to your car." I keep my voice low before raising it slightly and turning to the children. "Thank you for being such good passengers."

I wait until they're all settled in her big red SUV and have turned out of the road before turning my engine on. I lock the car doors from inside. My eyes are watching for action from Eric's house, but all is quiet, except for a twitch of curtains from an upstairs window. I take a deep breath. My mouth is suddenly dry. It's time to go home. There are several things I need before my meeting this evening.

SIX

Joanna

WEDNESDAY

As soon as Becky leaves to go to her surveillance job, Will heads upstairs with his laptop. He's halfway up when I think to ask, "Why aren't you working in the kitchen?"

"No offence, Mum, but I need a bit of peace. I have to concentrate."

"You can do. I'm going out shortly."

"Anywhere interesting?" He looks down at me from his elevated place on the staircase.

"I'm popping into the library and going to meet a friend or two after that. I'll be back in time for dinner."

"Great. I'll sit in the kitchen then. It's warmer, and I'll have constant access to the kettle and biscuit tin. Have fun."

I let him pass me in the hall, then head to my bedroom to get ready. I change quickly into a black pencil skirt and cream silk blouse and straighten my usually curly hair into a bob, covering it with a red beret. It's a bit nineties, but I want to look classier than usual. I add red lipstick and eyeliner. A short rummage in the wardrobe produces a pair of red patent court shoes with a three-inch heel. I totter downstairs and into the kitchen. Will's pouring himself a large mug of tea and hasn't started work yet.

"Do I look okay?"

He frowns. "Sorry, Mum, but that's not a good look. What are you trying to achieve?"

"Smart and professional. Stylish would be good too."

"Ditch the hat and shoes. The skirt, blouse and hair – all fine."

"Bugger. Okay. Thanks." I return to the bedroom and swap the red patent for black leather boots with a two-inch heel. I find the jacket that goes with the skirt. Suited and booted, I check the mirror. Will's right. I now look more like a professional, and less like an old pro! I select a neat black handbag and fill it with my purse, mobile phone, notebook and pen, keys, and emergency paracetamol. There's no space for anything else, so I extract a fawn-coloured trench coat from the wardrobe and transfer my phone and keys to the pockets, leaving room in the bag for the lipstick and some tissues.

"Do I look okay now?" I ask Will when I get back downstairs.

"Much better. Put the coat on and let's see the full ensemble." He waits for me to comply, then nods. "Yep, that works. Are you taking your car? I can insure you on mine for the day if you want to impress?" Will recently invested in a dark blue Audi with his share of the money from our last case. It's not new, but at only two years old, it's immaculate, and he cleans it at least once a week, inside and out. My car is a battered Ford Focus that's been around the clock at least once, and has so many bloody scratches that an observer could be forgiven for thinking I park it in a thorn bush every day.

"Thanks for the offer, but I'm only driving to the Metrolink. I'll get the tram into Manchester and do all my errands there. I hate driving around the city centre – and parking is even worse."

I regret my decision halfway into the city, when the Metrolink grinds to a halt because of an electrical failure. I use my phone to advise my contact about the delay, but it's more than an hour before we start moving again. At least I have a seat. Even with the lower heels, I wouldn't have appreciated standing up for so long.

When I finally reach Central Library, I call again.

"Hi Wendy, I'm finally in town. Do you want to meet now, or wait until I've been to the library?"

"Now would be good. I can come with you to the library and help you with your search, but let's have a coffee first. There's a Starbucks behind the library, next to the Friends' Meeting House. I'll meet you there. What would you like? I'll get the drinks in."

I thank Wendy, request a Skinny Latte and disconnect. It takes a few minutes to make my way to the back of the library – I suspect I chose the long way round, but I eventually find the right coffee shop, and Wendy is sitting in the window. She waves at me and I go in and join her.

"Thanks so much for meeting me like this. I hope you didn't mind me contacting you after all this time?" I glance at her anxiously before taking a sip of my coffee. It's been about thirty years since we last spoke.

"Of course not. You sounded on the phone as though you needed some help. What can I do? And is there any reason you've not asked Becky?"

I hesitate. "You know that thing when it's easier to talk to someone you don't know so well?"

"Absolutely. You and Becky were such good friends at first, and I know there was a long time before you caught up again, but she told me only a couple of weeks ago when we met up that she's so pleased you've become close again."

"I am too. Becky's wonderful, but she's got her own stuff going on. I still don't know the details of why she left the police, but she was pretty damn traumatised when I tracked her down, and she's still jumpy at times. I figured my problems wouldn't ease that situation."

"So talk to me then. Hopefully, I can help."

"Thanks. How much do you know about my background?"

"Not a lot, I'm afraid." Wendy shakes her head, so I assume Becky's not filled her in. I'm relieved. Whilst I don't want to talk about it too much, it's good to know that my friend is discreet.

"I was married to a bastard named Lou MacLeod for far too many years. He's Will's dad, but he used to…" My throat clams up and I can't continue for a moment.

"Did he abuse you?" Wendy's gentle tones ease my predicament slightly, and I nod and force down a sip of coffee.

"How did you escape?"

This is a little easier to answer, and my voice is only a bit hoarse as I reply. "He left me when I was diagnosed with breast cancer. I was well shot of him, but not before he'd nearly bankrupted me with his gambling and drinking habits. He left me with nothing. Will was grown up by then." The story is flowing more freely now. "Lou moved in with a new girlfriend so quickly that it was obvious he'd been having his 'bit on the side' for quite some time. I think I was more bloody upset that he hadn't left me for her earlier than because he was being unfaithful. I'd long wanted him out of my life."

"I'm not surprised," says Wendy.

"Anyway, his troubles started when he began running through her money, and eventually the bailiffs turned up. The stupid git attacked one of them and got arrested for GBH. The girlfriend had him sussed out by then and added a few extra offences, and he got put away for five years in theory."

"When will he be out?"

"He's out now, on parole. While he was inside, I got an injunction against him. He's not supposed to contact me or anything, but I got a phone call from him last night. He's trying to find me." My voice cracks again, and my hand trembles as I go to pick up my latte glass.

"It sounds like he's broken his parole. Do you want me to contact the relevant authorities and get him put back?" She grins. "I still have the power."

"That sounds promising. I'd appreciate that. He still scares me, to be honest." I shiver. I'd rather not go into details of the threats Lou made when he was in prison. My injunction, and the reasons for it, had also added time to his sentence, and I know him well enough to realise that's cause for revenge.

"I'll need some information please." Wendy rummages in her capacious brown handbag and retrieves a notebook and pen. She notices me watching and laughs. "I carry everything in here. Half the medicines from Boots, a quarter of the toiletries, my Kindle, purse and notebook, plus about a dozen pens. It weighs a ton." She zips it back up and puts it back on the floor, under the table and out of easy reach of would-be thieves.

I delve into my bag for my phone and find her the information she asks for – his full name, date of birth, prison number and the prison where he was being held.

"How long is it likely to take to get him put back inside?" I rub my nose. Anxiety always makes it itchy.

"It depends. If he's turning up for his parole meetings, then not long. If he's done a runner, then it will take longer. Let's hope he's pretending to be good." Wendy's tone is dry. She seems to have his measure.

The chances of him behaving properly are slim.

SEVEN

Becky

WEDNESDAY

I collect Will at 8.15, following texted instructions from Anastasia, and drive to her house.

"Apparently the kids are in bed now, so it's a good time for us to come along." I park fifty yards up the road, near a kosher deli. It's shut now, of course, but the smell emanating from the back gives me a craving for a smoked salmon bagel. I suppress the thought and focus on the job at hand. I briefed Will earlier on the situation, and he's calm and reliable as always.

"Sensible, Becks. Far enough away to not alert the neighbours, and close enough to run to if we need a quick getaway." He grins at me.

"Exactly. Come on. I might need to get closer if we have to rescue Anastasia and the kids, but let's see. Hopefully, it won't come to that." I hesitate before speaking again, unsure how Will would take my request. "How do you feel about taking the lead on the questioning tonight? I'll do a bit, but I want to observe reactions, and it's easier to do that if I don't have to think about questions. It will be good experience for you too."

"Yes, sure. Happy to do that. Jump in if it looks like I'm about to say something wrong."

"You'll be fine. I trust you." I grin at him and we head towards the house.

I already had the address, as Simon Blackstone had provided it when he confirmed the job, but I've not been here before. The house is large, smart, detached and well cared for. I recognise the red SUV on the drive, and there's also the black BMW 5 series that Simon drove when we met him at our HQ. I glance at Will. I'm sometimes a little self-conscious of such ostentatious wealth amongst the Jewish community here, but my friend seems oblivious. As we stand outside waiting for the door to open, I wonder what to expect, and whether Anastasia has had to provide any explanations yet.

As she opens the door, I can see the sketchy make-up from earlier has been replaced by a much more thorough application of thick foundation. Only the wary look in her eyes gives the clue that she's less self-possessed than she first appears.

"Becky, Will, thank you for coming. Please come inside. It is cold out."

"Thanks. It is chilly. Spring hasn't quite got going yet." I smile reassuringly at her as we pass into the spacious entrance hall. A quick glance around takes in the mahogany grandfather clock, a smart cabinet in the same wood, displaying framed photos of the children, and several closed doors. There's also an open door, and our hostess indicates we should go in.

We find ourselves in a generously proportioned lounge-diner, which echoes the mahogany theme from the hall. Simon is pacing, but stops as we enter.

"Becky, thanks for coming. And is this Will?" He smiles congenially when Will nods, and invites us to sit on an immaculate brown leather couch.

We obey, but the leather smells new and I don't feel able to make myself comfortable. Anastasia joins us a moment later and sits on one armchair. Her husband has taken possession of the other, but now we're all seated, everyone seems reluctant to start.

I glance at Anastasia, and she takes a deep breath.

"Thank you for coming, both of you. I believe we need to get this all sorted out now, hopefully in a calm and reasonable discussion where no tempers will be lost." She gives her husband a quick nervous look, which he seems not to notice. "Simon, I don't know why you chose Eric as your partner. He's a vile pig, and a blackmailer."

"Bloody hell, Ana, do you think I don't know that?"

The shocked silence that answers this outburst seems to go on forever. Then Will takes control.

"Mr Blackstone, perhaps you could expand on that. I assume you mean he's blackmailing you? How long has it been going on?"

"I've known him a long time, but we moved in different circles. He's a couple of years older than me, and I was happy with my friends from school and university and with my family. I didn't look for any extras. But a few years ago, he came to me with a job that he wanted doing. It all seemed very innocent on the face of it, and I prepped the accounts and submitted them like I always do, but something niggled. I remember going back to them in the middle of the night – must have been five years ago now, but I've not forgotten. After a couple of hours, I found it. He'd snuck a dodgy fifty grand through under my bloody nose. Well, I rang him up the next day and asked him about it. The slimy bugger said he'd made a mistake, but it would look bad for both of us if I went to the Inland Revenue with it after I'd already submitted the accounts. It was a difficult time for the family. Ana was on maternity leave from her job as an interior designer, and I'd tweaked my own books a bit. Nothing major." Simon backtracks hurriedly, despite me and Will keeping our expressions neutral. "I just deferred a couple of payments on to the next year when I knew things'd be easier. Eric had a smarmy grin on his face when he said everyone tweaked things a bit – he was sure I was no exception – but I wouldn't want the Revenue sniffing around, would I? Bloody git had me over a barrel, so I agreed to stay silent."

Simon is clearly nervous. I'm pleased I can observe and leave Will to do his bit.

"Do you think he knew things were hard for you?" asks Will.

"I'd probably told him about Ana being off work. Git put two and two together, didn't he!" Simon grimaces. "Anyway, that made it too easy for him. He came to me a few weeks later with a 'proposition' as he called it. I was to come in with him as his business partner and no more would be said."

"What was the nature of the business?" I ask – as much out of curiosity as anything else, but it could be important.

"Imports and exports mostly. Business stuff. But basically, he wanted someone who could fiddle the books at the grassroots level. I didn't feel I had any choice. If I said no, he'd lay an anonymous tip with the Revenue, and they'd be round to check me out before you had time to say 'HMRC'. So I went along with it. But then, this last couple of months, he started making comments about Ana and her 'skills'. All kind of innocent in themselves, but it was the way he said them. I employed you to find out if they were having an affair, or if he'd just found another way to bloody torment me."

Anastasia has been sitting quietly through all this, apparently shocked at the extent of her abuser's villainy. As Simon finishes his narrative, I turn to his wife and gently invite her to share her side of the story.

"I didn't know any of this until tonight. I am sorry, Simon. Perhaps we should have talked earlier, and trusted each other with our secrets."

"Well, you've heard mine now. Time for you to reveal yours." The dry tone in her husband's voice seems to unnerve Anastasia, and she swallows and takes a deep breath before speaking.

"I disliked Eric from the moment I met him. His eyes seemed to undress me whenever I came into contact with him, so I avoided him as much as possible. Then, at the beginning of the year, I got a letter from him. The envelope was typewritten, and looked as though it was something innocent. Perhaps he guessed that Simon and I never open each other's mail. The mail arrives late morning usually. I work from home when I'm not visiting clients, so I was alone when his letter arrived. He said he needed to meet with me in private, as he had something to discuss with me – an incident of which he knew I would prefer my husband to remain in ignorance. I could not think of anything that fitted this criterion, but there was a number on the bottom of the letter, so I called it. He set up a meeting for the next day, while the children were at school and Simon would be in the office. We were to meet in a hotel in the city centre." She stops and runs her tongue across her lips. "Excuse me. I need to get a drink." She leaves the room and returns a moment later with a glass of water.

Will rolls his eyes at me, and I suppress a grin. Neither of us has been offered a drink, but the atmosphere is so tense, it seems wrong to ask for one.

Seated again, Anastasia takes a gulp or two of water.

"Sorry. My mouth was dry. Anyway, we met, and he explained that during a business trip to Moscow, he had uncovered some information about some relatives of mine who had remained there, despite the difficulties of being Russian Jews. My father left Moscow in the late 70s with his wife, my mama. He left behind his parents and younger sister, who refused to leave. The authorities imprisoned his parents soon afterwards and they died in captivity. However, my aunt married just a few days after my father left, and ostensibly converted to the Russian Orthodox Church, of which her husband was a member. They had two children – my cousins Boris and Mikhail. I believe they are twins of around my own age. I am thirty-three."

"You've never told me any of this," Simon interjects. "Why wouldn't you tell me?" He looks furious but also shocked.

"Because I only found out when your pig partner told me, in a terrible hotel room he dragged me to, insisting I would want privacy for his information."

I reach over and rest my hand on her arm for a moment. "It's okay. But I still don't understand why the existence of your aunt and cousins should be so secret, and how Eric discovered them?"

"The last bit is easy. He is a disgusting weasel who thrives on discovering secrets he can use to hold over people." She takes another mouthful of water. "He is so vile. He physically leaves a horrible taste in my mouth." She glances down at the carpet. "The secret, though… That is the awful thing, and by telling you, I may be condemning them to death. My aunt and cousins have not only been practising Jews throughout their childhood and into adulthood, but they have been underground operatives, assisting other Jews to escape to Israel, particularly during the Soviet years. These days, Jews live openly in Russia and are allowed to practise, but my family moved from assisting the emigration of Jews to supporting the anti-Putin movement. According to the pig, they have been very active, and if their government found out, my family would be shot. Eric has a cousin in London – Viktor Kazakov – who has contacts in the Russian secret service. Eric threatened to bring him into this and bring my family down. I cannot do this to them, but the day he told me of their activities, he insisted I should provide him with sexual favours in order to preserve his silence."

"And you agreed?" Simon's tone is scathing.

Will hastens to intervene. "What would you have done in her place, Mr Blackstone? In fact, what did you do when Eric tried to blackmail you?"

In a heartbeat, Simon's face goes from scarlet to white.

"Sorry. Yes. You're right. I suppose you wanted to protect them, and maybe even your parents."

"Of course. Mama and Papa would not stand by while my aunt and cousins were at risk. And then their own lives would be in danger."

"Surely they'd be safer over here in England?" Although as I speak, I remember, from last year, the poisoning of a man and his daughter by the nerve agent Novichok. The Russian government continues to deny involvement, but it seems highly likely they were responsible. I'm suddenly aware of another link with Russia that I'm getting involved with — the disappearance of a Russian jewelled egg. Is there a connection between the two? It's too early to say yet, but otherwise, it's a very bizarre coincidence.

Meanwhile, Anastasia continues her story.

"I cannot guarantee they would be safe anywhere. Eric's requirements grew from that initial time, until today when they became intolerable, and I revolted. I am now terrified about what he'll do to my family. His contacts in Moscow know where they live and have been keeping them under observation. I know virtually nothing about them, although I have pleaded for information beyond their names, which are relatively common ones in Russia. I also fear for my parents here in Manchester. They know nothing of this, although I wonder if Papa keeps in touch with his sister. I know during the Soviet years there was nothing. My aunt could not risk any association with a Jewish family anywhere in the world. She needed to keep hidden, and her marriage helped her to disguise her true nature and identity."

"Has Eric told you all this?" asks Will.

"Yes, but I knew from Papa that he had a sister that he left behind with his parents when he came here, and that she was due to be married. Everything adds up. And now I don't know what to do."

EIGHT

Will

THURSDAY

Having spent most of the night digesting Anastasia's story, I wake up late and go down to breakfast feeling grumpy. Mum's already in the kitchen, eating toast and reading the newspaper.

"Morning," she says chirpily.

"Morning, Mum. You okay?" I put the kettle on and make myself a coffee. I definitely need caffeine this morning.

"Yes. Wendy's going to help find your bloody father and stop him hassling me."

"And put him back behind bars?" I should be pleased for Mum, but it's not nice having a parent in prison, even though he is a violent bastard. This has been conflicting me for far too long. I don't want him near either of us, but having him back in prison is not my preferred option.

"That's the only way we're going to be safe from him, Will." She now sounds as grumpy as I feel, adding guilt on to my worsening mood. I force myself to change the subject.

"I know. Anyway, we had an interesting evening yesterday." I fill her in on the revelations of the Blackstones. She listens attentively, appearing to have pushed her own troubles into the background for the moment.

"So what happens next? Was that decided at all?"

"Eventually, we agreed Anastasia would speak to her dad and find out if Eric told her the truth. If there's a safe way for her dad to get a message to the relatives in Russia, he'll do so, warning them that their activities are about to be exposed."

"She'll stop… erm… servicing Eric then?"

"Bloody hell, Mum. What an awful expression! Yeah, she's pretty much told him to stuff his blackmail. I guess we need to wait and see what his next step will be, but we need to stop him doing any damage if we can, without bringing the tax authorities down on Simon."

"Do you think it would be worth asking Wendy or Finn?"

"Not yet. Let's see if we can come up with another solution. Becky wants to discuss it with Roger though. She thinks he might be able to help with the Russia connection, but also she mentioned to me after we'd left their house last night that there might be a link with the egg disappearance." The coffee seems to be kicking in. My bad mood is dissipating with the interest in the discussion.

"Bless her! I love Becky to bits, but how the hell does she make that assumption?"

"I didn't say she assumed; just that she thought it was possible. I gather it was more the strangeness of having two cases at the same time with connections to Russia."

Mum looks thoughtful. "Maybe. While we're talking about the egg, have you looked at the CCTV yet?"

"It's on my list for this morning. This afternoon, I'm due to pick Chloë up from school and take her to the park if it's warm enough. Otherwise it'll be McDonalds. Do you fancy coming with me? It's been a while since you saw your granddaughter." Time with my little girl is precious, but it was worth making the suggestion to see Mum's face light up so much.

"Oh Will. Thanks so much. I'd love to." She pauses. "I'd

better get on with some work this morning then. I'll phone Becky and see if she wants any help with the Blackstones."

"Brilliant. I'm going to work upstairs for a bit. I need to concentrate on this CCTV."

An hour later, I'm in the spare room swearing. I've managed to access the images that I hacked from the bank, and also the ones Iain sent me. They're mostly the same, but not quite. I scroll through the images again, slowly this time; first the originals, then the copies from Iain.

The CCTV from the bank shows a man fiddling with the lock at the back door. It's not possible to see if he has a lock-picking device or a key. The man is dressed all in black, including a balaclava, but is of medium height and slim build. Difficult to pin down for an identity parade. For Christ's sake, that could fit my description if I'd been dressed like that! A moment later, two similarly-dressed individuals appear in the frame, and enter the now open back door to the bank.

But when I look at Iain's saved images, the man at the door appears fatter and is wearing a bowler hat. I pinpoint the frames where he appears and enlarge those images. It would need an expert to be sure, but I think it's the set from the USB stick that has been tampered with. There's a fuzziness about the extra fat and the bowler that looks unreal to me.

It's time to phone Becky. I just hope she's not tied up somewhere with Mum.

She answers on the second ring. "Hi Will. Everything okay?"

"Not entirely. Hello, by the way." I can almost sense her grin in response to my late greeting.

"What's the matter?"

I explain about the differences in CCTV images.

"Interesting. I'm seeing Finn this afternoon. Do you want me to discuss it with him?"

"Blimey, Becky. You could get me into serious trouble. It is illegal to hack into the CCTV of a bank, amongst other things."

"I could go at it from the angle that you've looked at the USB images you've been given, and they look suspicious, as though certain bits have been faked. Then I can ask about the images they've seen from the bank. Let me take the USB stick and give it to Finn."

"I suppose that would work. He'll have access to labs to check it out. The alternative would be to go to Roger." I think for a moment. "What do you think about going down both routes? I can make another copy for Roger. We'd have to tell him it's a copy from me, but I think he'd want the police to have the original."

"Give me a few minutes. I'll give Roger a call and get back to you."

While she's making her calls, I save everything to my laptop and open a fresh USB stick. I always keep a supply just in case. I name the different images as *ORIGINAL FROM BANK* and *COPIES FROM BANK MANAGER*. There's no need to make Roger's team hack the bank again, and he won't mind about legality or otherwise. He was the one who told me to teach the others how to hack, for Christ's sake! I've just about finished when the phone pings. Becky's sent me a WhatsApp message.

'Roger's fine with copies. I'll collect them in half an hour if that's okay. Finn isn't to know about Roger.'

Of course not. We can't have government organisations knowing about each other. Perhaps Finn doesn't have security clearance. He's only a Detective Inspector. I'm not sure of Roger's role, but I think he's a fairly senior operative in the Secret Service. He had that air when I met him.

I check my watch. Nearly eleven. I head downstairs to find Mum and the kettle.

NINE

Becky

THURSDAY

It'll be a relief to get out of the house to collect Will's data. Matt woke up with a headache, and consequently has been a bad mood all morning. It doesn't improve when he overhears my conversation with Roger.

"Why would you hand over those images to Roger?" he asks, frowning.

"Why not? You've been working with him longest. I thought you trusted him?"

"Bloody hell, Becks. You can't talk about trust in connection with people like that. They have to trust you, but never ever make the mistake of trusting them."

I restrain the urge to throw my coffee over my husband's head. An impressive show of self-control helps because I'm sitting at the kitchen table, and he's lurking in the doorway.

"How can he trust me if I don't share information with him, and what is the problem with passing the images to him? I'll be sharing them in a slightly different context with Finn later." The thought of seeing my ex-police partner brings on sweaty palms and palpitations. I've not seen him since the last case wrapped up a few weeks ago, and I've had plenty of time to dwell on what he told me – his betrayal of me during my last days in the force, and his selfishness in putting my life in danger to protect his own reputation. I take some deep breaths to quell the fight-or-flight reactions, and shove the increasing anger to the back of my mind to deal with later.

Matt seems lost in thought for a moment. But then, in a sudden spurt of decisiveness, he plonks himself on a chair opposite me.

"I need to tell you more about Roger, and my past dealings with him, then you'll see." He launches into a tale of dark alleyways, suspicion, and withholding confidences from the people he loved. But then it gets darker. "So he betrayed my trust. I thought he would look after me, but then Joanna made her mistake, and although it wasn't clear that it was her fault, I didn't know her that well then. I told him my suspicions. He said he would deal with it, but I heard nothing from him for months. Next thing I knew was Joanna turning up on our doorstep."

"I still don't see how that would have had the reaction it did." Matt had collapsed with a heart attack on seeing Joanna, and it had taken a lot to convince me they hadn't been having an affair.

"My immediate thought was that Roger had told her of my suspicions and she'd come to kill me." He glances at my horrified expression. "Yeah. I know it sounds ludicrous now, but we knew very little about each other, and there is the general belief that every agent is dangerous in some way."

"Yes, but you know now that Joanna wasn't here for that reason. So what makes you think Roger betrayed you?"

"He acted on my suspicions and effectively suspended us both. That information I discovered much more recently. Joanna and I have discussed things properly and pieced together what happened. Then Roger got involved with us all again. I'm not sure, but I think it's because of you. You've got a lot of skills that he's very interested in."

"So, because of me, he's forgiven you and Joanna?"

"That's about the sum of it, yes. But you can see why I'd hesitate to trust him again." Matt gets up and walks round the table. He squeezes my shoulder briefly and is about to leave the room, but I haven't finished yet.

"Hang on a minute. Don't you think there's a difference between sharing some data from a case and discussing suspicions about another operative?"

"Maybe." He pauses. "Yes, probably. I would just be careful what you share with him." He disappears into the lounge, and I'm left wondering who I can actually trust.

It's a sobering thought, when the only ones I can come up with are my immediate family (Matt, Cheryl and Alison) and Joanna and Will. I can probably add Wendy to the list, but that leads my thoughts to Finn, and bile rises in my throat at the thought of his betrayal. I push away the emotion as far as I can. It's time to collect the USB stick from Will.

I don't stay for long – only the few minutes it takes for Will to pass me two clearly-labelled envelopes and remind me not to get him into trouble with Finn. I've schooled myself not to flinch when I hear the name, but I still can't help the increase in heart rate. He used to have that effect for a different reason. I wish I could go back to that time, but some things are unforgivable. We were partners in crime-fighting for over twenty years, but I wonder if I ever really knew him.

I stow the envelopes in separate sections of my handbag so that neither one is within view of the other, although Roger knows I'll be giving data to Finn. My next stop is a park bench in one of Bury's many green spaces. Roger's there before me, reading a newspaper and eating a sandwich, even though it's only 11.30 and a bit early for lunch. The weather is sunny, if a little cold, so it's not too conspicuous sitting outside. I take a seat next to him on the bench, leaving a comfortable distance. A plastic Tupperware box lies roughly equidistant between us. He appears to continue to read his paper and I survey the area. The bench is at the edge of a path, but with no trees or bushes in the vicinity. There is nowhere for an eavesdropper to hide. Due to the slight chill, the park is reasonably quiet, although a playground a hundred metres away is full of pre-school-aged kids and well-wrapped-up mums.

"I think we're safe to talk, don't you?" I say to Roger.

"We're never fully safe, but this seems as good a place as any. I'll keep my newspaper raised though. A lip-reader with binoculars can do a lot of damage."

I think about this for a moment. It seems a little far-fetched, but if it keeps Roger happy, I'll go along with it. I take my Kindle from my bag and open it so I appear to be reading.

"How's that?" I sneak him a quick glance and get a hint of a smile in return, although his gaze remains firmly fixed to his paper.

"That works. Do you have the package?"

"Yes. What do you want me to do with it?"

"Lay it down next to my lunchbox. I'll pick it up unobtrusively when convenient." He waits while I put my Kindle down and extract the envelope from my bag. "That's right. Just pop it down beside you, as if you've removed it to remind yourself to stick it in the postbox. Now pick up your Kindle again and pretend to continue reading."

I obey him. It seems like the easiest path, but I feel a bit silly. It's all so cloak-and-dagger. All because of a USB stick with some CCTV footage from a bank.

"When will you have time to look at the images?"

"I'll get it to my team this afternoon, and get back to you in good time, when I have reached a conclusion. I believe you're handing some information to your police friend this afternoon."

I'm about to say that Finn is no longer a friend, when Matt's advice pops into my head and I decide to hold my tongue. My history is none of Roger's business.

"Yes, but he's only getting the USB stick that was provided to us by the bank manager. He should already have the information from the bank's own CCTV, and I don't want to get Will into trouble. You might be okay with him hacking into the bank's systems, but the police wouldn't see it like that." I take advantage of this reminder to check that I've put the correct envelope on the bench. It's clearly marked with Roger's name, and I allow myself a mental pat on the back for getting this right.

"That's very true. It's good for Will to practise his skills on banks and similar moderately high-security institutions. There will come a time when I will need him to get into more challenging environments." He lowers his paper a fraction and flashes me a quick sideways glance. "You mentioned in your call that you had another case that was of some concern to you."

I explain about the complicated situation with Anastasia and her family. Then I add, "The problem really is that we don't know if Eric is bluffing about the trouble her family is in, or if there's even more to it than we've been told. I'm also disconcerted by the coincidence of two links to Russia in separate cases at the same time. If we had a hundred cases, I would say 'fair enough', but we only have two. It seems strange."

"Coincidences happen. However, I will look into this chap, Eric, for you. Send me a report about your meeting with Mr and Mrs Blackstone. Leave nothing out. I need full names, addresses, descriptions, insights, and any other information you can provide on everyone who could be relevant. That includes Mrs Blackstone's relatives. You know how to send encrypted messages to me, I believe."

"Matt can show me if I get stuck, but I think I can manage. We had to encrypt everything when I was in the police. Thanks. I'll get that report done later this afternoon. I've got another meeting straight after lunch."

"Of course. With the gangly inspector. Enjoy. I believe now would be a good time for you to pack up and leave, forgetting to take the envelope next to you. I will pretend to notice it when you're out of sight, and will pick it up with an apparent view of returning it to you until I am out of sight of anyone in the park."

"One quick question before I go. Why couldn't you just pop in and collect this from my house?"

I see a hint of a smile forming at the corner of his mouth.

"We like to check you can follow instructions, Becky. It might be important one day."

TEN

Joanna

THURSDAY

I've completely failed to get anything useful done this morning, so it's a relief when Will pops his head round the kitchen door.

"Mum, do you fancy leaving now, and we'll get some lunch in Preston? If Deb lets me pick up Chloë a bit earlier, we can take her to McDonalds. She'd love that. We can get her a Happy Meal."

"Sounds bloody brilliant. Not McDonalds exactly, but getting out for lunch with Chloë." I close my laptop and stand up.

"Don't you have anything to finish?" Will seems surprised, and I reflect guiltily on the online shopping channel I've been idly perusing for the last hour.

"Nothing that can't wait. Come on. Why don't you phone Debbie while I brush my hair and make myself fit to be seen? If you give her enough notice, she's more likely to say yes to us taking Chloë for lunch."

Heading upstairs, I change into skinny jeans and a long-sleeved flowery top. Perfect attire for meeting with my model ex-daughter-in-law. I've always felt slightly intimidated by her, and can only retaliate by looking as slim and attractive as possible. Although I've filled out a bit since I've been in Manchester, it's only enough to disguise some of the ugly angles created by the intense weight loss during chemo. The cancer treatment made me appallingly sick for most of the time, and the anti-sickness drugs only eased it towards the end of each cycle. I know I was unlucky. Most people tolerate it better than I did. My hair came back last year – ridiculously curly – and it didn't really suit me. I kept it cropped until I got here, but somehow Becky's acceptance of me, coupled with the joy of Will's company, has eased my concerns about appearance, and I allowed my hair to grow into a tousled mop. I managed to straighten it for my meeting with Wendy, so I have another go. It doesn't settle quite as well today. Typical. I'm about to have another go with the straighteners, when Will shouts from downstairs.

"Mum, are you ready? Deb said yes."

"Two minutes. I'm nearly done." I give my hair one more quick shot at straightening, then brush it through. It'll have to do. The beret won't work for today, but I look okay. My hair still has grey streaks. I've not got round to having it coloured since it came through. I was so relieved to have thick hair back, despite the weird curls, that I didn't want to do anything to jeopardise the growth. But maybe it's time now to move on.

Downstairs, Will already has his leather jacket on, with a blue checked shirt and black jeans.

"You look nice," I tell him.

"Thanks, Mum. So do you." He glances at his watch. "We need to get going though. Deb said she'd see a friend for lunch if she'd be free, so we need to get cracking."

We arrive in Preston in good time and pull up outside a smart, modern detached house with a double driveway. There are two cars parked in front – a black BMW and a beige Range Rover.

"Bloody hell, Will. I hope you're not still paying maintenance if they've got all this."

He turns the engine off and gives me a grin. "It got written into the divorce settlement that payments would stop if she got married. The wedding was three weeks ago. They didn't invite me."

"She seems to have done well for herself. Is she still modelling?"

"Part-time. Which is why it worked for me to be visiting today. It's teacher training today and tomorrow, so Chloë's off. Apparently, they want to take her to meet his parents this weekend." He grimaces. "Not happy about it, but he's now her stepdad, so I suppose he has some rights." He opens the door and gets out, so I follow suit. I want to see the house where my granddaughter is living.

Will's pressure on the doorbell elicits a speedy response, but it's not Debbie who answers. The man who opens the door is a tall slim chap with gingery hair and a moustache. He doesn't smile.

"You must be Chloë's dad." He nods toward Will, then glances at me. "Who are you?"

My jaw clenches at his rudeness, but I keep a grip on my anger.

"I'm Chloë's gran, Joanna. I assume you're Peter?"

"Yeah." The hostility emanating from him is so thick that you'd be hard put to cut it with a meat cleaver.

Will clearly senses it too, as he flashes me a quick nervous glance. "Is Chloë ready?"

"Where are you taking her?" asks her new stepdad.

"I'm not sure what it's got to do with you, but I'm taking

her for some lunch then to the park. We'll get her back in time for her tea."

"You'd better. Five o'clock sharp. We're driving up to Glasgow as soon as the rush hour is past to see my parents. I don't plan on driving all night, so you'd best get her back bang on five, if not sooner."

As he finishes his instruction, a beautiful little girl of five appears. I've not seen her for nearly a year, and she's grown so much. She's dressed in jeans and a SpongeBob SquarePants sweater, which matches her blonde hair and blue eyes. She flashes me her sweet smile – so like Will's – and exclaims with a squeal,

"Gran! You've come to see me. I've not seen you for ages. Do you like my jumper? It's brand new. Daddy Peter bought it for me yesterday."

I glance at my son in time to see his jaw tighten at the name assigned for his daughter's step-parent. He takes a deep breath and then smiles warmly at Chloë.

"Come on, Poppet. Let's get going. We're going to have some fun this afternoon."

The time with Chloë passes quickly – too fast really. We all seem to enjoy McDonalds, and then make our way to a playground in a park. We take turns on the see-saw, and do the swings and slide. Chloë finds it hilarious seeing Gran go down a slide and land at the bottom with a cheer, and is still giggling when we get ice-creams and sit on a bench. It's a bit cold for ice-cream really, but it's a lovely treat before we go over to a pond and watch the ducks for a while. The afternoon is only marred by Chloë's occasional announcements of "Daddy Peter bought me…" The list of articles includes a TV, a sweater, a rocking horse and a new doll. Will is still "Daddy" though, so we try not to stress about it too much. I sit in the back of the car with her when we go to drop her off and she holds my hand, chattering excitedly about ice-cream, the ducks, and a couple of dogs that we saw playing together.

Debbie answers the door when we get back. She glances at her watch, but it's ten to five. Under the circumstances, we felt it would be safer to be early. She nods at us both, and holds out her arms to Chloë, who goes to her, but blows kisses at me and Will before going inside.

"Thanks, Deb," says Will. "Have a good weekend."

Debbie seems to thaw a fraction. She gives something that could pass as a smile.

"Cheers. Nice to see you, Joanna. You're looking well."

"Thanks, hen. So are you."

We head back to the car, relieved not to have seen Peter again. Without saying another word, Will starts the engine and drives a hundred yards or so until we're around the corner and out of sight of the house. He pulls up outside a school, deserted now because of the time.

"So, do we go straight home, or do you want to do another recce around Preston?"

"A recce wouldn't hurt." I check my phone in case Becky's been trying to contact us, but there's nothing. I know she's been busy this afternoon, so I don't stress about it. "Actually, it makes sense to have a look now, rather than battling the tea-time rush hour."

Will agrees with me and restarts the car. He doesn't bother with satnav, so I assume he knows the way. He's been coming here every week since he came down to Manchester.

It's easy to park in the town centre. Most people have left to go home, and the evening diners haven't driven in yet.

We stroll casually around the town centre, chatting about the improvement in the weather, the frustrating politics in the UK and around the world, and climate change. Anything except for the things we need to discuss: the case, and our obviously equal dislike of Chloë's new stepdad. We both glance around us frequently, giving the appearance of tourists, curious about the area, but not unduly so. Our wanderings lead us to the bank.

It's nearly half past five, and the area is still quite busy with workers walking back to their cars or bus stops, and a few late shoppers. Pizza Express is open and nearly empty, and I turn a speculative gaze on my son. He notices and laughs.

"Yeah, we might as well get something to eat. The traffic will still be horrendous."

Ninety minutes later we emerge from the restaurant, to find the streets around the bank are much quieter. We can hear noise from further away, where most of the bars are situated, but we're now safe to do a bit more discreet snooping. There's also the advantage that it's dark. The clocks haven't gone forward yet, and seven o'clock is past sunset. That will change next week, so we've timed our visit well.

But it's still important to appear innocent, as you never know who's watching. CCTV is everywhere, and Will's hackings haven't reached the point of disabling the council's cameras. Not that we would want to. It's more important to see images than to prevent them.

"Given that Iain could tweak the images from the bank, do you think you could do that too?" I ask.

"Why?" Will sounds suspicious. "What do you have in mind?"

"I was just wondering if it would be useful to check out the locking mechanism on the back door of the bank."

"It might not be necessary." He reaches into his pocket and extracts a miniature pair of binoculars. "I always carry these now. Ostensibly for birdwatching, but actually they're pretty damn useful for checking out details from a distance. Do you want to have a look?"

I take them and raise them to my eyes. The image is blurry, so I feel for a focusing device.

"Here, let me show you." Will takes the binoculars and shows me the small wheel that changes the focus. I try again with more success, and get a clear image of the door.

"It doesn't help that it's dark. I can see the door easily enough, but I can't actually see a lock." I hand the binoculars back to their owner. "You try."

Will fiddles with the focus for a moment, then gives up and gets out his phone.

"There's this app. I wrote it myself for Android, but haven't bothered to sell it. I'm not sure if it's something that should be out there, although if it works properly, I might sell it to Roger for his team."

"What does it do?"

"It combines light with zoom – so basically in a situation like this, we should be able literally to shed light on the door, but with no one else being able to see the light."

"Wow. That's clever. Does it work?"

Will grins at me. "Let's find out, shall we?" He gestures for me to get into a position where we can both see the screen, then points his phone at the door. He taps an icon on the screen, and the door lights up in the image. I glance up, but in reality it's still in darkness.

"Wow. That's quite impressive." I watch as he zooms in, and we see the enhanced view of the door lock, somehow lit up in the image, but with no light showing anywhere else. "How did you do that? Is it real?"

"Good question. There's a bit of AI in there – artificial intelligence. It works out what it can see, then adds the light, and uses machine learning to work out what it's likely to look like if it was lit."

"So it's kind of made it up?" I'm disappointed, but I glance again at the image. "I'm going to risk getting closer. Just keep an eye out for passers-by. I'll try not to look too suspicious." I wander casually towards the door. There's a huge bin not far away. I feel in my coat pocket and extract a couple of tissues. They'll serve the purpose. I walk over to the bin (incidentally triggering a lighting system), put the tissues in, and then bend down to fiddle with the buckle on my shoe. Once done, I stand up and manage a quick look at the door. The lights are still on, so I daren't linger too long, but I see enough to realise that Will's app was remarkably accurate. The door has a keyhole that looks suitable for a mortice-type deadlock. I force myself to stroll casually back to Will.

"Well? Does it look the same close up? I noticed you set off the security lights."

"It looks identical. I'm very impressed." I pause for a moment. "How easy would it be to pick a mortice lock?"

"Why? Are you considering breaking in? I don't have a set of lock-picks." He grins. "Is it necessary equipment for private detectives?"

"God knows. Ask Becky! No, I was just wondering if any decent burglar could break in, or if this suggested an inside job."

"Hmm. Interesting question. If it was the mortice by itself, I reckon anyone could have broken in, but don't forget I checked the CCTV." He glances round, prompting me to do the same. There are a couple of young men hanging around, lighting up roll-ups. "Let's discuss this in the car. The traffic should have died down by now."

We walk back to the car in companionable silence; I don't want to break the chain of thought, and I suspect Will feels the same. It's not until we're in the car that he speaks again.

"Okay." He puts the keys in the ignition and starts the engine. "I think we need some heat. It's cold out there now."

"Yes. Now come on, tell me."

"Right. The CCTV showed that as well as the back door, there was an inner door – made of silver-coloured metal. It wasn't possible to see the opening mechanism to that, but it looked more hi-tech than the outer one. I think it's safe to assume that either they were very accomplished burglars, or that there was some sort of help from people who worked there." He grimaces at me before putting the car into gear ready to set off. "Particularly, as the only thing of real value that was stolen was that egg. £3 million pounds is nothing in comparison."

ELEVEN

Becky

THURSDAY

Eating lunch is harder than usual today. My stomach refuses to cooperate, and my throat isn't much more helpful. Matt's made some soup – a thick vegetable concoction – and home-made bread. It's delicious. My husband's culinary skills have improved dramatically since his heart attack nearly six weeks ago. He's due to return to work next week, and I'll have to resume cooking duties myself.

Unfortunately, I'm due to meet Finn in an hour, and all our history is coming back to haunt me. This will be a difficult meeting. I could pretend that he didn't tell me at the end of the Troy case that he'd been responsible for the whole setup in the warehouse last summer. I saw him in the days that followed his revelations, as we were tying up loose ends of the case, but I was too numb to take in properly what he'd said. My longstanding crush on him had died an immediate death that day, but it's difficult to obliterate the past completely. He'd been my best friend for such a long time, and his betrayal is almost too painful for me to face.

I try again to swallow a mouthful of soup. Matt's watching me.

"What do you think, Becks? I've changed the recipe a bit. Is it too spicy?"

"No. It's great. I'm not feeling particularly well. My throat hurts and I feel queasy. I hope I'm not coming down with a bug. Finn and I need to talk about the bank case this afternoon." My tone is neutral. I share a lot with Matt, but my emotions are too intense for me to reveal on this occasion. Although I told him when I discovered Finn had set me up, I made sure my horror was in line with that of a friend's betrayal. I would hate to hurt Matt. It's not his fault that my feelings for Finn are so complicated.

"Why don't you leave it for now? It might be psychosomatic. You've got a pretty traumatic meeting ahead of you. I know you've played it down, but Finn was your partner and friend for a lot of years. If it was me, I'd be bricking it just now. Whether you decide to pretend it hasn't happened, or you go for the throat and bash it all out, either way it's pretty damn stressful."

Maybe he gets it more than I give him credit for.

"Which would you do if you were in my place?"

"I'd probably chicken out, and pretend it had never happened, and try to carry on as usual. But you're not me, Becks. I think you need to get it out in the open. Discuss it. Yell at him if you have to. Look, Cheryl's at school and is going round to Joel's afterwards, and I need to go shopping for some new trousers for work. My old ones are hanging off me. Ask Finn to come here instead of meeting him in a pub. You'll be able to speak openly and say whatever you need to. I won't come home until you let me know he's gone. I can always drink coffee for an hour or two and read my Kindle in Costa's in Bury."

I consider his offer. While I'd rather not see Finn at home, Matt makes sense, suggesting that a private conversation would be more beneficial. Frankly, even the discussion of the case would be better taking place without risk of eavesdroppers.

"Thanks. Good plan, if you're sure you're okay being out all afternoon?"

"Yeah. Good practice for work. Put your soup in the fridge. Heat it up afterwards. I reckon you'll need it then." He drops a kiss on my forehead and leaves me to message Finn to change the arrangements.

Finn rings the doorbell at exactly 2pm. He's been waiting in his car for five minutes – I know because I've been looking out of my bedroom window. As soon as he got out of the car, I rushed downstairs, so I take half a minute to get my breath back. It won't do him any harm to wait.

When I open the door, Finn stands still for a moment, looking uncertain.

"Hi Becky. Thanks for arranging this."

"No problem. Come in." My tone is abrupt. I'm not sure how this will play out, but I haven't forgiven him and I don't know if I ever will.

"I think we should go for a drive, actually." He won't meet my gaze, and my heart pounds erratically. Something is not right here, and it's not just the past. Instinct warns me to be careful.

"I'd prefer not to. I'm more comfortable here in my home."

"Then I need to make a call." Finn gets his phone out of his pocket, but I reach out and grab it from him before he has a chance to react. "What the hell…?"

"Why would you need to make a call, Finn? We're old friends and you've come here for a chat about a case. There's no good reason for you to need to do anything other than sit and listen."

"Put the kettle on then." He gives me an agitated glance then wanders into the lounge. I follow and take the cordless landline phone from its base.

"Sure." I keep out of Finn's reach as I take both phones into the kitchen with me. I lock them both into the medicine cabinet and slip the key into my jeans pocket. With the kettle on, I make two cups of coffee. "Do you still take sugar?" I shout through.

There's no answer. I go into the lounge. The patio door is open, and my ex-colleague and ex-friend is gone. An engine roars – the sound coming from the front of the house. I go in, locking the patio behind me, and rush upstairs. Sure enough, Finn's car is gone.

What on earth just happened? I make sure all doors are locked, then remove the phones from the cabinet. Will's out this afternoon, so I need to do this by myself. My time as a police detective taught me how to search the Dark Web. It doesn't take long for me to find what I need, but the first thing to try is to get into his phone by moderately legitimate means. His passcode used to be the year of the Battle of Hastings. I try that first. No success. The next number to try is his birthday. A couple of different combinations lock it. I have to wait for a minute before I can try again. The phone prompts me to wait but I know this is my last chance before it locks completely. A sudden weird thought prompts me to try my own birthday. The lock screen clears. I have access. And sweaty palms and palpitations.

I pick up my phone and call Matt. "You can come back. He's gone."

"What? He can't have been there long." Matt sounds confused.

"He wasn't. I'd really like it if you get back soon though." My voice is shaky, despite my best attempts to sound calm. I'm not sure what I escaped from, but it feels as though there was a big bullet with my name on it.

"Sure. I've just paid for two new pairs of trousers, so it's perfect timing. Give me fifteen minutes. Get yourself some tea and biscuits, and calm down."

Relieved to hear he's on his way back, I focus instead on the job at hand: that of checking Finn's phone. It's still unlocked, so I go first to the recent calls. There are many people I don't recognise, and a few contacts from the police. I've got a few options, but I'm not planning on trying any of them until Matt's home. I spend a bit of time checking Finn's internet history. There's nothing particularly outstanding on there – a bit of porn. Quite a lot, actually. I think back to some of the times we spent before Matt came along. A short fling, but nothing too significant. Looking at his viewing, I'm pleased I didn't get further involved with him. Although maybe if I had, he wouldn't have been tempted to set me up. It's an irrelevant question now, but I'm feeling as though I never knew the man I'd thought of as my best friend for nearly three decades.

The phone in my hand vibrates, and a message comes through.

*"Where the f*** r u? Should be here by now with that bitch. Call me."* The name that pops up as the sender is Jez. It means nothing to me, and I can't help but wonder what Finn said to him to inspire such apparent hatred.

A ringtone – straightforward, no frills – sends me into a sudden panic. Should I answer? I really don't know what's going on here, and I'm alone in the house. The screen shows that it's Jez again. He's getting really impatient, but I'm not going to answer. Let him stew for a while. Meanwhile, I need to make a call on my own phone. I fumble as my shaking fingers struggle to use the touch screen properly.

"Wendy, are you working today? It's Becky."

"Are you okay, love? You sound… anxious." She's right, but that's a bit of an understatement.

"I've got a bit of a problem. Have you got a few minutes to pop in and pick up Finn's phone? He's left it here, and there are some… aggressive messages coming through."

"Sure. Don't respond to them. I reckon I'm about twenty minutes away, traffic permitting. See you soon, love. Now get yourself some tea and biscuits. You sound as though you need them."

As Wendy's now the second person to make that suggestion, I decide to obey. About the tea, at least. The thought of eating anything makes my stomach churn.

Finn's phone rings half a dozen times before anyone arrives, and when I hear the key in the door, it takes all my effort not to pass out with relief.

"Becks?" Matt calls out as he opens the front door. "Are you okay? Where are you?"

"Lounge." My voice is muffled because my head is between my legs. The room has done a kind of kaleidoscope effect around me. Matt and Wendy must have arrived at the same time, because they're soon hovering over me, making soothing sounds and letting me know how concerned they are. My husband has me lying on the couch with my feet elevated on cushions, and Wendy brings me a fresh cup of tea, which she won't let me sit up to drink yet. After a few minutes, during which Finn's phone rings twice, and is ignored both times, Wendy squats at my side.

"Okay. You've got a bit of colour back in your cheeks. Do you want to sit up? Slowly!" She puts her hand behind my back and eases me into a more upright position. The room stays in one place, and I smile at her, relieved. "All good?"

"Yeah, thanks." I point to Finn's phone on the table. "You might need to deal with that. I tried to have a look but…" I tail off, not wanting to admit that I hacked into it but got freaked out when it started ringing. "The person who keeps ringing is called Jez. Does that mean anything to you?"

"It's not a name I recognise. How about you tell me everything? There's clearly a backstory here that I'm not aware of."

"We might need more tea and biscuits, Matt. This is going to take a while." I smile at Wendy. "Sorry. It's a long story. Make yourself comfy."

Wendy knows roughly what happened in the warehouse. She was on another job at the time, but the death of a colleague at work always rippled through, and Wendy was as appalled as the rest of us. But not as much as I was. I was less than three feet away when DS Rachel Brooks was shot.

So I start my narrative with Finn's admission of betrayal. I see the anger in her eyes, and the pursing of her mouth, but she says nothing until I've finished describing today's events.

"Sorry, Becky, but I'm not as shocked as you. I know he was your partner for a very long time, but I never entirely trusted him, and a few times I had to intervene to prevent him from putting you in danger. If only I'd spotted this situation, though. Rachel might still be alive."

"You were busy with that special project. I'm sure you didn't have time to worry about what Finn was up to." I can't keep the bitterness from my voice, but it's not against Wendy. It wasn't her fault. Should she have told me her suspicions about Finn's integrity? Possibly. But then I probably wouldn't have listened. I would have doubted her judgement over mine. The fact that I'd been a little in love with him for all those years had skewed my vision. I'm silent for a while as I think back over several times when he'd failed me. He'd always had a great excuse – or reason, as I'd thought at the time. Bile rises in my throat as I realise I've been his dupe for over twenty years. How many times has he used me to cover for nefarious activities?

Wendy interrupts my mental wanderings. "The most

important thing to do now is to deal with the current situation. We have a few things to worry about. First, what is Finn up to, and how much danger are you in from him? Second, I need to access the original CCTV files for the bank; and third, I should be able to help with your Russian lady, with a bit of digging around."

"Erm, I wasn't going to tell Finn this, but I do trust you. Will has a copy of the original CCTV from the bank too." I've already given her the USB stick with the data from Iain.

"Hacked?" she raises an eyebrow and shakes her head. "He's a naughty boy, but I guess… Is Roger involved?"

"How the hell do you know about Roger?" Matt's been quiet until now, but can't seem to help himself from interrupting at this point.

"He has his finger in a lot of pies, and when last year I worked on a special project, I was liaising with him rather closely. He asked me for a reference for Becky, you know. Even though he already knew you, Matt."

"Why didn't he tell me he's been working with you?" I ask.

"He's a man who likes to keep secrets. I suppose it's part of his job, but sometimes I think he hides things for fun." Wendy grins. "Okay, so if Roger's involved, I assume he knows about your Russian case and the hacking?"

"Yes, to both. He's promised to do some digging himself." I've calmed down a bit. Unburdening myself to my longstanding mentor and friend has helped, particularly as I don't seem to have any secrets from her. It's strange that she knows Roger, but it's a great help for me. Unlike Finn, Wendy has never done anything to let me down.

"Great. Between us, we're likely to find something useful. Meanwhile, I need to take Finn's phone back to him. And I will use it to extract some information. He might be an inspector, but I outrank him, and I can bring him down if necessary. I just need to make sure it happens in a way that doesn't put you at risk."

"I feel as though I'm in danger anyway. This Jez seems to expect Finn to deliver me to him. I don't want to be delivered."

"Use Will and Joanna to keep yourself safe. Be vigilant, and only go out with people you totally trust."

"I trusted Finn once." Tears threaten, and I blink them back fiercely. I need to keep calm and hold myself together until we know what's going on. My life might depend on it.

TWELVE

Will

FRIDAY

Becky phoned yesterday. Mum put her on speakerphone so we had a three-way chat, and heard all Becky's news. It sounds as though Finn has completely screwed her over. I gave strict instructions that she mustn't leave the house without Matt, Mum or myself. She sounded dubious, but Mum backed me up.

With that sorted, I set off to meet Glen, the chap I met the other day when I rescued his dad from the middle of the road. We've arranged to have a pie and a pint in a local pub, and I'm looking forward to a good chat. I have other motives, though. I recall Glen mentioned that he's an accountant.

Once we're sitting in a quiet corner, with lunch ordered and frothy pints on the table, I glance at my new acquaintance. He looks a bit tired.

"How are you doing?" I'd already asked him this on saying hello, but he gave the typical "Fine, how are you?" response, and I didn't believe him.

"I'm all right." He glances at me, and must see my sceptical expression. "Okay. I'm not great. It'll probably take a few months before I'm properly okay, but it's nothing worse than normal."

"Okay. As long as that's all it is. My mum had cancer a year ago. She's okay now, but I know it took her a while to get back to being herself. She's still too thin really."

"Do you see much of your mum, or does she live in Scotland?"

"I live with her. I moved into her spare room a short while ago. We live about half a mile away from you."

"You live with your mum and I live with my dad! Funny. You're young though. I'm guessing your mum must be closer to my age than you are, Will."

"How old are you, if you don't mind me asking?"

Glen grins. "Probably younger than I look, mate. I'm 52."

"You're a year older than Mum then." I refrain from commenting on how old he looks. In any case, I find it hard to tell when people are bald. It's time for a change of subject. "You said the other day that you're an accountant. Do you know a chap called Simon Blackstone?"

"I do, as it happens. Friend of yours?"

Both Becky and my mum have impressed client confidentiality on me several times, so I hesitate before saying, "Just someone I know through work. I don't know him well though. How well do you know him?"

"Enough to know he's dabbled in some shit I wouldn't touch with a barge pole."

I raise my eyebrows. "What do you mean?"

"I've met Simon a few times. To be honest, he seems like an okay sort of bloke, but his partner is scum. Eric Yanov is a complete shit."

I dig back into my memory. The name differs slightly from my recollection. It comes to me after a moment. Ulyanov. "Has he always been known by that name?"

"Who? Eric? I'm not sure if Yanov's his real name, but it's what he's known as on the circuit."

"What circuit?" My knowledge of accountancy includes nothing of that kind.

"There's a bit of a crowd round here – twenty or thirty accountants with a bit of a *quid pro quo* attitude. You know, the old 'you scratch my back…' attitude. I got in with them when I first started, as I was working with a firm that was part of it." He glances round, and seems to relax a fraction when he sees that we're alone in our section of the pub. "I thought it was nice at first, but I quickly got a bad feeling about it. There was some stuff going on." He halts, and I follow his gaze. A waitress is coming out with our lunch. I wait for it to be set on the table, and for her to return with cutlery and sauces, before I prompt Glen to continue.

"What sort of stuff?" I dig into my steak and onion pie while I give him time to respond. It's delicious, but not enough to distract me. I glance at my companion and raise my eyebrows.

"Dodgy dealings, mate. I got asked to do something I didn't like. It was about five years ago, and jobs were ten-a-penny. I said I'd think about it, then called a recruitment agent. I had an interview that afternoon and handed in my notice the next day when they offered me the job. The dodgy boss put me on gardening leave and sent me home that day. I reckon they didn't want me rootling around, but I'd already done some research. There were links to drugs and arms traders, and they were covering stuff up, left, right and centre."

"Why didn't you report them?" I think I know the answer, but I'd like to hear it from Glen.

"Bloody hell, mate. I value my life, and that of my dad. He wasn't in such a bad state at that point, but he was living with me. When I resigned, the boss said something on the lines of

'You know that little job we asked you about yesterday? You'll keep schtum, won't you? You wouldn't want any harm to come to your old dad?' The bastard had the cheek to threaten me, but I probably wouldn't have said anything anyway. I just wanted to get away from them all. The next place I went to was clean, but after a couple of years, the partners closed down. One was retiring, and the other wanted to emigrate to Canada. I decided to go out on my own, and they were decent enough to send most of the clients my way. It was good until I got ill, but even before that, Yanov and his cronies sniffed around me a bit to check me out. Simon was one of them. He tried to recruit me to a job, but he kind of seemed half-hearted about it. When I said no, he thanked me, and backed off. Yanov was a bit more direct and threatened to send in the heavies if I declined, but I was older by then, and Dad wasn't well, so he wasn't really going out. I installed a good alarm system and started training in judo. I reckon I can handle myself. Or at least, I could before the bloody cancer got to me."

I'm fascinated by what he's told me, but I figure I won't get any more information from him in the pub. I need to get him to ours, where he can feel a bit more relaxed. It's a good start though. For now, I pick up on the judo, as it's something I have in common with him, and we indulge in an interesting and highly technical discussion before moving on to competitions and comparison of trophies. By the time we've finished our pies and pints, we're pretty comfortable with each other, having achieved a similar level of attainment and the knowledge of a shared hobby.

"Do you fancy coming back to mine for a coffee? I can introduce you to Mum." I reckon it's time Mum knew more people round here than just me and Becky.

He looks quite keen on the idea, but claims he has to go

home and see his dad. So we make arrangements for him to pop in on Sunday afternoon for tea and cake. I'm pleased. It will give me a chance to get more details about Simon and Eric and the intriguing dodgy deals.

THIRTEEN

Becky

SUNDAY

It's been three days since Finn's strange departure. Wendy reported that she'd returned the phone and given Finn a warning, but she didn't go into details. I've been stuck indoors for all those days. Matt has offered to come out with me, and so has Joanna, but the paralysing fear that I felt after the death of Rachel has returned to keep me indoors. I've spent a lot of time staring at a page in my Russian language textbook, but nothing has gone in. This morning, while I was fiddling with my spoon, looking at a bowl of cereal, Matt came in.

"We're going out this morning. I have to go back to work tomorrow, but I can't leave you in this state. It's either back to the doctors for some meds, or you come out with me for a bit of fresh air." He knows I hate the meds the doctor put me on for anxiety and depression, so it's not much of a choice really.

I give up on breakfast, just finishing my tea, and then go upstairs to get my trainers on. My pulse is racing, and I feel as though I need the option to run – just in case. Matt's waiting in the kitchen when I get back downstairs.

"Are you okay? You look awful. Are you sure you're up to this?"

"No. It was your idea. You didn't give me much of a chance to back out." I hate being so stroppy with him, but I'm nearly hyperventilating and on the verge of a panic attack, and we've not even made it out of the door yet.

"Okay. But you can't go out like this." He takes my hand and guides me into the lounge. "Sit there and turn around."

I sit cross-legged, facing away from him, and his hands start a gentle massage on my neck and shoulders. I feel myself relax under his healing touch, and after ten minutes my head is drooping.

"Lie down," he whispers. I obey, and he continues with his treatment for a while longer…

I wake feeling confused. Why am I lying face down on the sofa? I try to get up.

"Take it easy there." Matt's voice is quiet but firm. I turn my head to look at him. "Are you feeling better?"

"I think so. Fuzzy, that's all."

"That's expected. You've been asleep for half an hour, and you rarely nap during the day. Are you more relaxed?"

"Spaced out really, so I guess that's a yes." I sit up properly and get my bearings. Weren't we supposed to be going for a walk? Have I got out of it? I glance out of the window, and the sun is shining. It might be nice to get some fresh air. Surely nothing bad can happen if I'm out with Matt. He'll protect me. Actually, I can protect myself. I'm a black belt in several martial arts. I take a deep breath. "So when are we going out then?"

"Whenever you're ready. Shall we go now?"

I nod, but it takes me a few minutes to get my head together. But I need to leave before the anxiety erupts again.

Matt's idea of a walk is to drive to Heaton Park, a huge expanse of parkland a couple of miles away. He grumbles about the parking fees, but I'm not sorry to be sticking to such public areas. We wander for about half an hour, making our way down to the lake and starting a stroll around the back of it. We're about halfway round when my neck hairs prickle. I get my phone out, as if to take an innocent photo, and turn around. There are a few people about, mostly mums with buggies, older couples and a few joggers. But one man seems familiar. I take a snap of the lake, making sure I catch him in the photo. He is about fifty yards behind me. I quickly turn back to Matt.

"Come on, let's go," I say in a low voice. "I recognise that man over by the lake, near the swans. No idea where from, though."

We continue walking, taking the pace up a few notches. My heart is racing now, and nausea threatens to overcome me, but I want to get back to the car as soon as possible.

"Worry about it later. Let's have a coffee in the lakeside café."

I stare at him. "Seriously? We're being followed, and you want to stop for coffee?"

"Yes. There are loads of people around. I think our follower will retreat into the background, and if he doesn't, we can observe him easily."

I can see the sense in his suggestion, but my instinct is to retreat home. I indulge my 'fight-or-flight' reaction slightly by speeding up towards the busier part of the park, but Matt takes my hand and tries to force me to slow down.

"Come on. Can we get a move on?" I'm on the edge of panic. Matt glances across at me and relents, to the extent of lengthening his stride to match my current fast pace. We continue in silence until we reach the café a few minutes later. I make him stand with me in the queue to get our coffees, while I scan the area, looking for Mr Familiar Stalker. I don't see him just yet. Either he's retreated from such a busy area, or he's watching me from a greater distance. Matt carries the drinks to the table; my hands are shaking too much to be of any use. I'd end up spilling most of the hot liquid and scalding myself. We sit inside, with our backs to a wall, so we can see the area clearly.

"Is he around here?" Matt asks between sips of his drink. He seems calm and mildly curious. I have an urge to hit him, until I meet his eyes and realise the concern behind the apparently placid demeanour. As a pharmacist, putting a calm face on amid chaos has become a habit for him.

I'm about to say no when I spot someone standing outside on the tarmac between the café and the lake. He's smoking, and has a casual stance as though he's just stopped to enjoy the scenery.

"Becks?" Matt follows my gaze. "Who? The guy over there by himself, smoking?"

I glance round the area. There's no one else who could fit into that category. Everyone else has company or is jogging or cycling.

"Yes. I still can't think why he's familiar though." I'm puzzling it out when a miniature train comes into view. It stops outside the café and deposits some parents with young kids in front of us. The man is blocked from view for a moment, but the transport has jogged a memory. It was only a few weeks ago, but a lot has happened since then. I was on a train, and a man had sprawled out next to me, and then harassed me after I'd moved away. Seeing him here raises a lot of questions. Roger's boss, Sylvia, claimed that there was no connection with her team, and I'm inclined to believe her. This guy sets my hackles on end. Roger's odd, and a bit intimidating, but not in a terrifying way. I don't believe for a moment that Roger would do me harm, whereas this stalker...

"It's time to go, Matt. I know now where I remember him from. Let's get back to the car and take the most complicated route possible back home."

FOURTEEN

Joanna

SUNDAY

Will's new friend has just left. Glen seems like a nice guy. Not classically good-looking; if I'm being totally honest he looks tired and unwell. He told me he's just finished chemo, and I know how that feels. He's got a nice smile though, with a cute dimple in his left cheek.

I shake my head. For Christ's sake, woman, pull yourself together. I've got Lou on my back and we're hovering on the edge of a new case – at that godawful stage where no one knows anything useful. A grin sneaks on to my face. Three months ago, the White Knight Agency was a concept that I hadn't even discussed with anyone, and now I'm moaning about the phases of a case. Ridiculous.

I force myself to turn my attention to the present. Will has gone for a walk, but it's time for dinner. I call him.

"Hey, can I interest you in pizza?" I ask.

"Sure. How about calling Becky and seeing if she wants to join us? I'll be back in five."

"Sounds like a bloody good plan to me." I disconnect, and click on Becky's number.

"Oh, hi, Joanna. You okay?" She sounds distressed.

"I'm fine, hen, but what about you? You sound awful."

"We had a bit of an incident in the park. We're okay, but I'm a bit shaken up."

"Anything that pizza couldn't cure?" It's flippant really, but nothing wrong with injecting a bit of humour.

"I don't feel ready to come out without Matt, and I don't think it would be wise to leave Cheryl at home by herself right now."

"Why don't you bring them with you? We'll have a little soirée. You need to get out of the house and tell us all about it."

***

Two hours later, we're all stuffed with food. Will picked up some Ben and Jerry's ice cream along with three huge pizzas and garlic bread – and we're up to date with the latest news on both sides. Cheryl looks pale, and as I clear up the boxes, I invite her into the kitchen to help me get some drinks. She nods and follows me in.

"Are you okay?" I start with the easy question. I find it's a good technique in all situations. "Sit down. I'll put the kettle on. They won't miss us for a while." I noticed Becky giving me a grateful smile as I passed her. They'll give us as much time as we need.

"Kind of." Cheryl manages a weak grin. "I guess that's not very helpful."

"Tell me some more then, hen. What's bothering you?"

"All sorts of stuff really. But I suppose the main thing is hearing that Mum has a kind of weird stalker."

"Your mum has the type of job that can attract attention sometimes, and not always from nice people. I know from our dealings so far that you're a kind lass, and it can be hard imagining that not everyone is as sweet as yourself." I pour out tea into two mugs and hand one to Cheryl. The others can wait for theirs. We settle down at the kitchen table.

"Of course, I know people can be horrible. I expect Mum told you what happened at school last month?" She looks at me questioningly, and I nod. "Well, it was pretty grim, but I got some great new friends out of it who are really cool, so it worked out fine. The girls who started the bullying though, they were… I can't think of a word bad enough."

I cup my hands around my mouth and whisper, "Shitty? How's that for a word?" I lower my hands and grin. My young friend giggles.

"Blimey, Mum would kill me if she heard me saying that, but it describes their level pretty well. So, yeah, they were pretty…" She mouths 'shitty' silently. "And I know, from things that were said by Mum and by Joel's mum at the time, that at least one girl had a dad who's a complete… well I can't say that word either in case Mum comes in, but it begins with a 'b' and ends in 'astard'. I know not everyone is lovely and kind, but you don't expect your mum to have a stalker." She pauses. "Do you think he's dangerous?"

Bloody hell. How do I answer this? Cheryl's fifteen, though. She's not a baby.

"I think it's really important that you all take care of yourselves and of one another. Your mum has agreed to not go outside alone. I know your dad goes back to work tomorrow, and you're at school, so Will and I are going to look after your mum and make sure she's okay. But you need to be careful too. Do you get the bus to school?"

"Mum takes me, and then I get the tram home and she or Dad picks me up from the tram station, or I go back to my boyfriend's house to do homework and then Mum or Dad will pick me up from there."

"I don't like the idea of you waiting at the tram stop by yourself, hen."

"I can go back to Joel's more often. His mum said I'm always welcome. Or he can come back to mine. A couple of times, if he was with me, we walked back from the tram stop. Would that be okay, do you think?" She looks at me anxiously.

"It's a possibility, but you must never accept a lift, or get separated and walk back by yourself. And if there's ever a change of plan; if Joel's off sick or something, can you message your mum or me or Will at lunchtime, and one of us can pick you up from school?"

I tap my number into her phone so she can contact me in case of an emergency. I realise I've done nothing to relieve her anxiety – I've most likely added to it – but it's more important to ensure she's safe. Becky's enemies may decide to use her daughter to lure Becky into a trap. Cheryl's face is set into a look of grim determination. The colour has returned to her cheeks, and she looks uncannily like her mum looked when I met her thirty years ago. I guess it's only uncanny, because I'd always thought Cheryl looked far more like her dad.

"I'll be okay, you know. You don't need to worry about me. Joel is fiercely protective and wouldn't let anyone hurt me."

I suppress the thought that her boyfriend might not be a match for these villains. We don't know what they're after, but if they sent Finn to bring Becky to them, they must be after something. I'm still shocked by Becky's revelations this evening. She told us that Finn had betrayed her. Her eyes were dark and flinty as she spoke. But even if they hadn't been, I wouldn't have dreamed of referring to her crush on Finn earlier this year. Not in front of Matt. She's never said anything to me about her feelings, but I know her well enough to have seen it in her eyes and the way she reacted to him on our first case together.

Thinking of Matt seems to conjure him up, as he opens the door and pokes his head round.

"Everything okay in here?" His body follows, and he rests his hand on his daughter's shoulder.

"We're fine, Dad. Did you want a word with Joanna? I can go into the other room. I wanted to speak to Mum, anyway." She stands and gives her dad a quick hug before turning to me. "Thanks for telling me. I feel better for knowing the truth. I'm nearly sixteen. It's about time I got treated like an adult." Her tone is one of affectionate exasperation.

"You might have to wait a while for that, poppet. You'll be our little girl for a long time." Matt grins and opens the door for Cheryl. She shakes her head and disappears into the lounge. He pushes the door to, but not completely shut. "Well, this is awkward," he says, and sits on the chair just vacated by his offspring.

"Why? It shouldn't be, you know."

"Last time I saw you, I collapsed with a heart attack. Becks has been trying to keep us separate throughout my recovery, but events seem to have overtaken us. I think she has other worries just now."

"Exactly. Becky knows the reason you freaked out. At least, I assume she knows you had concerns about my integrity."

"Never your integrity, Joanna. Your judgement, maybe. We can all make mistakes though. I figured you'd made an error, and Roger was going to create merry hell. Then you showed up, and I panicked. Last time I'd seen you, we were planning strategy, then it went a bit…"

"Tits-up?" I suggest.

"Yeah, something like that. But Roger seems to have forgiven you now."

"Perhaps. He seems to have decided Becky can fill my shoes, and probably more effectively now I can't even provide lab services to him. He's dumped me, by the look of it. I'm a necessary evil who's allowed to know a minimum of information and help you and Becky when needed." I note

Matt's look of concern. "Don't worry. My involvement previously scared the shit out of me. I always wondered why I was selected, given my bastard not-at-the-time-ex-husband. Why would a secret agent entrust any work to a woman who's being beaten up regularly by her partner? It seemed unlikely, and frankly a bit stupid."

"Why did you do it?" Matt goes to the kettle and switches it on – I think in a kind attempt to give me some privacy while I answer.

"Excitement. Desperation. A need to be doing something for me. Lou only allowed me to go to work because he'd run through all the money and couldn't be arsed working himself. Working gave me a sense of escape. Coming down to meet with you was an incredible high. It was a real escape from an intolerable situation. Will had moved out by then, so I felt no guilt at leaving him extra drink money while I went away on my 'business trips'." My speech is followed by silence for a couple of minutes while Matt deals with the boiled kettle.

"Did Roger know what you were escaping from?" Matt returns to his chair with two cups of tea. I'm not a fan of tea but accept it out of politeness. Particularly as my old spy partner looks haunted.

"I suspect so. He once reassured me he'd 'take care' of Lou while I was away. All I know is that when I got back, Lou was round at someone's house, hung over after celebrating a win on the horses." I pause on seeing Matt wince. "Are you okay?" I take a sip of the tea and suppress a grimace at the bitter taste.

"I should have seen that something was wrong. I'd thought we were friends, even though you knew nothing about me other than the few details Roger allowed us to share. It was very cloak-and-dagger, but probably not that important in the grand scheme of things." He shakes his head. "You couldn't even know that I was married to a woman with whom you'd been close friends. Crazy."

"I don't know who was more shocked that day when you got home from work, when I was visiting Becky. I know you had a more severe reaction, but I felt pretty freaked out too. Of all the people to have been married to Becky…" I glance at Matt. He's looking uncomfortable. Time to move on. "Anyway, that's all water under the bridge now. I'm glad we've had a chance to chat about it, but I think the more important thing now is to protect you all from this creep who wants to harm your wife. I don't think he'd let a husband or daughter get in his way."

"Daughters. Alison comes home from uni in two weeks. It's nearly time for the Easter holidays. I don't know whether to suggest she stays there. Do these people know that I've got more than one child?"

"We can't possibly know that, but how about I send Will to pick her up? She's only in Nottingham, isn't she?"

"She's planning on getting the train. I can't take a Saturday off work so soon after returning. And obviously it would be a bad idea for Becks to go by herself. I'm not sure how Ali will react to us sending a stranger to pick her up though. Or if it's a good plan. Supposing someone turned up pretending to be Will?"

"Fair point. How about Will goes with Becky to pick her up?"

"That would work. Thanks Joanna. Let's tell them. They may not like us planning their time for them."

Our return to the lounge seems to spark a flurry of coats and goodbyes. I clear up the empty takeaway boxes, then retreat to my room, where I find an image of Glen appears to have imprinted itself on my retina.

Once in bed, I try to banish it with thoughts about the case, but that doesn't help with the end goal, which is to get some sleep. I must doze off at some point, because I wake at seven, bleary-eyed and feeling grumpy. Some people across the road are doing renovations and have started drilling already. The urge to shout out the window to shut the **** up is strong, but I need to stay here a while and can't afford to buy my own house yet. I can keep a low profile for now I suppose.

I don my dressing gown and head downstairs – coffee is an urgent need. With a large mug of it in front of me, I drop Becky a quick message.

"Are you taking Cheryl to school?"

"I will be shortly. Everything ok?" she replies less than a minute later.

"Just checking you're following rules." I follow it up with a smiley face.

"I'm not going to put Chezz at risk. We'll be fine. I'll lock my doors while driving. Don't stress."

After the chat, I finish my coffee. I can't decide what to do for the day, but once showered and dressed, I start on accounts. That lasts about five minutes. Concentration is screwed. I give a thought to cleaning up, but after years of living with Lou, old habits are hard to get rid of. The house is spotless already.

Will comes down and throws some bread in the toaster.

"Morning, Mum. Do you want some?"

"No thanks. What are you doing today?" I'm not sure what I'm hoping for, really.

"Shadowing Becky mostly. As soon as I've checked she's made it back from the school run, I'm going to sit in the car outside her house and make sure nothing untoward happens." He grins at me. "I expect I'll be bored rigid, so don't even think about complaining."

"Wouldn't dream of it."

As soon as Will's gone, it starts raining. It suits my mood though. I get my coat out and put on some hiking boots and go for a walk. With everything that's going on, it's probably not the cleverest idea to walk in the woods, but I need to commune with nature. It's a half-hour walk to get to Philips Park, and there are a few people about, mostly dog-walkers. It's a chance to relax and enjoy the gentle rainfall and the smell of greenery around me. I've been meandering for about an hour when I notice something. I'm not sure what alerts me; perhaps a footfall on fallen twigs, maybe just instinct. I walk on for a few moments – on edge now. All my senses are ready to receive any signal that I'm in danger. Now that I'm listening carefully, it's clear that someone is behind me. Should I turn around and confront him or her? It could be some random stranger going for a walk who just happens to have come into my space. The not knowing is awful.

I turn around.

"Hi Joanna." Lou stands casually with his hands in his pockets. Rainwater streams off his jacket. His wet face shines with glee at having caught up with me – alone.

I try to stay calm, ignoring the erratic thumping in my chest.

"What the bloody hell are you doing here? You know it's illegal to be within a mile of me, due to the injunction?"

"Don't give a shit, sweetheart. I've broken so many fucking laws to get here. Do you think one more makes any sodding difference?"

"Why are you doing this?" I ask.

"Because I can." He leers and grabs at me, but I dodge out of the way, and start running. I'm not sure if I can outrun him, but I'm a lot fitter than he is. My lead is maintained to the edge of the park, but I can hear him lumbering behind me. I sprint across the bridge, but I'm going faster and for longer than I'm used to, and a stitch appears, making it hard to continue. I still don't know what's at stake, but after years of being beaten up by this lout, I'm not in a hurry to find out what he wants. At the end of the bridge I keep going, but drop my pace a fraction. Houses are in sight. The rain has eased off, and there are a few residents out and about now. A builder is on the roof of one of the nearby bungalows, and I consider shouting out to him. I pause in my run and look back. Lou is still on the bridge, but he's getting nearer, and looks angry.

"Excuse me?" I struggle to shout whilst catching my breath. No one hears. I try again, taking a deep breath first. "Hello, please can you help me?"

The builder continues with his work, and I realise he's got earphones in. Shit. Lou's only twenty yards away. I shake my head and resume running. I've only been going a couple of minutes when a car pulls up next to me.

"Joanna! Are you okay?" Glen, of all people, is looking at me with concern in his eyes. "Do you want to get in?"

I almost fall into the passenger seat with relief. Glen takes one look at the furious figure of Lou glowering at the car and drives off with an excess of acceleration noise.

"Where would you like to go? I'd take you for a coffee if you wanted, but you look as though maybe you'd rather be at home?" His kindness and sensitivity reinforce my already good opinion of him.

"You're right. I could do with going home, but I'd love you to join me for a coffee there if you've got time." No way am I going to turn down a coffee with my new knight in shining armour – even if he doesn't quite match the standard physical job description.

"That sounds great. My neighbour is in with Dad at the moment, so I don't need to rush back."

"What were you doing in that part of Whitefield? If you don't mind me asking, that is."

"I'd just picked up some files from a client. Chemo doesn't stop the bills coming in, worse luck, so I need to crack on with some work. I've been feeling better this week. My final cycle ended last Monday. Still a long way to go, but it's a start. There's just this tiny increase in energy levels, you know."

"I remember. I think Will told you I've been through it myself?"

He nods, and I continue. "It took me a couple of months before I could function reasonably well, but there was definitely a slight improvement after that first cycle. It was about six months before I got my energy levels back properly, though." I'm relieved that Glen hasn't asked me about Lou. I don't feel ready to discuss that yet.

He parks the car outside my house. "Are you sure you're okay for me to come in?" he asks.

"Yes, please do. I'm not sure I want to be alone just yet." As I say it, I realise my hands are shaking and I feel sick. Reaction is setting in.

FIFTEEN

Becky

SATURDAY - THE FOLLOWING WEEK

Apart from taking Cheryl to school and picking her up again, I've not been out of the house since Sunday. It's now Saturday and the walls are closing in. I've seen quite a lot of Will the last few days. Wednesday afternoon, I saw him trailing me in the mirror on the way to the school. I phoned him when we got back and invited him to join me for the journey the next day. Cheryl was okay with it. I think she likes Will. She seems to be chattier when he's there, and is happy to talk about her day and even to mention Joel.

Now it's the weekend though, and I can't dredge up the energy to get out of bed. Matt's working an early shift in the Pharmacy today, and won't be back until lunchtime, and Cheryl is being a typical teenager and is likely to sleep until Matt's home. I pick up my Kindle from the bedside table and immerse myself in a historical romance.

I've been reading for about an hour when I get a call on my mobile. I check to see if I know the caller and see that it's Anastasia Blackstone. Instinct tells me that this is urgent. I answer the call, but barely have time to say hello, when Anastasia's voice, nearly hysterical, bursts in.

"Becky? They've got Tania. You must help me!"

It takes me a few seconds to recall that Tania is the name of her daughter, their older child.

"Tell me what happened. I'll be with you as soon as I can, but you can talk while I get ready." I put the phone on speaker and I'm already out of bed, and dragging on clean underwear, black trousers and a light blue shirt as fast as physically possible.

"We were in the park, and I turned round and she had gone. I looked everywhere for her, and then another child, an older boy of about ten or eleven, said that if I was looking for my little girl, a big man had dragged her away from the park and into his car."

"Which park were you in? Did he give a description of the man?" I finish buttoning my shirt and put my watch and rings on.

"It was Philips Park. The playground is right next to the car park. I'm so stupid, but I only took my eyes off her for one minute to push Zach on the swing." Guilt and despair mingle in her voice.

"I'm sure there was nothing you could have done. When people want to take a child, they watch like hawks for the slightest opportunity. Was the boy able to describe the man at all?" I ask again. I'm used to having to repeat questions. When in shock, people are apt to only give half an answer.

"He just said the man was big."

Knowing that Anastasia can't see me, I roll my eyes. To a ten-year-old, everyone seems big. However, I'm now dressed in record speed.

"I can be with you in five minutes. Are you back home, or are you still at the park?"

"I came home in case there were any messages and so at least Zach would be safe." She sniffs. "Please come as soon as you can. I do not know what to do."

Before setting off, I make two more calls. The first is to Will, who's instructed me to call him any time I need to leave the house. He promises to meet me at the Blackstones' house. I then phone Wendy and explain the situation.

"I don't know if this is a kidnapping, and there'll be instructions for 'no police', so let's play safe and not go in all guns blazing. You wouldn't do that anyway, but..." I trail off. I don't need to mention that Finn has occasionally endangered victims by not taking proper precautions. It happened twice, and both times I was shocked and had serious words with him. He'd sulked, but eventually apologised. Each time, my trust in him dropped a notch, but the ever-present crush always had me making excuses for his shortcomings.

"That's fine, Becky. You go round first and find out the situation. If you can bring the mum to your house at 11.30 today, I'll meet you there. It will be more discreet."

"Well, possibly, except that I have a stalker. I don't think it's connected, but I wouldn't like to put a child at risk on the strength of it." I fill her in on the events of the preceding week.

"Bloody hell, woman. You do find trouble, don't you?" The affection in her voice negates the exasperation in the words. I grin.

"A bit, yes. Perhaps we should meet at Joanna and Will's? Will is coming with me to see Anastasia anyway."

She agrees and rings off. I dive into the garage, open the front, and get in the car. Since Tuesday, we have kept the car in the garage every time we've been home. Much safer and easier, and it makes it harder for anyone to see whether we're out.

One of the first things we did after the Troy case, when I had a suspicion that I was being followed, was to change the garage door to an electronic one. So I don't need to get out of the car to shut the door; I just hit the button on my remote control. I glance around outside but can't see anyone other than the neighbours. All the same, the hairs prickle on the back of my neck. I know he's out here somewhere. But the house is locked up, and I've left Cheryl a note on her bedside table to tell her I've had to go out for work, and to remind her to stay indoors until her dad gets home. I can't afford anything bad to happen to her.

Will is outside Anastasia's house when I pull up against the kerb. I get out of the car.

"Have you been in and seen her?" I ask in a low voice.

"Not yet. I've only been here a couple of minutes. I thought I'd wait for you."

"Did your mum not want to come?"

"Mum's been busy this week – she's seeing a lot of this chap, Glen, that I met a couple of weeks ago. Oh, and trying to avoid Dad, who's evading the police and make Mum's life hell at the same time. She said she'll catch up with us later, but she'll be on hand if we need her." Will turns towards the door. "Shall we knock on?" He sounds reluctant.

I know how he feels. I've always hated missing child cases. The horrible reality of dealing with the parents can be debilitating, particularly when you can imagine how you'd feel if it was your own child.

I nod and lead the way to the front door.

Anastasia answers immediately, before I've even had time to ring the bell.

"I saw you through the window. Come in." She looks awful. Her face is streaked with mascara-infused tears. She's always seemed like the type of woman to wear make-up to take the children to the park. It's not something I would have done, but we're all different. Her eye make-up is all smudged around her eyes, where she's clearly rubbed the tears away. She leads us into the lounge where we'd been before. Her younger child, the little boy, is sitting on the floor playing with some Lego. He looks up when we come in, and then gazes at his mum.

"Mummy, when's Tania coming home?"

Her eyes fill with more tears, and she turns away from him, presumably so he won't see her upset. Her voice is only a trifle wobbly as she responds.

"She should be home later today, darling. Why don't you find Daddy and ask him to watch telly with you?"

"I assume Simon knows?" I ask, once the boy has left the room.

"Of course. He's on the computer, trying to work out where she can have got to by now, but… Oh God… maybe the police can do that. Is it safe to involve the police?"

"I have a close friend – very high up – she's a Chief Inspector. She will meet us at Will's house," I check my watch, "in about forty-five minutes. She'll be able to help without increasing any risk to your little girl."

Anastasia nods slowly. "I suppose that's okay. We just don't know what this is. Have they kidnapped her? Will we get her back?"

My phone rings. It's Wendy. I make an 'excuse me' gesture, then press *Connect*.

"Hi."

"Are you with the mum, Becky? I've got one of my sergeants at the park. Xanthe's very discreet, and has her ten-year-old nephew in tow. They've both been asking questions, and Luke, Xanthe's nephew, got talking to the lad who saw the man taking the girl."

"Wow. What did he say?"

"Luke found out the kid has a photographic memory and noted the registration of the car they took her into. We're tracing the car now, but hopefully we'll have an address soon, and we can find this poor young lass quickly."

"Fantastic. Well done. Do you still want to meet us all?" I glance at Anastasia, who's watching intently.

"I don't think so at the moment. Let's see what happens

when we get those car owner details. I'll call you if anything changes. Thanks, Becks."

I explain to Anastasia what's been discovered, and she sways, suddenly white. Will catches her and lowers her to the sofa, sitting her with her head between her knees. After a moment or two, she lifts her head.

"Thank you. It was the sudden relief."

"It's good news, but please don't get too hopeful just yet. There may be twists and turns before we find Tania. Sometimes these things are less straightforward than they first appear. It's a great start though. We at least have a lead now." I watch as she looks at me incredulously, so I sit down next to her and put my hand on her arm. "I don't want to seem cruel. Sorry. This is a hugely traumatic time for a parent, and the only way to cope with the ups and downs is to treat them with caution."

She nods. "Of course. I suppose my reaction just now indicated the importance of being calm. I will try."

"Thank you. While we wait for a call-back, can I take some details about Tania please?"

We go through the mundane, such as description, what she was wearing and any distinctive marks, then proceed through medical history, as I need to know if there are any additional risks over and above the usual. I once had a case where the abducted child was a Type-1 diabetic, and had died because the kidnappers didn't know, and we didn't get to him in time. Everyone involved in the case was devastated, and ever since, have made it a priority to know the victim's medical background. Fortunately, Tania is in good health, although if she makes it out of this safely, she's likely to have nightmares and symptoms of PTSD for the rest of her life. However, it's better than the alternative.

We're just finishing up when Wendy calls again.

"Hi Becky. We've got the car owner details, and there's a strange connection to your agency."

"That sounds odd. What is it?"

"The car is owned by a man called Peter Donaldson – stepfather to Will's daughter, Chloë. Break the news gently to Will, but meanwhile, we need to get up to Preston and find out if he's got Tania safe."

SIXTEEN

Will

SATURDAY

When Becky breaks the news to me that Chloë's stepdad might be involved with Tania's abduction, my legs nearly give way. I sit down heavily on an armchair across from Anastasia and Becky.

"Are you okay, Will?" The bearer of the news looks at me anxiously.

Judging from the faintness and nausea that are assailing me, I guess that I've gone pale. I take some deep breaths and dredge up a faint smile and a nod for the ladies. Anastasia asks for more details about the connection, but I leave Becky to do the explanations. I duck my head between my knees. I'm not the coolest guy around, but fainting at this point would really not be very professional. A moment later, the nausea passes, and I'm able to sit up. Anastasia has left the room, and Becky's watching me with concern in her eyes.

"I'm okay." I rush to reassure her. "It was just a shock and sudden fear of what he might subject Chloë to if he's involved in this."

"Of course. Anastasia's just gone to tell her husband. I think she should come with us to speak to Peter, but Simon will need to look after the little lad properly, rather than trying to bury his head in work."

"Is Wendy going to come along too?" I don't know the Chief Inspector well, but the fact that Becky trusts her so implicitly gives me confidence. A small voice in my head argues that she trusted Finn too, but I'm not totally convinced that she did. Her feelings towards him always seemed complicated.

"Wendy's going to meet us up there. She said she won't come in unless we think it's appropriate, but we can see when we get there."

Anastasia returns at that moment, accompanied by Simon.

"I want Ana to stay here with Zach. I'll come to Preston with you." He stands a little too close to me and jabs his finger into my chest. I back off a fraction.

"I understand you're angry and upset, Mr Blackstone, but we need your wife and son to stay safe. We feel she'd be better protected with us than at home here by herself. You're well placed to protect your little lad." I watch as this sinks in, and he retreats a few inches. His hand falls back to his side.

"I can't sit at home and do nothing. Can't we all come?"

Becky comes over and puts a hand on Simon's arm.

"Don't you think Zach would be happier at home with his toys, with some normality of sorts? I don't think it's healthy to subject him to the strain of that journey. Also, we need someone reliable to stay here in case the kidnappers leave a message. Please stay, Simon. I think it's the best thing you can do for Tania and Zach. Ana will come with us in case Tania is being held in Preston."

I nod as Becky finishes. Her experience in handling difficult situations shines through, as Simon concedes.

"All right. That sounds fair. But I want to be kept up to date. Ana, you'll phone me when you arrive and when anything happens, won't you?"

Anastasia nods. Her face is white, and fear shows in her

eyes. They both look haunted by the terrible possibilities. I want to promise that we'll get their little girl back safely, but I don't think it's fair to give false hope.

"Shall we go? We'll take my car. It's bigger than Becky's." Also, I don't want to risk us being followed by her stalker. The whole bloody situation is so complicated now. I'm beginning to feel paranoid that there are enemies everywhere. God alone knows how Becky feels about it – it must be even worse for her.

The roads are fairly quiet, with it being Saturday, and we make good time to Preston, getting there just before midday. I park round the corner and out of sight of the house, as Wendy instructed us to wait until she arrives in the area.

"I've just had a call from Xanthe," says Becky. "She's the sergeant who's with Wendy. They're about a mile away. They'll join us on this road and want a quick word with me and Will before we go in."

"Don't I get to know what's being said? This is my daughter we're trying to rescue, and she could be suffering while we wait." Anastasia sounds close to tears.

"This man we're going to see is my little girl's stepdad. He's not a guy I would want to go to the pub with, but I don't think he's the type to be cruel to kids. My Chloë likes him, and she wouldn't if he was horrible to her. Hold on to that for now. If she's here, she'll be safe." Talking it through, I become convinced that Tania wouldn't be here. I can't envisage Peter kidnapping a child and then bringing them to his home. If he's here, then she isn't. I didn't see his car outside, but they have a garage, and probably use it.

Ten minutes later, Wendy pulls up behind me in a black Audi. Becky and I get out, but Anastasia, as directed, stays in the car.

"Thanks Wendy." Becky goes over to her friend. I'm a bit more hesitant, but they beckon me over.

"Hi Will. Nice to see you again." Wendy smiles and we

shake hands. "This is my colleague, DS Xanthe Matthews. Xanthe, this is Will, and I think you already know Becky."

"Yes, we worked together before Becky left." There's an edge to her voice, and I wince. What did Becky do? I glance across and see that she's noticed it as well.

"We did indeed. You've probably heard a lot of things from different people. Don't believe all you hear. There was a lot that went on that day that shouldn't have happened, and a lot of mud has been thrown indiscriminately." Becky sounds calm, but I know her well enough by now to know that she's upset by Xanthe's attitude.

"Maybe. Anyway, it's irrelevant now. Wendy wants you and your colleagues to be treated as part of our team. It's unconventional, but she's the boss." Xanthe shrugs.

"Absolutely. I am indeed," Wendy says. "We're a team now, working together on this. Now, Will and Becky, I want you to go in first and see if Peter's in, and if so, what he has to say. If there's any hint that Tania's there, call us in. Meanwhile, if it's okay with you, we'll sit in your car and keep the mum company." Wendy holds out her hand for my car keys.

I hand them over reluctantly, but with a grin. "You're only getting them in case of an emergency. I don't allow anyone to drive my car, you know."

Becky and I head down the road towards Peter's house and Chloë. My heart's thumping, and I think my friend must be able to hear it, because she touches my arm briefly.

"It'll be okay. I've got a gut feeling that Tania's not here, you know."

"Thanks. So have I, but… something tells me he's involved." I rub at a spot between my eyes where a headache is beginning.

"Let's see. Do you want me to take the lead on the questions, Will? It might be easier for your future relationship."

"Sure." I manage a grateful grin before Becky rings the doorbell.

Debbie answers.

"What are you doing here? It's not your day. And who's she?" She doesn't invite us in.

"This is Becky, my colleague and friend. We're here on business. Is Peter at home?"

"He's in the study, calling the insurance company. Someone nicked his car last night."

"Has he contacted the police?" asks Becky.

"Not yet. He will do. He needs a courtesy car straight away though, so the insurance company was the priority." Debbie is defensive, perhaps a little too much so. I was married to her for three years and can tell when she's not entirely truthful. I think she's being honest up to a point, but there's something not quite kosher here.

"Is your daughter here, Mrs Donaldson?" Becky stands a little taller, and exudes authority. I don't think I've seen the change so obviously before.

"She's out at a friend's house. She's staying there for lunch."

"Do you have any other children on the premises?"

"Why the hell would we have another child here, if our own is out?" My ex-wife glares at me. "What the fuck is going on, Will? Why've you brought this miserable cow to ask us stupid questions?"

I take a deep breath and make an effort to unclench my fists. Aggression isn't going to help me find Tania. Becky casts me a reassuring glance.

"Perhaps we can come in, and then we can explain. It would help if we can speak to Peter as well." I succeed in my effort to appear calm, but inside, my stomach is doing judo with my intestines. I'm not sure who's winning, but it feels bloody uncomfortable.

Debbie reluctantly opens the door wider and steps aside so we can get in. Becky goes first and I follow.

"This isn't personal, Debs. Don't make it into more than it is."

"I don't bloody know what it is yet," she mutters, then raises her voice to direct Becky into the lounge on the right. We're grudgingly invited to sit down, but she doesn't offer us a drink. "I suppose I'd better see if Peter's free. Stay here."

It feels odd sitting in my ex-wife's living room when my daughter is out of the house. I've been here a few times, but always to see Chloë. Becky and I sit in companionable silence until Debbie returns a moment later, her new husband following her into the lounge.

"What's going on?" He directs his question to me, anger and distrust in his tone, but it's Becky who replies.

"A child was abducted this morning. Your car was used. The child was dragged into your car and taken away."

"Well, as my wife no doubt informed you, my car was stolen last night. Now get out of my house."

His anger and aggression are disproportionate to the information he's just received. If he'd been totally innocent, I would have expected shock, or even horror, that they had used his vehicle in such a way.

"As you're clearly innocent, you won't object to us having a look around your house, will you?" Becky smiles.

"I do fucking object. Get the police and a sodding search warrant if you believe I'm lying."

"Oh, if we find you're lying, the police will be here before you've had time to contact your solicitor. Come on, Will. I think Mrs Donaldson would know if there's a strange child in the house." Becky nods at Debbie and walks into the hall. I glance at my ex and see fear and defiance in her eyes. She obviously knows something, but at this stage it's hard to tell how much. I follow Becky, and we go outside.

"So, what do you think?" I ask as we head back to the car.

"Tania's not there. If you're a crook, and you're allowing your car to be involved in an abduction, you wouldn't bring the victim to your own house, in case your car gets traced. Having said that, I'm damn sure he's involved in some way. Why would a kidnapper go all the way to Preston to nick the car that they're going to use to abduct a child in North Manchester? It doesn't make sense. There are plenty of other cars in the vicinity."

"They might hold a grudge against Peter and want to implicate him. Hell, I'd want to bloody implicate him – he's a git, and I can't bear that he's got access to Chloë." My fists clench.

"I get that. I didn't take to him either, but I still think he's directly involved." Becky pauses before asking me a question to which I have absolutely no answer: "Why do all paths in our current cases lead to Preston?"

SEVENTEEN

Becky

SATURDAY

The journey home is quiet. Before leaving Preston, I tasked Wendy and Xanthe with finding out as much as possible about Peter. I'm convinced he's involved in this. Will and I had a quick check around the back of their house and in nearby garages to check for any signs of either the car or a missing child, but there were no indications of either, so we had to leave without a real lead.

Will is driving. I think being at Chloë's house and not seeing her has upset him. I'm sure it's not great for his relationship with Chloë's mum and stepdad either to accuse them of child abduction. The visit didn't go well. At least I've been able to offer Anastasia some hope that we're on the right track, but she's sitting in silence in the back, her face pale and taut, and wearing an expression of anguish that tears at my heart. If it had been Cheryl or Alison, how would I feel? I know I would be beyond distraught. The stab of pain I feel, just thinking about it, prompts me to turn my head towards the back of the car.

"We'll find her, Anastasia, I promise. Today's visit has given us some hints, and we're following them. Have you spoken to Simon yet?"

"No. I suppose I should, but I do not think I could get the words out."

"Do you want me to call him?"

"Please, if you would."

I have his number in my phone already, so make the call. He sounds frantic when he answers.

"Becky! Why are you calling me? Is Ana okay? Did you find Tania?"

"We've not found her yet, but there are some clues that we're following in conjunction with the police. Ana's with me, but she didn't feel able to break the news that we've not got Tania back yet. I don't suppose you've had any communications from the kidnappers?"

"Nothing. It's bloody torture. Can I have a word with Ana?"

"Of course." I hand the phone to her.

"Simon? Is Zach okay?" She sniffs and seems to make an effort to pull herself together. I can't hear the other side of the conversation, but a moment later, she says, "Fine. I'll see you soon." She returns the handset to me.

"Did he have anything important to say?"

"My son's playing, but he keeps asking when his sister will be home. Oh God, when's this going to end?"

With a bit of contortion, I reach behind to take her hand.

"Let's get you home, and then Will and I can follow up on some of the clues we've got. We'll be in constant touch with you and Simon, and any information on either side will get shared immediately. Okay?"

"Thanks." She removes a tissue from her handbag and blows her nose. "Yes, of course we'll be in touch if there's anything."

An hour later, I'm sitting in my kitchen with Will and Joanna. Matt is back from work and watching football in the lounge. Cheryl is in her room doing some homework. Both popped in to say hello and then left us alone to talk.

"What did you make of my ex-daughter-in-law?" Joanna asks me as she takes a chocolate biscuit from the plate in the middle of the table. Her expression is neutral at the moment, but I don't think that will last.

"She was frightened. I'm not sure whether it was of her husband, or of what she knows about his activities, but there's something not right there."

"Silly bitch." The neutrality didn't last, and her eyes are filled with anger now. "She should have stayed with Will, shouldn't she, instead of slutting behind his back? If she'd kept her bloody knickers on, she'd be fine now. Settled down with a decent man, instead of that slimy prick."

"I guess you don't like Peter either then?" I pick up a pen and open the A4 pad I have in front of me. "Shall we make some notes and see what we've got?"

Will reaches across – he's seated opposite me and next to his mum – and extracts the pen from my grip. Joanna pulls the pad across the table and settles it in front of her son.

"Let me do the writing, Becky. I've seen your scrawl. We need to be able to read this afterwards." Will smirks.

"Bloody cheek. Go on then. I'm happy not to write. I seem to recall you didn't like the way I lay things out, either."

"Well, I didn't want to rub salt in the wound, but now you mention it…" He draws a neat table on the pad, using the edge of his wallet as an impromptu ruler. "Right, so we've got suspects, motive, opportunity, and where each one might hold Tania hostage."

"Suspects – I suppose the first one then is Peter, because it was his car that took her, even if it did get 'stolen'. Motive – no idea." I look at Will. "You probably know him better than the rest of us. Why would he do something like this?"

"Money? He seems to have a lot of posh stuff, and I reckon that house they're in is well above his pay grade. I always thought he had a bit of a dodgy side, so maybe he takes handouts to get involved in shady dealings – like allowing his car to be used for an abduction."

"So, if that's the case, it's not personal against the Blackstones, and the slimy git's probably not holding her hostage," says Joanna.

"I'd guess it depends on how much money he's being paid. And who knows what's going on in the background?" Will frowns. "I feel as though I'm missing something."

"What does Peter do for a living?" I ask. "They have a lovely house."

"He's an accountant," says Will.

"That's not a badly-paid job. If he's independent, he could make a killing on that, depending on who his clients are."

"Shit! That's it." Will turns to his mum. "Do you remember what I told you about my conversation with Glen? About the racket going on involving Eric Ulyanov?"

"Yeah, but surely there are enough accountants in the Manchester area, even ones who are dodgy, without expanding into Preston?" She looks at me. "What do you think?"

"Okay. Suppose, just suppose, Eric Ulyanov is looking to get his hands on a Fabergé egg. He wants some handy accomplices in the area where the heist is going to take place, so he enlists Peter, who he might have heard of through some of his other cronies as being always ripe for a payout."

"Interesting theory, but it sounds far-fetched, even for you." Joanna gives me a quick grin. I stick my tongue out at her. "Very mature, Becky."

"You deserved it. Come on, back to the case. I know it's far-fetched, but is it possible? Will, what do you think?"

"I reckon it's possible. Peter is almost certainly dipping his toes into several unsavoury things. I don't think he'd stop at kidnapping, even if he's only on the edges of it." Will writes on the pad. *Peter. Money. Allowing his car to be used.* "The only thing is, I can't see where he'd keep Tania. He wouldn't take her to his house because of Chloë. There were no signs of her being there."

"Maybe there's a plan to move her to his house after a few days when the fuss has died down?" I hope for Ana's sake that we've sorted this long before then, but I don't need to say it. The look of horror on the faces of both Will and Joanna shows they're in complete agreement.

"Bloody hell. We'll find her before then. That whole family is being more traumatised with each passing hour." Joanna looks at the pad in front of Will. "Who else have we got?"

"I guess without the car, Eric is the most obvious suspect. We know he's got a grudge against Anastasia, and he's a right villain. He seems to have his fingers in all sorts of dodgy pies. I'm just wondering if Tania would know him. Would she have got into a car willingly with him? She's about eight, isn't she? Old enough to know not to go off with strangers." I think back to my car journey, picking the kids up from school. "She seemed like a bright kid when I met her."

Will picks up his phone. "Shall I give the mum a call and find out if Tania knew Eric?"

I nod, and he makes the call. He speaks for a moment or two, then disconnects.

"Ana is sure that Eric's involved somehow. She said he's met the kids a few times. But he's been making threats ever since she stopped sleeping with him."

"Why the hell didn't she mention that sooner?" Joanna

frowns. "You probably didn't need to traipse up to bloody Preston."

"Yeah, but I still think Peter's involved. He has to be. Otherwise, why would Tania have been taken in his car? I just can't believe that little slimeball is stepdad to my daughter!"

"We can choose our friends; we can't choose the step-parents to our children, unfortunately. Have a biscuit." I push the plate towards Will. Poor guy. It's an awful situation for him. I can't imagine how I'd feel if I was in his position. "So, do we only have two suspects?"

"Given the information we have about Anastasia, do you think it could be some crazy Russian mafia gang?" Joanna grabs the last biscuit from the plate after her offspring has removed the penultimate one.

"I hope not. It's much easier to trace people we know than unknown gangs, but let's see what we've got. Will, do you want to scribe? Motive: connection with Ana's Russian cousins, who may have been causing anarchy in the Russian underground. It's pretty tenuous. Opportunity is even more so. We have no idea who they are or where they are, let alone where they might have taken Tania."

"I agree," says Will. "We need to keep them on the list, but let's hope it's not them."

My phone vibrates on the table. I check the screen and answer the call.

"Hi Wendy, is there any news?"

"Hi Becky. We've got a tap on Peter Donaldson's phone. He was speaking to someone in Russian. I know Roger asked you to learn it. How have you got on?"

"It's not the easiest language to learn, but I've got the basics and some vocabulary. Is it a file you can send over, or do you need me to come in?"

"Under the circumstances, it will be better if I come to you. Are you at home?"

"Yes. Joanna and Will are here too." I smile at my partners' curious expressions. I know how frustrating it is when you can only hear half a conversation.

"Great. Get the kettle on, love. I'm not far away. I can be there in ten."

I relay the gist of the conversation to the others, and confess that I've spent a lot of my free time over the last couple of weeks battling with an online Russian language course.

"How on earth does Peter know Russian?" Will looks at me with a puzzled expression. "I get why *you*'d learn it, but frankly he doesn't seem like the sort of bloke to want to learn a difficult language for the fun of it."

I'd left out the information that it was Roger who had asked me to learn it – he'd wanted me to keep that a secret for some strange reason. Letting Will and Joanna believe I was crazy enough to learn for fun seems the easier option. Will's right, though. Peter doesn't seem the type.

"I would say his reasons are definitely nefarious. But I guess we'll find out more shortly. Wendy will be here soon."

EIGHTEEN

Joanna

SATURDAY

Frankly, I don't know if I'm more shocked that Becky's been learning Russian on the quiet (and I have a sneaking suspicion there's a reason she's not shared that information with us), or that my granddaughter's slimy stepdad can speak Russian. I guess we'll find out his level of proficiency any minute now, because that's the doorbell.

Becky gets up to answer it, and returns a moment later, followed by Wendy, with whom I exchange a friendly smile. I haven't told her yet about the encounter with Lou in the park, as I've been… shall we say, a bit busy with Glen over the last few days. He's such a lovely guy, but I won't go into that just now; it's enough to say that I feel protected when I'm with him. After the shitty time I had with Lou, Glen is a novel experience.

I shelve the thought for now, though, because Wendy is sitting at the table opening her laptop. She glances over at me.

"Everything all right with you, Joanna?"

"All good, thanks." I hesitate, but decide to mention Lou after all. "My delightful ex-husband showed up in the park the other day when I went for a walk. He must have been following me. He was quite aggressive, but I got away with a little help from a friend." I feel my cheeks go pink. Bloody hell. I'm not a teenager – this is ridiculous. Thankfully, Wendy doesn't appear to notice.

"We're still trying to track him down, but he's being elusive. Do you want us to keep a watch on you in case he shows up again?"

The thought of being under surveillance makes me shiver.

"I'd rather not. My friend – the one who rescued me – will come with me if I go out for a walk again. We could call you if we see him and give you a location so you could catch him. Would that work?"

"I would hope so. You might need to engage him in discussion until we got there. It could still put you in some danger."

"I'm prepared to take the risk." I glance at Becky, who's just placed a fresh mug of coffee in front of me. "Thanks, hen."

Once everyone has a hot drink, Becky sits down.

"I've told Will and Joanna that I've been learning Russian. Do you have the recording, or, better still, the transcript with you?"

"I've got the recording on my laptop. Do you want me to play it now?" Wendy presses a few keys on her laptop. The result sounds like gibberish to me, but Becky is frowning with concentration. She scribbles on the notepad that she's snaffled from Will. The call lasts about a minute and a half. I glance at the pad when it's finished. Becky's written about three words. Her handwriting is too bad for me to read upside-down.

"Did you understand any of that?" I ask, hoping she'll enlighten us.

She frowns. "Just a bit. It was very quick. You know what language courses are like. They say everything slowly and clearly. When you come to listen to a real conversation, it's completely different."

"Do you want me to play it again?" Wendy smiles at Becky. "I can repeat it as many times as you need."

Twenty minutes later, I've lost track of the number of repeats, but Becky now has a few sentences written down.

"Okay, I think this is the gist of the conversation. Peter is speaking to someone called Boris. They're quite formal with each other, and it doesn't sound as though they know each other well."

"How can you tell?" I interrupt, despite my eagerness to know the full conversation.

"The words are slightly different depending on whether they're used formally or informally. Anyway, they're discussing a child – it sounds as though they're talking about Tania, as they mention food and drink to keep her alive, and a house in Bolton where they're keeping her." Becky gives Wendy a grim look. "We need to locate that house, because Peter and Boris have created a code. If the police come to arrest Peter, he sends Boris a message, and they'll lock the little girl in the cellar and leave her to starve to death. We can't let that happen."

"Of course not," says Wendy. "We're not going to put her in any danger. Now I know where to target the search, I'll get my team to review all the traffic cameras in Bolton until we can pin that car down to a specific location. Let's see if we can find her that way. I assume there was nothing else of any interest in their conversation?"

"Only a discussion about payment. Boris told Peter he'd get the money as soon as the family was co-operating. Peter asked if they'd been contacted yet, and Boris said it would happen soon. Whatever that means – soon could mean in twenty minutes, or in a couple of days."

"It's obviously not happened yet, otherwise Anastasia would have called us," says Will.

"True." I stand up. "I think someone ought to tell her what's going on. Bloody hell; I can only begin to imagine what she's going through."

"Sit down. I'll phone her. I don't want her to get too excited for the moment." Becky waves me back to my seat. "Let's not get her hopes up too much. I'm not a hundred per cent confident that I've interpreted correctly."

She makes the call and gently tells Anastasia that we have a lead and hope to get her more news later today. It's all very calm and low-key, but I'm buzzing. I want to get to Bolton and have a look around, even though I know we don't really have enough information to get started yet.

"While Wendy's got her troops looking for number plates, there must be something we can do, surely?" I send a pleading look to Will and Becky.

"I've got a hunch that Eric Ulyanov is involved in this somehow. He's the one who told Ana about her family in Russia. He's the leader of the accountancy ring, whatever it is they're doing." Becky turns to Will. "Do you think you could pump your friend Glen for a bit more info on that? It sounds as though he was on the fringes, but got blocked when they realised he had some integrity."

I feel myself going warm again, even before Will says blandly, "Mum might have a better opportunity. She's spending quite a bit of time with Glen at the moment."

Three pairs of eyes are gazing with interest at my face, which feels like it's burning.

"Good luck to you, Joanna," says Wendy with a smile. "Is that the friend who rescued you from Lou?"

"Yes." I force my attention to the job at hand. "I'll have a chat with him about Eric and see if he can tell us anything else, but I'm sure he'd have told Will everything he could think of." I can see Will's about to tease me, and I hold my hand up.

"Enough. I said I'll ask him. Now what else can we do? Is it time for us to have a chat with this Eric chappie?"

"Not yet," Becky looks at Wendy. "Could you check him out in the files, please? See what there is and get back to us."

"I've left Xanthe at the station, running traces on everyone remotely concerned. Eric is one of them, so I'm expecting a call from her shortly."

The phone doesn't quite ring on cue, because Wendy sends her pal a message, but a minute later the desired call arrives. We have to wait patiently (or impatiently in Becky's case, as she's tapping her fingers on the table), but eventually Wendy disconnects and smiles at us.

"Well, that was fascinating. Eric is an ex-con. He did time in his twenties for fraud, and seems to have made the most of his time inside, learning tricks from his fellow-cons. He's managed to stay on the edges of legality, exploiting loopholes and appearing to be reasonably clean, but when Xanthe dug deeper, she found there's a file on him that requires special permission to access. She's applied for it, but knowing how long these things can take, it might be an idea if Becky gets on to Roger and sees what he knows."

"I can do that." Becky looks thoughtful. "I guess Eric's under special ops. He seems to have fingers in enough pies that MI5, MI6 and any other security forces might be interested – particularly if he's dabbling in Russian affairs."

"Yes, there's too much at risk not to keep a close eye on people like him," says Wendy. "But it doesn't get us any closer to finding that little girl."

Becky's phone pings. She glances at it, then picks it up and looks more closely.

"It's Anastasia. They've had a message from the kidnappers. She wants me and Joanna to go round, looking innocent and unofficial." She grins at me briefly. "I'll get my jeans and hoody on. Have you got something equivalent? We can pop into yours on the way, so you can get changed."

"I've got jeans. I don't really do hoodies, but I'm sure I can find a casual sweater to throw on." I don't want to be gaudy, but also not too maudlin. I have a burgundy woollen tunic that will go well with skinny jeans and boots. Hopefully casual enough to deceive the bad guys into thinking Anastasia just has a couple of friends visiting for support.

Fifteen minutes later, we're ringing Anastasia's doorbell. Becky's parked a little way up the road, out of sight of the house, in case the kidnappers are watching and recognise her car.

The woman who answers the door is tall and would be attractive in normal circumstances, but currently her face is drawn and haggard, and she looks much older than the thirty-five years we have documented in our files.

"You had better come in. We do not have conversations on doorsteps any more."

We step inside and follow Anastasia into a plush-looking lounge.

"Here you go. I received an email. I have printed it out." She hands Becky a sheet of A4 paper. No one is invited to sit down.

I wait a moment for Becky to read the message, then as soon as I see her eyes lift, I grab it from her hands. Her expression is troubled. I lower my gaze to the paper.

'We've got your little girl. You've got money. Get us a million quid and you can have your kid back. If you're good, we'll leave you alone after that. We'll give you three days to get the dosh together. You'll get another email with more details of where to bring it. Don't get the cops involved or you'll never see your kid again.'

There are no clues in the email address – it's a jumble of letters and numbers. Will may be able to extract some meaning from it. I take out my phone, photograph the message, and send it via WhatsApp to my clever son.

"What are you doing?" Anastasia's voice is sharp from fear and suspicion.

"You've met Will, I believe?" I wait for her to nod and see the tension in her face ease a fraction. "He may be able to trace the email address. He's brilliant with computers." I add an explanatory message in my phone and send that to Will too. While Anastasia is assimilating that, I also forward the photographed message to Becky with a brief text saying, '*For Wendy?*'

Becky glances at her phone, then nods at me.

"We need to get working on this, Anastasia. We're hoping to get you reunited with your daughter long before those three days are up. Meanwhile, please can you pretend to be getting some money together? You should reply to the email if it allows you to do so. It's important to negotiate, otherwise they might think they can get more money from you in the future." Becky hesitates, then asks, "How much could you afford?"

"I do not know. Simon would know this. At a guess, if we sell investments, maybe fifty thousand, or a little more." She disappears for a moment, and then returns, several shades paler. "We have nothing. My husband's business has been struggling, and he has sold shares and gone into debt to rescue it. He says we are on the verge of bankruptcy." She sits heavily on the couch and drops her head into her hands. "Oh, God! What are we going to do?"

My heart goes out to her. I've struggled enough with debt over the years, thanks to my bastard ex. That was without the added complication of a kidnapped child on top, with a hefty ransom needed to rescue her. I sit next to Anastasia and put my arm around her thin shoulders.

"We'll rescue your little girl, I promise." All the same, a lead weight sits in my stomach. How can I make a promise like that? Wendy's doing her best, but there are so many variables; so many things that could go wrong.

Becky is more practical.

"Simon needs to go into the bank and explain the situation. I'll type a letter for him to give to the bank manager."

"If you're going to rescue Tania anyway, why do we need to go to the bank?" The question seems a fair one.

"Two reasons. First, we need to convince the kidnappers that you're doing all you can to pay the ransom. Second, they may have links with the banking staff. Let's not take chances." Becky pauses. "Erm, if it's okay with you, can we have a look at replying to the email to see if we can get the figure down a bit? Again, it will convince them you're serious about paying, enabling us to concentrate on a rescue."

Anastasia leads us into back into the large entrance hall, and then to a little office on the other side of the staircase. There's a computer and printer on top of a mahogany desk. She moves the leather swivel chair aside and turns on the screen before typing in a password. The email application is open on the screen, with the offending email taking centre stage.

"What should I say?" she asks Becky, who stares thoughtfully at the screen for a moment.

"How about, '*Please don't hurt my little girl. We can't possibly afford that sort of money. We may be able to get a loan for thirty thousand.*' Does that sound reasonable?"

"It sounds like the sort of thing I might say, but I do not think we can even get that sum of money together."

"If we start lower than that, they may feel they're not going to get paid. Frankly, I'd rather offer more, but I don't want to get you into trouble either." Becky looks at me. "What do you think?"

Shit. Why is she asking me? She's the ex-policewoman. There's a glint in her eye, though, and I won't challenge her in front of our client. I consider what we know, and what we don't know. My gut is telling me it's not about the money, but I can't pinpoint why.

I nod at Becky. "Offer the thirty. See what comes back. Hopefully, it will buy us some time. We have a lot of checks going on in the background."

Becky agrees, and Anastasia sits down to type. She shows us the finished email. Give or take a word or two, it reads exactly as suggested by Becky.

"That looks fine," I say.

"Go for it." Becky puts her hand on our host's shoulder. "Hit *Send*."

With the email gone, we offer words of reassurance, then take our leave. We say nothing more until we're back in the car.

"Bloody hell!" I fasten my seatbelt. "Do you think we've done the right thing?"

"Let's hope so." Becky's tone is grim.

NINETEEN

Becky

Joanna and I head back to my house, where Will is chatting with Wendy and Matt, and Cheryl is putting the kettle on.

"That's good timing. I could do with a coffee. Thanks, Cheryl." My grin gets even broader when she produces chocolate digestives. I sink on to a chair and grab a biscuit before noticing that everyone is looking expectantly at me. "Joanna can fill you in. I need to eat." I get a glare from her, but she gives them the gist of our visit to Ana.

She finishes by saying, "We sent you the email, so you've seen what they said. Any thoughts?"

"I've checked the email address," says Will. "It won't be easily traceable. I've sent it over to Roger to ask if any of his experts can help. We're a bit time-critical here; otherwise I'd do it myself. I think I can better spend the time searching Bolton for likely places."

"I still think Eric is our best lead. Is anyone following him?" I ask Wendy, as everyone else involved is sitting in my kitchen.

"Not directly. We don't have the resource, but also it could put the child at risk if he's feeling pressured. His mobile number is being monitored, and we're checking records."

Wendy looks at me. "Come on, Becky. If you were in charge of the case, you wouldn't want to risk him seeing that he's a suspect, either."

"No, I suppose not. I just don't want that little girl to be away from her mum for another day. It doesn't seem right if we've got a hunch that we know who has her."

"She's not at his house though. We know from your translation that she's in Bolton. Eric lives in Whitefield." Wendy reaches over and clasps my hand. "Be patient. We'll get her back and we'll do it safely. We're still waiting for Xanthe to get access to those files. I've called Roger and asked him to help and he's working on it, but it's a bit of a challenge to get things moving on a Saturday night." She looks at her watch. "No – Sunday morning. Did you know it's nearly 3am?"

I finish the coffee and put down my mug with a sudden burst of decisiveness.

"Right, why don't we get a couple of hours' sleep, and then at first light we'll go and suss out Bolton. We've enough space for you all to get your heads down."

Everyone agrees. It's been a bloody long day, and nothing is going to be achieved by staying awake all night.

It's eight-thirty by the time we re-convene at the table with coffee and toast. I look at Wendy, who's perusing her phone. "Have your team had any success with those cameras?"

"Locating the path of the car, you mean? Let me check now before we head out." Wendy makes the call to the station. "Any news? Yes... okay... that sounds promising... obviously... brilliant, thanks. Yes, we'll head over there now. Very casual and discreet. Thanks again, Xanthe. Great work. Have you had any sleep yet? No? Then go home. We'll catch up later." She disconnects, smiling. "They've pinned the car down to an area between Raikes Lane and Leverhulme Park. So we can go down there and search. I suggest we go in two cars and try to make it look as though we're out for an early morning stroll. Perhaps Becky and Cheryl, Matt and me, and Joanna and Will?"

"I don't want Cheryl coming along. We don't know what we're going to find. She can stay here with Matt and help with any information we need while we're there. I'll pair with you, Wendy. We only need to go in one car, but if we park near the big shops on Raikes Lane it'll be easy enough to wander from there fairly unobtrusively."

My younger daughter looks a bit disappointed at not being allowed to join us, but the promise of being able to help clearly pacifies her. She's not stupid, and understands that danger can come from unexpected directions. I'm sure she's not forgotten the conversation we had at Joanna's house the other day.

Matt meets my gaze, then turns his attention to Cheryl.

"Come on, poppet. If Mum keeps her phone on, we'll track her on the computer. That way, we can see where she's up to and provide support if she needs any."

"Okay. That's cool. Be careful though, Mum. That bloke might be around somewhere and waiting for you to go out. Even if he's got nothing to do with this little girl that's missing."

"That's why I'm pairing with Wendy." I force a grin to hide the fact that my insides have turned a bit jelly-like.

Twenty minutes later, Will's parked up outside Aldi. We decided on only one car with just the four of us coming here. As agreed, Joanna and her son head off first to Raikes Lane. It's only a short walk from here. Wendy and I pop into Aldi, which has just opened, to get some supplies. She has a small rucksack with her, and we fill it with the sort of snack food a child would like – milkshake, apple juice, chocolate, cheese strings and *pain au chocolat* – easy ways to get energy into Tania quickly if we find her.

By the time we leave, the others are out of sight, but during the car journey we agreed on routes. Wendy and I head to the edge of Leverhulme Park to check out the warehouses near the entrance.

As it's Sunday morning and not all the shops are open yet, the area is fairly quiet, but not completely without activity. There are several buildings on the road leading to the park, and a few further back, off the road. These look more likely candidates for hiding places for kidnappers, but it's not impossible for them to have paid a large sum of money to a business owner to hide Tania in plain sight; maybe upstairs over an open garage.

While we're wandering along the road quietly discussing possibilities, my phone pings at the same time as Wendy's. I check it. There's a new WhatsApp group containing the four of us and Matt. I'm pleased to see Cheryl's not included. Will has sent a message.

'*Lots of likely buildings but no car. How r u getting on?*'

"Shall I reply, or do you want to?" I ask Wendy.

"Go for it, Becks."

I grin and start typing.

'*Same here, but there's still time. Not checked all the streets yet.*'

"*Where r u*'

His reply irritates me. He's a lovely boy, but I need to teach him to use punctuation in his texts. It's a pet hate of mine.

'*We're at the entrance to Leverhulme Park – by the river. Are you going to join us, or search round there a bit more?*' I make sure my message is fully punctuated and grammatically correct.

'*We'll come to u*'

I try not to grind my teeth. Wendy reads the messages through and laughs.

"You'd forgive him the abbreviations if he ended his

sentences with a full stop or question mark, wouldn't you?" She shakes her head in obvious amusement.

"Possibly. You know me too well." I grin back. "So what now? Do we wait here for them or explore a bit more?"

Her face turns serious as she peruses the yard to the right of us.

"We'll wait. There's a car there that looks remarkably like Peter's 'missing' vehicle. Let's not rush in without being careful. We could put that little girl's life at risk. We need to get closer and check that registration plate."

"Agreed." I look to where she pointed and see a car parked opposite a commercial storage facility. I glance around where we're standing – at the end of a bridge on the threshold of the park. "If we edge round a bit, do you think we might get a better view of the building without being seen ourselves? There's a fair bit of foliage further on."

"That's not a bad idea. We're a little too visible lingering here, anyway. I'll message the others to let them know where we are."

Concealed by bushes and trees, Wendy and I have a good enough view of the storage facility where we believe Tania may be located. I extract a pair of miniature binoculars from my handbag, and grin at my friend.

"Do you want the first look?" I offer them to her.

"Go on then. Thanks." She takes the binoculars and raises them to her eyes. After a bit of fiddling with the focus, she surveys the area. "Becky, have a look at the upstairs window. Not the one directly above the shutters, but two to the left of that." She hands me back my kit, and I have a look.

I check out some of the other windows first to orientate myself and to provide a baseline. I need to see what's normal in those upstairs rooms. Mostly they seem to be offices, although there's an area that looks like a lounge or common room, and another room that's almost certainly a kitchen.

Finally, shifting to the window in question, I can see very little because it seems to be boarded up. There's intact glass in the frame, but inside that is a panel of plywood or some such cheap wood that can be easily obtained and nailed to a wall. I lower the binoculars.

"I see what you mean. Why board up one window when the glass is unbroken? It raises interesting questions."

"What questions?" Joanna appears beside me and reaches for the binoculars. Will is a few steps behind her.

I direct her to look initially at the building as a whole, then focus in on a few windows, before fixing her gaze on the window to the left and above the shutters. I wait for a moment or two as she follows my instructions.

"Bloody hell! Do you think she's in there? That room that's boarded up?" Joanna turns to look at me, then offers Will the binoculars. He waves them aside.

"I don't need those things to see that one window has boards across the inside. Some of us have young eyes." He looks smug. I refrain from retaliation, but store it up for future use.

"So what do we now?" I ask Wendy.

"I call for discreet backup, and then we go in," she says. Her expression is grim, but there's a hint of excitement in her voice. I think she's been office-based for a little too long – the perils of seniority – someone else is always available to do the dirty work. She makes the call and advises we need to wait for her team to get into place.

"Should we all go in?" I look around at our little group. "If there are people in there, it might be useful to have the extra support, and one of us could look for Tania while the others deal with…" I trail off. I'd rather not spell out what we might need to deal with – there's already enough anxiety in this situation.

Wendy pauses for a moment before answering. "Yes, I think

that's probably best, unless one of you would prefer to wait out here and message us if there's any action out here?" She looks mostly at Joanna, who nods and looks resigned.

"I can do that, I guess."

I hate waiting. I always have. Action is much preferable, and this still feels too much like the trauma of last summer – going in for a rescue and not knowing what we'll find. Obviously, on this occasion, we hope we're going to find an unguarded little girl, but I'd feel a lot happier if the car known to be involved was not parked outside the building we're about to raid. My mouth is dry and my heart is hammering so loud I reckon Tania could hear it, but no one comments. I glance round at my friends and colleagues, and see evidence that they're as nervous as I am. Will runs his hand around the back of his neck and pulls at the top of his polo shirt as if it's constricting his breathing. Joanna runs her tongue over her lips. I guess I'm not the only one with a dry mouth. Only Wendy looks more excited than nervous, but even she keeps checking her phone.

After several long moments, her phone pings. She glances at it and looks up with a smile.

"They're in place. It's time for us to go in."

TWENTY

Will

SUNDAY

The women are all so calm. Maybe Mum's nervous. She's not done this sort of thing much either, and now has her own special task of being a lookout. This is our second time, but I'm not sure it gets any easier. I tell myself that a little girl's life is at stake. It could so easily be my own daughter. That brings difficult thoughts too. She's in the care of the man whose car is involved in the kidnapping. My heart rate increases yet another notch. I need to focus. We're moving towards the building, and are about to lose the cover of the trees, when there's some action below. The shutters open and three men emerge from the front entrance. They close the shutters again and head towards the car – Peter's car. A moment later, it's gone. Wendy speaks to one of her colleagues asking for the car to be discreetly followed, but our job has just become a lot safer and easier. After standing still watching the men leave, we can now go in knowing there are three fewer people watching over the little girl. Mum will let us know if the car comes back while we're inside.

I'm hoping that those three men were the only ones in the building, and whilst I wouldn't want a child of that age to be left alone in normal circumstances, it would be great if that's the status right now. Meanwhile, Wendy's beckoning for us to follow her. We take a circuitous route to the front entrance, keeping to the edges of walls and shadows where possible. But if someone's watching, we're probably behaving strangely enough to raise alarms. When we get near the entrance, Becky asks the question that's been in my head for the last few minutes but which I haven't been brave enough to voice.

"How do we get in? Do you want to force the shutters?"

"I think so. Then, if we need backup, the troops can get in easily and quickly. I know there's a disadvantage that if those men come back, they'll see pretty fast that there's a problem." Wendy grimaces, but bends down and fiddles with the padlock on the shutters. Her fiddling is successful, because a moment later, she's raising them to reveal the front door.

Wendy's lock-picks come in handy again, and in a very short time the door is open. The lights are off inside, but it's bright enough with the early morning sunshine streaming through the glass in the door.

We're in a small reception area – empty due to it being Sunday, I assume. A lift and staircase are within a few metres, and corridors flow from the reception area to the left and right.

I've remained quiet so far, happy for Wendy to take the lead, but while she's looking around the reception, opening drawers in the desk that faces the door, I speak up. My anxiety to get this over with is taking over, and Wendy's calm perusal of the area is stretching tension to the limits. What if someone's been watching and has called those men back? I'm not keen to wait for that to happen. I might be the only man in the group and a black belt in various martial arts, but at heart I'm a wimpy nerd.

"Shall we go upstairs? The boarded window was above here and a couple of windows across." I turn as if looking at the building, and then point in the direction of the room we want. "It will be that way. Let's use the stairs. I think it will be easier to get our bearings at the top, rather than coming out of a lift."

By unspoken agreement, we're all as quiet as possible on the stairs. I'm sure I'm not the only one who's wondering if the men would leave their young hostage alone in a big building. When we get to the landing, Wendy takes the lead again, beckoning us silently to follow her along the magnolia-coloured corridor. Windows looking out to the back of the building light the way. I glance out, but all seems quiet immediately outside. A little further afield, on an otherwise deserted backstreet, there's a van. My eyes are not quite sharp enough to see who's inside, but it doesn't appear to be empty. I point it out to Wendy, and she nods. I interpret the gesture to be confirmation that her team is waiting inside that vehicle.

The first door along the corridor is open, and the room is empty, but the second — the one we believe Tania to be in — is locked. There's still no sign of anyone around, but my mouth is getting drier by the minute; in contrast to my hands, which are really clammy. It's as well that Wendy is the one unlocking doors. My hands would be too slippery to operate the lock-picks.

Inside, the room is dark from the boarded window. The only light is coming from the door we've just opened. Despite the dimness, it's easy to see the little girl crouched on a mattress in the corner of the room opposite the door. In another corner is a bucket, covered over with a square of wood. Next to the mattress is an empty plate and a cup. The girl looks scared at first, but I shoulder open the door further to let in more light, and Becky crouches down next to the mattress.

"Hi Tania. Do you remember me? I'm Becky. I gave you and your brother and your mum a lift home a couple of weeks ago."

Tania nods and reaches out a hand to Becky, who takes it, then envelops the child in a hug.

"Shall we get you out of here?" Becky swaps the hug back to a handhold and pulls Tania to her feet. She's a bit wobbly at first. I doubt she's had enough to eat or drink for the last 24 hours. It's a bloody miracle we've found her so fast. Hopefully, there won't be too many lasting effects, but the important thing for now is to get her home.

"Are you okay with walking? I can carry you if you like. I'm Will. Becky's friend."

Tania shrinks back against the only one of us she knows and shakes her head.

"I can walk," she whispers.

"Great. Let's go." I give a quick glance to the other adults in the room; a silent reminder that we may not be alone for long. We make it to the bottom of the stairs before the front door opens. My phone pings but there's no time to check it. I don't recognise the man who comes in. Fortunately, there's only one, and he's short, overweight and balding.

"Who the fuck are you? What are you doing here? This is a private building." His accent is pure Lancashire. I don't reckon he's the one who was speaking Russian to Peter.

"I'm Chief Inspector Lucas. These are my colleagues. You're wanted for questioning in connection with kidnapping. Are you going to come quietly, or do I need to use the handcuffs?"

He co-operates, but as Wendy opens the door to escort him to the waiting police car, he suddenly makes a run for it. I'm half-prepared, having foreseen the possibility, and I leg it after him. He's middle-aged and obviously unfit. As I may have already mentioned, I'm a martial arts expert, and at the peak of my game. It takes me about half a minute to catch him and wrestle him to the ground. The handcuffs are on in an instant, and as Wendy steps back, I haul him to his feet.

"Do you have a name?" I ask.

He gives me a dirty look. I didn't think I was too rough with him, but he may have a few bruises. It's difficult to knock someone to the ground without inflicting some discomfort.

"I'm going to take this young lady back to the car. Joanna, will you come with us?" Becky calls to Mum, who's now heading towards us and nods. "Are you two going to deliver this idi…er… man to the troops?"

I stifle a grin and look at Wendy while I dig out my car keys for Becky. Her lips twitch a bit, but she looks otherwise stern and professional.

"Yes, of course. My team will get him to the station and set him up in one of the interview rooms." She turns to face him. "I'll come and see you in a little while."

We deliver our slightly subdued prisoner to the waiting police, then return to the front entrance of the building.

"We'll seal off the building and the car for now. I can lock it up and put up some crime scene tape." Wendy flourishes her lock-picks with a grin. "Xanthe and I can come back tomorrow with a search warrant and sort out any evidence that we might have left today. I think the priority is to get Tania back to her mum."

TWENTY-ONE

Becky

SUNDAY

Tania clings to me as we make our way to the car in the Aldi car park, and I wish we'd parked closer. When we eventually make it back, Joanna and I sit her between us in the back seat. Her teeth are chattering. I grabbed Wendy's rucksack from her before we parted, and I dig out a blanket, a carton of apple juice and a Freddo chocolate bar. I wrap the blanket around Tania's shoulders and give her the food and drink to eat. Her hands are shaking too much to put the straw in the carton's hole, so I do it for her. Meanwhile, Joanna gets out of the car and makes a phone call. She's only a moment, then she returns to sit back on the other side of Tania.

"Hey, I've got your mum on the phone. She wants to speak to you."

Tania grabs the phone, spilling a bit of apple juice on her jeans.

"Mummy?" Her voice is just a whisper. I've not heard anything louder from her yet, and my heart goes out to her. Poor kid – she's probably traumatised. She sniffs. "Yes. Becky and her friends got me out. There was this man that tried to stop them. He's the one that got my food and gave me a bucket. Can you imagine, Mummy? I had to wee and poo in a bucket. It was horrid." She starts to cry.

Anastasia's voice is barely audible on the other end of the phone and I can't make out what she's saying. I can hazard a guess, though, because Tania's next words are, "Yes. I'll be home soon."

Joanna takes the handset back and confirms that we'll be bringing Tania back as soon as our driver gets back to the car. We should be with them in less than an hour.

At that moment, Will and Wendy turn up.

"All sorted. Shall we get this young lady back home now?" Wendy provides an update on the man they've handed over to Xanthe and the rest of the team. "The guy's name is Freddie Carpenter, and he's got a criminal record for fraud and misconduct. He's a trained accountant – now disbarred. Very interesting, considering our suspicions, don't you think?"

"Absolutely." I agree with her. "We can do some more digging after we've reunited Tania with her mum." I want to remind them not to say too much in front of the little girl. I think it works, as Will starts the engine and we head back to Whitefield to drop her off.

At the start of the journey home, Tania's quiet, but she clings to my right hand as if to a lifeline. I wrap my left arm around her shoulders. I want her to feel as secure as possible. The car is almost silent until Will turns on the sound system and presses a button. Music from the *Frozen* movie fills the car, and Tania relaxes a fraction.

"Ooh, great music choice, Will. I love this movie." I smile at Tania and squeeze her shoulders and get a shy smile back in response.

Frozen keeps the atmosphere in the car calm until we arrive at the Blackstones' house. The front door opens as Will parks up, and Anastasia bounds to the car to wait for her little girl to emerge. We don't waste any time. Joanna is on the kerb-side of the car and gets out as soon as the vehicle comes to a halt. I release Tania's hand and she's out of the car and in the circle of her mum's arms within seconds. While they're hugging, the rest of us step outside too and watch the reunion. Although I've seen kidnap victims reunited with family in the past, somehow this one feels more emotional. I blow my nose and blink a few times. It's not for me to be crying. Anastasia is doing enough of that for all of us. She's entitled to that release.

After a minute or two of us standing watching, Anastasia seems to notice we're here. She stifles her sobs before speaking.

"Thank you. From the bottom of my heart, thank you all so much." She points to the house. "Do you want to come in?"

"I think we should, yes." I glance round, questioning the others. Seeing their assent, I add, "It would be good to fill you in. So you know what you could expect."

Once seated in the lounge, Tania sits on her mum's knee and cuddles her as if she'll never let go. Her younger brother comes in and sits next to them, and Simon perches on the arm of the sofa. Joanna and Wendy distribute themselves between the armchairs and I take the other end of the sofa, within reasonable distance of Tania, who occasionally looks up and offers shy smiles. Will perches on the arm of the chair that his mum is using, until Simon notices.

"Hey, you'll spoil the chair like that. I'll grab you a seat from the dining room."

Will glances over at me and I try not to laugh. Neither of us mentions Simon was doing the same thing. It's his house and his furniture, after all.

Once everyone is comfortable, Wendy summarises how we found Tania, and I add in some precautions that they should take to keep them all safe. As they've paid no ransom, there's a likelihood that the kidnappers would try again.

As I'm finishing up, Simon's phone pings. He looks at it,

then passes it to me; presumably because I'm closest. His expression is grim. I focus on the screen.

"*You got the fucking police involved, you stupid bastards. You'll regret this.*" The message is in the form of an email from the same address as the ransom note.

"Charming!" I hand the phone back to Simon. "Can you screenshot that please, and send it to me? We'll need that as part of the evidence." As soon as I receive it, I forward it to Wendy, Joanna and Will.

"I'll arrange for some police protection for you all." Wendy tries to reassure them, but it's hard to offer protection without alarming people. Tania clings harder to her mum, and I don't blame her after what she's been through.

After a few more words of advice, including an instruction to not leave the house or allow the kids out to play until we say it's safe, Wendy thanks them for their hospitality, smiles at Tania and says goodbye.

Simon escorts the others to the front door, but I hang back and crouch down next to Tania.

"You're such a brave girl. Be good for Mummy and stay indoors until we've caught the bad men who took you, okay? They can't hurt you in here, and we're going to put them in prison very soon."

"Very, very soon?" she whispers back.

I rest my hand on her shoulder. "Yes. Very, very soon. Can I come and see you again when we've caught them and tell you about it?"

She nods, and lets go of her mum for long enough to give me a quick hug. As soon as she releases me, I say "Bye" and escape from the room. Tears are threatening. I don't like making promises I can't keep, but there's no room for failure here. We have to catch those men.

By common consent, we return to my house. Matt has been tracking me on his phone and has ordered a Chinese takeaway for all six of us. While we're waiting for it to arrive, we fill him and Cheryl in on the events so far. Personally, I'd rather she wasn't interested enough to join us for the discussion, but in some ways she's very like me, and curiosity is clearly a dominant gene in our household.

When Wendy finishes the narrative, Matt asks the key question.

"What's the plan for catching those men? That family won't be safe until they're locked up."

"Well, Xanthe is interviewing Freddie Carpenter as we speak. She'll threaten him with a long prison sentence if he doesn't cough up some names. He's already got a record. I don't think he'll want to go back inside." Wendy glances round at us. "I also don't think he's a leader in this. He's not the type. More of a 'do-as-he's-told' type of chap."

"I'd agree with that," Will chips in. "Mum, you and Becky didn't see him, but he was bald and flabby. Nothing wrong with either attribute, really, but I felt he was flabby-minded too. He might be an accountant, but I'd guess he didn't sail through his exams the first time. Chartered accountancy exams are tough."

Wendy glances down at her phone. "Apparently, according to the info Xanthe sent me, when he was disbarred they looked into his past, and found that when he did his exams there were accusations of cheating. They couldn't prove anything, so granted him his certifications, but there was always a bit of a cloud over him." She looks at Will. "You might be right about him not being the brightest knife in the drawer, but he's a piece of work. I've just messaged and asked Xanthe to let me know when she's finished interviewing him. Whatever he says, though, I'm beginning to think it's time to bring Mr Ulyanov in for questioning. What do you think?" Her gaze rests on each of us, even Cheryl.

"He's the one you reckon's in charge, isn't he?" My daughter takes advantage of Wendy including her in the conversation and gets her question in first.

"Probably. He's got fingers in a lot of places they're not supposed to be, and thanks to Joanna and Will's friend Glen, we know he's involved in dodgy dealings with several accountants. Not least Simon Blackstone, and most likely Freddie Carpenter."

"Why haven't you arrested him yet?"

Wendy smiles at Cheryl.

"It's a matter of timing. The more evidence we can gather, the more chance we have of building a case against him that the prosecutors can work with. If we bring him in too early, there's a risk that we'll have to release him again without charge."

"So, have you got enough evidence now?" asks Cheryl.

Wendy grimaces, and I intervene.

"Possibly not, but there's too big a risk to the little girl that was kidnapped and her family. If we don't get him arrested, he could do them more harm. As always, these things are complex."

There's a ping, and all six of us reach for our phones. I can't help but laugh.

"Modern times!" I say before glancing at my own. I have no new messages, so look around the lounge where we're all gathered.

"It's Xanthe. She's finished the interview. He refused to mention anyone, but when she raised the name 'Yanov' he clearly knew who she meant. Apparently, he went whiter than paper, but clammed up even further."

Interesting.

"Are you going to send her out to arrest Eric?" I ask.

"I'll just phone her now. Do you mind if I go into the conservatory to make the call? I don't think she's happy about me working with you all. I'm going beyond protocol, but it's not against the rules to work with consultants and specialists. It's not worth stressing her out about it though." Wendy returns a few minutes later. "She'll phone me back shortly. They're heading over to his house now to make the arrest."

The doorbell rings, and Matt goes to answer it. I've avoided answering the door since I recognised my stalker in the park. A moment later, my husband pops his head into the lounge. "You'd better come into the kitchen and grab plates and forks. There's enough food here to feed an army."

For the last half an hour, my stomach has been making enough noise to wake the neighbours, so I dive into the nearest foil tray without waiting for the others to tuck in and tuck into what turns out to be chicken chow-mein. My friends and family follow my example, and for a few minutes only the sound of chewing fills the room. Once the worst of the hunger is alleviated, conversation gradually resumes, but we avoid work topics. It's not until about twenty minutes later that Wendy's phone rings.

She answers it, and a moment later her expression becomes grim. As she disconnects, she looks round at us all.

"Xanthe and her team knocked on his door. When there was no answer, they used the authority of the arrest warrant to break into his house. Eric Ulyanov has fled. We have to assume that Anastasia and her family are in danger."

TWENTY-TWO

Joanna

WEDNESDAY

With Eric gone, Wendy arranges for a police guard to be left watching the Blackstones. We all agree that they're in significant danger. Meanwhile, the rest of us need to get on with our lives. I turn my attention back to the egg heist. We have no clues to date, and a meeting with Roger is planned for Friday to update him on our progress.

It's now Wednesday afternoon, and my research from the last two days has felt like a waste of time, except that I'm now considerably more knowledgeable about the Fabergé family and their link to the Romanovs. It's been hard to concentrate this week. I've been checking in with Anastasia at least twice a day, and I know Becky has too. Despite Wendy's team of guards, I'm twitchy about Eric being on the loose. His disappearance has hitched him up the suspects list, and it's almost certain that he was involved in the kidnapping of Tania.

I check my phone for the hundredth time since I sat down at the laptop an hour ago. Glen has booked a table at a local restaurant for this evening. He's got the neighbour lined up to watch his dad, and everything is organised and ready, so there's no reason for him to message me again, but I'm like a bloody teenager expecting some sort of sign that he likes me enough to say hello for the sake of it.

I roll my eyes, frustrated with my stupidity. Glen's lovely, and we're getting on great, but he's got far more important things to worry about than my anxieties.

With a considerable effort, I return my attention to the screen, and I actually get absorbed in a description of the Coronation Egg, presented by Nicholas II to his wife in 1897. My phone rings, and my heart rate seems to double in an instant. I check the screen before answering. It's an unknown number. Bugger. Probably someone else wanting to fix internet issues I don't have, or offer me compensation for the car accident that never took place. I don't answer, but a minute later the caller rings back. I shrug mentally and hit the *Connect* button.

"Joanna! You've been avoiding me." Shit. It's my bastard ex-husband. I blocked him last time.

"You've changed your number." There's plenty more I could say, but this will do for starters. Heart rate increases further – the essential organ is pounding so hard I feel sick. Too much history and far too much of a threat. "And while we're talking about it, you're not allowed to contact me. So what the fuck do you think you're doing?"

"Burner phone, love. And I wanted to let you know I've got some money coming in. One of my pals has got me a couple of fake passports, and one of them has your photo on it. We're going on a little trip."

"I'm going nowhere with you. Get out of my life. You ditched me at the one time I could have done with your support. What right have you got to come back demanding my company now? I have scars from you that will never go away. They are constant fucking reminders of what a bastard you are. Now piss off and get back to prison where you belong. The police are after you."

I'm about to hang up when his voice – quiet and threatening – comes through again.

"I will take you with me, you fucking bitch. You thought you'd escaped me, but I'll get you back." He ends the call as I stare at the phone in horror. A sudden burst of nausea sends me to the bathroom where I empty the contents of my stomach. It's several minutes before I'm able to remove myself from the embrace of the porcelain goddess, and I wobble unsteadily to my bedroom and lie down under the covers, shivering, miserable and terrified. All those years of being controlled by that bastard, and now he wants me back. I can't do this.

I huddle there for several moments, before common sense creeps back in. I still have my phone with me, having automatically stuffed it in my jeans back pocket as I ran to the loo. Without leaving the comfort of my bed, I select Wendy's number and call her.

"Joanna, are you okay, love?" Wendy's always had a great instinct about whether it's a social call, and she seems to know before I speak that something's wrong.

"Oh god. No. Lou just called. He's got a new phone. He wants to take me away with him to another country. The bastard has fake passports and one of them has my photo on it. Shit, Wendy! I'm so bloody scared."

"Okay. Have you got the number of the phone he called you from?"

"Yes. Do you want me to send it to you?" I feel some of the tension leave me as Wendy's calm practicality works its magic.

"Please do. We should be able to locate him, or at least to identify where he was when he made the call. That will give us a chance to arrest him and get him back behind bars. If that doesn't work, there are other avenues we can try. Send me that number, Joanna, and I'll call you back shortly. Is there anyone who can stay with you? Is Will there?"

"He's out. I can call Glen."

"Do that. Don't let anyone else in, unless Becky shows up, and she's not supposed to be wandering around alone either." There's a moment's pause, then she adds, "One day, you two are going to stay out of trouble."

I can picture her amused expression as she speaks.

"Yeah, one day… when you see a sky full of flying piglets."

Ending the call on a chuckle – remarkable under the circumstances – I take a deep breath and select Glen's number.

"Hey, sorry to bother you. Do you have a couple of minutes?"

"As it's you, sure. Are you okay?" His voice comforts me even more than Wendy's, but I'm nervous about overstepping some invisible boundary. His tone suggests nothing but welcome though.

I explain about Lou's call and Wendy's advice about not being alone.

"Are you working?" I ask.

"Nothing urgent, but with the neighbour coming over tonight, I can't ask her to pop in now. Unless you wanted to have a takeaway here? I can ask Pat to pop in now for a few minutes while I pick you up, and you can spend the rest of the day and evening round here. If you're okay to watch telly with Dad for a bit, I can get my work out of the way, and you'll be safe enough here."

"That would be great. Happy to sit with your dad for a bit too, as much as you need."

"Thanks, love." His endearment renders my insides slightly squishy, even though it's the sort of thing he might say to anyone. "I'll check Pat's okay to pop in, then I'll be with you in a few minutes. Don't open the door. I'll phone you when I arrive, so you know it's safe."

With that call ended too, I pace the floor, until I realise I've not sent the burner phone number to Wendy. I remedy the omission before resuming my pacing. A car door slams. I jump and go to the window. Partly obscured by the curtains, I glance outside. A neighbour is emptying shopping from her car boot. My skin tingles. Am I being paranoid, or is someone watching the house? I don't dare to move now in case the watcher sees a change in shadows or glimpses me behind the curtain. Nausea returns. I don't think I'll be eating much of that takeaway tonight. Probably better than going to a fancy restaurant though.

Glen's car comes into view and he parks directly outside my front gate. He gets out and looks around, then gets back in the car and phones me.

"All right, love, I'm here. Something doesn't feel right though. Call Wendy and get her to send some of her team down here. I'll stay here in the car. Where are you?"

"I'm in my bedroom. Behind the curtain." I want to ask him what's put him on edge, but I'm not sure I want to hear the answer. "Anyway, I'll phone Wendy. Lock your car door. I don't want anything bad to happen to you."

"Me neither. Phone Wendy, then call me straight back."

I do as I'm told. I've got quite good at that over the years, although more recently, I've become better at figuring out when it's in my interests to obey, and when it's better to rebel. Since Glen's instructions seem to be entirely for my benefit, I call Wendy and explain the situation. She offers to send a team down immediately, although she's keeping back an officer who's working on the burner phone number, trying to locate Lou.

"I've got a feeling Lou might be here," I say.

"You might be right. My lot will be with you in about fifteen minutes. Do not leave your house; tell Glen to stay in his car until they arrive. I'll message you once they're in position."

"Sure. Thanks Wendy."

I disconnect and call Glen again. I've not taken my eyes from his car the whole time I've been talking to Wendy. At least, I didn't think I had.

Glen's voice when he answers is a little breathless.

"I was a bit slow locking the door. So sorry, Joanna, love. I've got company." The voice changes to one I know far too well. "I've got your little boyfriend here, slut. If you don't do as you're told, he'll be getting his throat cut. My knife's all sharp and ready."

My blood runs cold. I put the phone on speaker and hold it away from my ear so I can send Wendy a message.

"Help. Lou's in the car with Glen. He's threatening him with a knife if I don't do as I'm told. Can't wait for your guys, but I'll stall as much as I can."

Meanwhile, Lou's issuing instructions. I've got to get outside immediately and go to the car with my hands in the air as though I'm being arrested. As I'm listening, I grab a Swiss Army knife from my bedside table drawer and slip it into my pocket. I've donned a red ski jacket for warmth, visibility, and the convenience of deep pockets, so the knife is well hidden. I add a matching woolly hat and conceal a hatpin in its bobbly bits. Lou's still talking. Telling me to get a move on.

"I'm just putting on my coat and hat – it's bloody cold out there. You wouldn't want me to freeze to death, I'm sure. I'm no good to you dead." My voice sounds remarkably calm; years of practice of pretending when I'm a gibbering wreck inside. I walk downstairs – more terrified about what he'll do to Glen than to me – and open the front door. They're still in the car, but I can see Lou's got a knife resting against Glen's throat. I disconnect the call as soon as I'm sure they've seen me, and put my hands on my head as I walk towards the vehicle. My fingers nudge gently against the blunt end of the hatpin. Glen's window winds down, presumably under instruction as the knife makes no progress towards his throat.

"Get over here, you fucking bitch, and get in the back of the car." Lou's face is as aggressive as his tone.

Okay. This is going to be trickier than I thought. I take a deep breath and push the hat and pin off my head towards the rear wheel.

"Bugger." I bend down. "Just need to pick up my hat." The pin is on the ground and I shove it into the tyre with as much force as I can muster. I yank it back out and leave it by the kerb at the edge of the road. There'll be no need for it again on this trip. I make a mental apology to Glen – obviously I'll pay for the replacement tyre for him. I get in the car and put the hat on the seat next to me.

"Fucking hell, woman. You take your bloody time don't you?" Lou turns his face back to Glen. "You, turn on the fucking engine and start driving."

Glen's eyes meet mine in the rear-view mirror, and I give him an almost imperceptible nod. He turns the engine on and releases the handbrake. We've moved about a hundred yards when I hear the hissing of air. Being in the back, I'm the first to hear it, but I don't have much time. In the minute that we've been moving, I've been fumbling in my pocket. I have the Swiss Army knife open and ready to go.

Lou's attention is still on Glen. He tells him to turn right on to the main road. That works for me up to a point, but it's restrictive. If all goes badly, there are too many people about for me to get away with plunging my knife into Lou's throat. It's damn tempting, but perhaps better not to go all that way. I just need to scare the man for the moment. I move quickly, and my blade is in position before my ex-husband realises.

"I think you'll find Glen will drive better if you take the knife away from his neck." I press slightly until Lou puts his free hand up and works out that he's not the only one using a sharp blade as a weapon. Due to angles, Lou isn't able to move my knife away from his own neck, and he releases his grip on the knife in his hand in his attempt to escape from danger. Glen stops the car. It's slowing anyway thanks to the now flat tyre. Without a knife against his jugular, he seems a lot more relaxed and in control. He puts on the handbrake. We seem to be at the top of a hill – no one wants to cause more damage than needed. I'd forgotten that Glen's a good match for Will in martial arts skills, until he does a complicated manoeuvre that leaves Lou's knife at his feet and Lou's wrist twisted up behind his back, somehow entangled with the seatbelt. As soon as the knife drops, I remove my weapon and put it back in my pocket. With a bit of luck, help should be on the scene soon, and Glen seems to be in control now. We're getting stares from passers-by. I would rather avoid their interference if possible, and my little sharp gadget is better off out of sight.

"What the fuck do you think you're doing?" Lou blusters and tries to pick up his knife with his free hand, but Glen yanks on the wrist in his grasp and his tormentor-turned-victim yells in pain. "You've fucking broken my wrist, you bastard. I'll get you for that. I should have shoved my knife in you when I had a fucking chance."

Someone knocks on the window. Glen's car is quite old and has winders for the back windows. I wind mine down.

"Everything alright, love?" asks a man in jogging gear.

"All under control thanks. Just a domestic. But if you see the police round the corner, please send them this way. The chap in the passenger seat is an escaped convict."

Lou's still swearing – partly about his wrist but also because he's realising he's beaten this time. A police car draws up behind us, waved down by the jogger. Their car door opens, and a PC is about to approach when Xanthe's car stops in front of us. We're surrounded on two sides, but if Glen loosens his grip, Lou will still be able to run.

Xanthe gets out of her vehicle and goes straight to the front passenger door, where Lou is sitting, still with his arm locked in Glen's relentless grasp.

"You can let go of him now, sir," she says. "Louis MacLeod, you're under arrest…"

I can see she's about to go into the full spiel, but she doesn't get a chance. Despite Glen's grip on his right wrist, Lou reaches down with his left hand, grabs the knife, and plunges it into Xanthe's right breast. I leap out of the car, shouting for the other police officers to come and help. The jogger, who's been standing for the last moments with his mouth open, joins me at Xanthe's side.

"Call an ambulance, now!" I shout at him. Lou's knife is still protruding from Xanthe's body. She's conscious, but barely, and red bubbles are escaping from around the blade. It's clearly penetrated her lung, but I've enough knowledge to realise that removing the weapon would do more harm than good.

Within seconds, one of her colleagues is with us, calling the situation through to her boss. Jogging Man is trying to explain the injuries to the ambulance controller, but he can't string a sentence together. I grab his phone from him.

"Hello. The police officer is losing consciousness. She's got a sharp knife stuck in her right lung, and needs urgent help if her life is to be saved. How far away is the ambulance?"

The man at the other end of the phone seems to breathe a sigh of relief – presumably at the prospect of speaking with someone sensible.

"I've got your location here." He gives a road name. "Is that correct?"

"Yes. We're at the top of the hill." Out of the corner of my eye, I see that Glen now has both of Lou's arms behind his back and is gripping on for dear life.

"The ambulance is five minutes away." I stay on the phone

while the controller tells me what to look out for. The jogger, whose phone I've now commandeered, is sitting on the kerb at the side of the road, looking pale and sickly.

Two of Xanthe's colleagues are next to her, one on either side. Others are milling round. I go up to one officer.

"Don't you think it might be an idea to arrest Mr MacLeod? Apart from anything else, he's just tried to kill a police officer."

The sergeant shakes his head slightly, as if to clear it. "Of course. Yes. Sorry, Ma'am. Bit of a shock seeing a friend stabbed. I'll sort it now. That chap with the vice grip. What's his name?"

"That's Glen Thorpe, a friend of mine." I can't keep the pride out of my voice. Glen's been a real hero today.

The officer goes to Glen and says something to him. I can't hear the exact words because I'm still keeping half an eye on Xanthe. Her friends are monitoring vital signs, and from their body language, she is still clinging to life. The officer leans over Glen and attaches handcuffs to Lou's wrists.

A minute later, the ambulance arrives. I thank the controller and disconnect, go back to the jogger and handing his phone back to him.

It takes some time to get Xanthe loaded into the vehicle, as the paramedics have to be careful not to worsen the injury and increase her risk of death – which is already pretty high. She looks grey and clammy, and more red bubbles are escaping from the corner of her mouth. I send a quick prayer, even though I don't entirely believe, that if anyone is up there listening, perhaps they can save this brave woman who was only doing her job – trying to protect a member of the public.

As soon as the ambulance is on its way to the hospital, the officer who used the handcuffs comes round to the passenger side of the car, and bundles Lou to his feet. My ex looks defiant and is swearing – expressions that I've not heard since I was living with him and had accidentally thrown out a winning betting slip. He'd made me rummage through the rubbish for hours until I'd found it, but had spent most of that time cursing. He'd then returned to the betting shop to collect his winnings – a measly twenty quid.

His current language takes me back, but I can see the fear in his eyes. He knows he's going down for a very long time.

TWENTY-THREE

Becky

WEDNESDAY

After receiving a call from Wendy this afternoon, letting me know that Joanna and Glen are in danger, I spend a lot of time pacing. I want to go to her rescue, but Will's out for the day with his little girl and Matt's at work. Wendy strictly forbade me from leaving the house by myself. She kindly reminded me that Finn's waiting to get me to his cronies and that I have a stalker. Thanks, Wendy. I'm feeling much better now.

I pace for about fifteen minutes, then extract my phone from my jeans pocket – an activity only repeated about every two minutes since Wendy called. Nothing has changed when I look at the screen again. I don't want to disturb Wendy, and I'm under instructions not to phone Joanna, Glen or Will. I don't entirely agree about Will. He'd want to know that his mum's in danger, but I know his time with Chloë is precious. I decide to wait for more news before ringing him. Meanwhile, I'm going stir-crazy here. I glance at my phone again. I've set my background to a picture of the missing Fabergé egg, and it catches my attention as I gaze at my phone. Maybe there's something I can do to move the case along. I click on my contacts and locate the person I need to speak to.

"Hi Roger. How are you doing?"

"I'm well, thank you, Becky. What can I do for you?" His tone is dry. To be expected, really. I suppose I only ever call him when I want something, but then he's not exactly a friend.

"I was thinking about the egg heist, and I'd like to get some background info about the egg. That jeweller, Wartski: does he still have a shop? Is he still alive?"

"The shop is still a going concern. I could arrange for you to visit if you wish. There's another descendant of Mr Wartski who may help you. I've been doing some research. I'll see what I can arrange, and call you back in a few minutes, if that's acceptable?"

I agree and disconnect. Now I have two calls to wait for. My pacing resumes.

Roger returns my call after about five minutes. Pretty quick, really, but most likely it's only because I'm more keen to get a call from Wendy or Joanna to confirm if everything is okay. Murphy's Law dictates Roger would phone first.

"I have a couple of appointments tentatively arranged for Monday for you. Can you get to London on Monday?"

"I think so. I'm picking my daughter up from university on Saturday, but I don't see any reason I can't go to London two days later. What time?" I ignore the fact that I'm not supposed to go anywhere alone. For goodness sake, what can happen to me in London?

A few minutes later, I have a detailed itinerary and train tickets on my phone. I thank Roger and hang up. At least it's an outing to look forward to, and a chance to get stuck into my case. Will can take me to the station and pick me up, and once I'm at Piccadilly Station I should be pretty safe.

An image of my stalker, who I first encountered on my last train journey to London, pops into my head. I take some deep breaths to fend off the lightheadedness that appears, hand-in-hand with its mates: palpitations and clammy palms.

I sit down for a moment and duck my head between my knees.

I stay there for a couple of minutes before rearranging myself and lying on the sofa. A few more deep breaths finally bring the anxiety under control. I've been dealing with these attacks since last summer. They don't get any easier, but I've become better at managing them. I've also learnt that hiding myself away doesn't help. Letting the demons win makes them stronger. I resolve to go to London alone and face down any villains lying in wait for me.

I've just made this decision when my phone rings. I answer it immediately, noticing that the caller is Wendy.

"Hi. Any news?"

"Joanna and Glen are safe." Her voice sounds very wobbly, given what she's just told me.

"But?"

"Xanthe's been stabbed. She's on her way to the hospital, and so am I. I need to be there for her and will have to break the news to her family."

"Oh my God! How bad is it?"

"Joanna told me there's a knife still in her chest and it looks as though it's pierced the lung. She's still alive though. Joanna is with Glen. Lou's been arrested for attempted murder, amongst other things. Glen's car has been impounded for now, so they're getting a taxi over to you. I hope that's okay. I thought you'd want to check on her in person." Wendy still sounds shaky and as if she has a cold.

"That's fine. I'll be pleased to have them here. You see to Xanthe. I hope she's…" I tail off. She's clearly not okay, but what can I say? Nothing that will come out right.

"Thanks, love. I'll let you know how she gets on." Wendy knows me too well – she understands my intention despite her own distress.

I've no sooner said goodbye and disconnected when the

doorbell rings. I go into the hall and check the door cam that Matt installed earlier this week. Joanna is there, with a man of around our age whom I don't recognise. She looks anxious and tense, but her proximity to the stranger suggests that he's not a stranger to her. I suspect this is Glen, and open the door to let them in.

Joanna closes the door behind them and introduces her friend.

"Becky, you've heard me and Will mention Glen a couple of times." She blushes, and looks annoyed at herself for doing so. I refrain from teasing. Now is not the right time.

"Of course. Come into the kitchen, both of you. I'll put the kettle on and make a brew. You can tell me what's been going on. I've just been hearing from Wendy about Xanthe." I usher them into the kitchen and gesture to them to sit at the table while I rummage for chocolate digestives. Tea and biscuits – the best cure known for shock. I can see it setting in – the pallor and shaking apparent in both of them.

I add a couple of teaspoons of sugar into the tea before setting the mugs in front of them, then make myself a decaf coffee and sit down. The tea and biscuits are working their magic and they seem to regain a little colour, although Glen still looks grey.

"Do you want to tell me about it?" I ask gently. If they prefer not to speak for now, I'll survive the suspense, but I know from long experience that bottling up trauma doesn't help it go away. Quite the reverse. It took me months before I could tell even Matt what went on in the warehouse that caused me to leave my job, and some of the details are still locked away. I tell myself I'll face up to them one day, but I'm not there yet.

Joanna starts the story, even including the clever use of her hatpin. Although Glen looks a bit put out when she tells us how she punctured his tyre.

"I'll pay for the replacement, Glen. Sorry. I didn't know

what else to do to stop him from taking us away from where the police were coming to help."

He looks thoughtful for a moment, then nods. "Fair enough. Pretty clever really. But yeah, if you wouldn't mind paying for the tyre, it would be a help."

"We'll reimburse you from the business," I say. "There's some money still from our last case, and we've got some coming for our current one too." I can see Joanna hesitating. "Seriously, don't worry about it. It's criminal activity that you were involved with and trying to prevent. It's irrelevant that it was your ex. Carry on with telling me what happened. I still don't know how Xanthe got injured."

A few minutes later and I have all the details. I'm shocked by Lou's action.

"Why would your ex be so desperate to avoid going back to prison? I can understand it's grim in there, but stabbing someone in the chest sounds a pretty drastic measure."

"He was never one to consider consequences. He would just lash out if he got backed into a corner. That's how he ended up inside in the first place." Joanna seems a lot calmer now the story's been told.

"So stupid though. If he gets convicted of attempted murder, he could get years in prison. It would be unlikely to be less than thirty for stabbing a police officer on duty. Particularly given he was out on bail."

"Actually, he'd skipped bail. He's already broken so many bail conditions, including doing a runner. It sounds awful, but I'll be pleased to see him back behind bars for a bloody long time."

"It doesn't sound awful," I say. "He treated you so badly in the past and all he's done recently is terrorise you. It would be incredible if you don't want him locked up." I turn to Glen. "Well done for keeping him restricted. It sounds as though they wouldn't have caught him if it hadn't been for you."

"Thanks. But I wish I'd captured both his arms behind his back at the start. Then Xanthe would be okay. I feel awful about that."

"Hindsight is wonderful." I'm about to expound on times when I wish I'd done things differently, when my phone rings. Caller ID shows it's Wendy.

"Hi. How's Xanthe?" I've known Wendy too long to waste time on niceties.

"In surgery. Likely to be there for several hours, I've been told. We nearly lost her. She flat-lined on the way to the hospital, but the paramedics brought her back to us. It's touch and go."

"Bloody hell, Wendy! I'll pray for her." It's rare for me to talk about my faith. I'm not overly religious, following only the Jewish traditions that fit with my lifestyle and family, but in the past, I had a strong belief that there's someone out there looking out for us. I guess they have a higher scheme that we can't see or even imagine, causing huge loss to life and major tragedies. Maybe we wouldn't agree with the decisions that are made on our behalf even if we were privy to the foresight and grand picture, but I had to trust in something. All the same, my faith was gravely shaken after the incident in the warehouse. I can't imagine why my lovely colleague, Rachel, had to die. But it was her or me. Perhaps that's a cause to believe in something – even if it's only that my guardian angel was on duty that day. Anyway, perhaps praying for Xanthe will do some good. It can't do any harm.

I avoid glancing at either Joanna or Glen. I know she's agnostic – bordering atheist. He's an unknown quantity in that area, but my beliefs are pretty personal, and I don't want to engage in a discussion about them.

Wendy asks after my guests and I reassure her they seem to be okay, if a little shaken. They can obviously hear my end of the conversation. Joanne mouths, 'How's Wendy?' She's got a point, and I take the next opportunity to ask.

"How are you doing?"

"Just worried sick. I'll be okay though."

"Are you going to stay there tonight?" I ask.

"At least until she's out of surgery and settled. All being well I'll be home and in bed before midnight. They'll be taking her to ICU. I've called her sister, and she's on her way to join me. She had to wait until her husband came home from work so she could leave their lad. Obviously, he's upset about his auntie. His dad left work early and got home about ten minutes ago, so Kelly messaged me to say she's on her way. It'll be good to have some company to be honest, although it's going to be hard explaining how her sister got herself so badly injured on duty."

"Don't you start feeling guilty, boss! There's nothing you could have done to prevent this."

"I wish I was still your boss, Becky. I might not have been able to prevent this, but I always have to think about what I can put in place to make sure it doesn't happen again. There's always something that could have been done differently."

"I know, but I've got Glen here worrying that he should have got hold of both of Lou's wrists behind his back."

"Glen was a hero. It's thanks to him we've got Lou down at the police station in a cell. I'm going to do some questioning in the morning, but I need to know how Xanthe is before I can concentrate on that."

"Let us know how you get on, Wendy. And if there's any news about Xanthe…"

"Obviously, I'll keep you posted. I'd better go. I said I'd meet her sister at the main entrance."

We say our goodbyes and I turn my attention to my guests. I give a quick update on the minimal information I've gleaned from Wendy. They still look stressed and anxious, so I fill them in on my plan for Monday. Glen looks a bit confused.

"Have you not told him about the egg, Joanna?" I ask.

"We've had a lot of other things to talk about. He knows about the Blackstones, but I don't think we mentioned the egg. It seemed relatively unimportant compared to Tania getting kidnapped."

"I know, but she's back now. Don't you think we have a lot of links to Russia going on here?"

"How do you mean?" Joanna frowns in thought, so I put her out of her misery and explain.

"Anastasia is Russian by birth. She was being blackmailed by Eric who has now gone missing. He appears to have links to her Russian aunt and cousins, who are apparently activists and at risk of imprisonment. He thinks he has something on them, and threatened to land them in it if Ana didn't sleep with him. We've moved on from that, but we don't know what's going on at the other end, if anything. It might have been an idle threat."

"From what I know of Ulyanov, I doubt it." Glen grimaces. "He's a scary bastard. I wanted as little to do with him as possible."

"Useful to know, thanks. I have asked… er… someone I know to look into his links in Russia. Meanwhile, we've got the fact that Will's daughter's stepdad was speaking to someone in Russian about the kidnapping of Tania. Why on earth is Peter Donaldson, a Scottish accountant, speaking Russian? Trust me, it's a bloody difficult language to learn."

"Which also begs the question, why are you learning it?" asks Joanna.

"I was told to." I give her a meaningful look. It's not that I don't trust Glen. He seems like a nice guy, but anything to do with Roger is top secret and on a need-to-know basis. Roger will need to vet Glen before we get to let him in on any of this.

Joanna shrugs. I'm not sure what that means, but I can't ask her just now, so let it slide and resume my list of Russian connections.

"Anyway, we also have a Russian Fabergé egg that's now gone missing; stolen from a bank in Preston, the same town that's inhabited by Peter. It's one hell of a coincidence if it's not connected."

"That's it, though, isn't it? There aren't any other Russian links, and even these are pretty hazy." Joanna gets out her phone, hits a few buttons and passes it to me. I take a look. There's an article on there from a couple of years ago, suggesting that the egg could be anywhere but is likely to be somewhere in the UK. There's no mention of the bank in Preston.

"What if the egg was never there in the first place, and we've been sent on a wild goose chase?" she says.

"There's a bad joke in there about geese and golden eggs, but let's not go there." I sometimes can't prevent my childish sense of humour from surfacing, but now really isn't the time. Even so, there's a quiet chuckle from Glen, and Joanna's mouth twitches at the corner. I hand back the phone.

"Definitely a bad joke! Seriously, Becky, what do you think? Could this article be correct?"

"We've been asked to locate the egg, so perhaps we should focus on that, whilst keeping in mind the possibility that it was never there. I'm still going to London on Monday. I'll have a chat with this guy who works in the Wartski shop and follow R... the other lead we've got. What can go wrong?" I ask this with some bravado. Inside, I'm still bricking it. Finn is out to get me, and I have a stalker. I don't even know if those two things are connected, but either way, I'm in some trouble. "I don't suppose Will could run me to Piccadilly Station on Monday morning and pick me up again in the evening?"

"I'm sure he would, but why don't you ask him yourself?

Isn't he going with you to collect your eldest on Saturday? You should have plenty of chance on the journey to discuss it."

"That's a good point. He said he'll drive me to Nottingham to collect Alison from Uni. Under the circumstances, I don't want her coming back on the train by herself, and I seem to be under instruction not to travel anywhere by myself, although the train to London seems to be exempt." I can't keep the dry tone from my voice.

"Only because Wendy doesn't know yet. And she's got other things on her mind. She'd bloody well freak out if she knew."

"Excuse me, ladies. Sorry to interrupt, but I'm going to need to get back to my dad. I've just had a text from Pat, my neighbour. She needs to get home and doesn't want to leave Dad alone. I've just called an Uber. Joanna, are you okay to stay here until Will gets back and can pick you up? We'll catch up another time. I'm so sorry." Glen looks genuinely apologetic; and also still unwell.

"Are you okay?" I ask.

"Yes. It's been a tough day. It will do me good to get back to the normality of caring for Dad. By the time I've made his tea and sorted out his bath and got him to bed, I'll be just fine." He turns to Joanna. "Will you be okay, love? Message me when you get home. Maybe we can chat on the phone later?"

A toot from outside makes us all jump. I guess everyone's edgy. Glen looks down at his phone.

"That's my Uber." He kisses Joanna on the cheek and holds out his hand for me to shake, before leaving abruptly. I lock the door behind him. We can't take any chances.

Matt and Cheryl arrive shortly afterward, and soon after them, Will shows up. We gave in and called him after Wendy confirmed Xanthe was in theatre and Glen had gone. We kept missing each other, but voicemail is wonderful. Joanna asked him to come here, as she didn't want to go back to an empty house by herself.

"It's ridiculous," she said to me after Glen had gone. "Lou's in custody, but I feel less safe today than I did yesterday."

"It's natural after today's trauma. You're bound to still feel shaken up." I don't mention to her that the stress of what happened this afternoon could haunt her for months or even years to come. My own PTSD comes close to incapacitating me regularly. Some days, I don't want to get out of bed. Others, I make a pretty good show of normality, like forcing myself to go to London alone, or comforting my friends with tea and biscuits. I want to be normal. I still remember the bubbly girl I was at eighteen and at various times since, before the challenges of being a police detective took their toll.

My phone ringing rouses me from my thoughts.

"Hi Wendy. Any news?" I notice everyone in the room stops talking and turns to look at me, but I choose not to put the phone on speaker. Cheryl is one of the room's occupants, and if the news is bad, I would rather she heard it from me.

"Xanthe's out of theatre. They've removed the weapon and stitched her up inside and out. There's some lung damage, and they've taken her to the ICU to keep her as well ventilated as possible. The doctor who came out to speak to me and Kelly seemed cautiously optimistic."

"That sounds promising. Are you going to stay there any longer?"

The faces around me relax as they infer the better news.

"Kelly's on her way to the ICU to be with her sister. I've said goodbye for now. Tomorrow, I'll pop in after I've interviewed the bastard that did this to her. But first I need to get some sleep."

When the call is over, I deliver the more detailed news. Joanna looks particularly relieved, but starts shaking again.

"I'm sorry. This is so stupid."

Cheryl goes over to her and takes her hand.

"Not stupid at all. You should have seen Mum a few months ago. There were days where she'd do nothing but sit and shake. She couldn't even lift her cup of coffee without spilling it. She's loads better now, but it took a long time."

"Thanks, love," I say drily. "I don't think that's helpful to Joanna just now."

"It is a bit. Doesn't make me feel less stupid, but it does make me feel less alone in being daft." Joanna sniffs and then grins at me. A shaky grin, but better than nothing.

Now that we have as much news as we're likely to get for the night, we adjourn. Tomorrow's going to be a stressful day, finding out the results of Lou being questioned and ongoing news about Xanthe. As I'm seeing Joanna and Will out, I remind Will of his promise to come with me on Saturday to collect Alison.

"Is it still okay for you?"

"Of course. I'm looking forward to meeting with a younger version of you that's old enough to be out of school." He winks at Cheryl who's hovering behind me.

"Bad joke," I say. "And you'll find that Ali's nothing like me. She most definitely takes after Matt."

"That's fine too." He glances at my face, which is probably showing signs of stress – it's been a long day. "Hey, don't mind my jokes. Just trying to lighten the load. We've all had a difficult day."

I manage a laugh and pull him in for a quick hug. I hug Joanna too. We don't have a lot of physical contact between the three of us, but this evening, it feels like the right thing to do.

TWENTY-FOUR

Will

***

SATURDAY

The last couple of days have dragged. After all the action on Wednesday, and I had a busy enough day of my own – more of that in a moment – Thursday and Friday were a fuzz of waiting for news. We checked in on Glen and his dad. Glen was fine, but stressed about being carless. The police still had his vehicle impounded. Mum and I liaised with Becky and decided the firm could afford to provide a hire car for a few days until his own was released, in addition to getting the tyre fixed. Other than that, we've spent most of the time drinking coffee and checking our phones. Xanthe is making progress, and has progressed from ICU to the high-dependency unit.

But to return to Wednesday. I had a couple of hours booked with Chloë and was due to pick her up from school that day. When I got to the school entrance, there was the usual mill of parents around, but amongst them was my ex-wife.

"What are you doing here, Deb?" I asked. I was pretty annoyed, because, as always, I'd been looking forward to some time with my little girl.

"Peter doesn't want you seeing her any more."

"Bullshit! I'm allowed to by law. He can't stop me. I've got rights."

Debbie rubs the back of her neck and looks shifty.

"He's said he'll claim you've been abusing her if you don't give up your claim on her now."

"What the…?" I notice some of the kids are out of school already, so I moderate my language. "He can't do that. He's got no basis for it at all."

"Mud sticks. A court wouldn't allow you access if there's any rumour that you're an abusive dad."

"That's utter rubbish. The courts sift through evidence. There's nothing to suggest…" I tail off, seeing my beloved Chloë come out of her classroom. She makes a beeline for me and comes over to give me a kiss and a hug.

"Hello, Daddy."

"Hi, precious. Have you had a good day?"

"Yes. I got a sticker for my reading. Look." She shows me a big unicorn sticker on her jumper, but then whispers in my ear. "Daddy Peter says you're bad and that you do bad things to little girls. Why does he say that?"

Christ – how do I explain this?

"It's because he loves you and wants you all to himself. He doesn't want me to see you, so he says things to make you scared of me. But you know I would never hurt you or any other child, don't you?"

She nods.

"So are you coming with me, and we'll go to the park and McDonald's?"

She holds out her hand to me. I glance at Debbie and shrug before leading Chloë back to my car. As we pass her, Chloë smiles at her mum.

"Bye, Mummy. See you later."

We have a nice time together, but it's when I return her home that all hell breaks loose.

I'm disinclined to go in, but knock on the door and wait for someone to answer. I hope it will be Debbie. It's not. The door is opened by a raging bull.

"Get inside, Chloë. Now!" Peter yells at my daughter and she scuttles indoors, looking terrified.

"How dare you yell at her like that?" I draw myself up to my full height of not quite six foot and try to look intimidating.

"I fucking well told her to go nowhere near you. I said you're not to be trusted with little girls, and that's what I'll be telling the courts."

"You're a sodding, stupid prick, then. You've already been linked with the kidnapping of another little girl. Why the hell would the courts believe you over me?" I guess I hit a nerve, because next thing, I'm being slammed up against the wall of the house with his arm against my throat. My mind goes blank for a few seconds – it was so sudden – but then my training kicks in.

With him now on the ground, I restrain my urge to punch him in the face. He's got murder in his eyes though.

"As you've just discovered, I'm a black belt in martial arts. If you hurt Chloë in any way, I will be back here to break every sodding bone in your body. If you go through the courts and try to keep me away from my daughter, you'll find yourself in such deep shit, you'll never get out again. I'm going now. Don't even think about moving until I'm back in my car." I carefully release him and return to my car, never taking my eyes off him. As soon as I'm in the car, I drive away, but I don't go very far. After about two hundred yards and a couple of corners, shaking sets in. I pull over and allow it to pass for a few minutes. I've only been in a couple of real fights previously, and each time this has happened. Violent shaking all over, followed by sweating and then shivering.

It takes about ten minutes to subside. Once the worst is over, I drive to the nearest pub. I'm not stupid enough to drink and drive, but it's a foodie pub. Although I order myself a sandwich and a cup of tea, I'm not really hungry. Actually, I feel sick. It's only an hour since I was indulging in McDonalds, but I need something to settle my nerves, and carbs will help. I've only been working with Becky for a couple of months, but her influence is becoming clear.

She's absolutely right too. I feel a lot better when I've finished eating and drinking. I decide to check my phone. It's been on silent while I've been with Chloë. Bloody hell. Six missed calls: from Becky, Mum and Glen. After listening to the three messages that have been left, I realise I need to get back as soon as I can and check Mum's okay. I'm in the car within a minute, take a deep breath and turn the engine on. Before I start driving, though, I call Mum. There's no answer, so I try Becky. Also, no answer. I leave messages for them to say I'm on my way.

Returning to the present, it's now Saturday morning and I have a day out planned, going with Becky to pick up her eldest daughter from uni. I'm quite intrigued as I've not yet met her, but I've heard a lot about her. I know she's nineteen and is studying Pharmacy in Nottingham. Becky always says Alison takes after Matt, but that her stubbornness has come through the female line. That makes sense. Matt is pretty easy-going.

A day out is just what I need to take my mind off Peter and his threats. I pick up Becky at 9.30 and we head off straight away. As usual, the journey is easy enough. We have plenty to talk about with the case and discussing Xanthe's progress. Traffic is about average for Saturday, maybe a little higher – it's two weeks before Easter, and Nottingham isn't the only university that's finishing for the Easter break.

As we get closer, I sense Becky getting nervous.

"Everything okay?" I ask.

"Yes. A bit excited really. Also slightly worried."

"Why are you worried?"

"I forgot to tell her I wasn't coming alone, and obviously I need to explain why. I thought it would be easier to have that conversation face to face, but now I'm wondering if I should have warned her."

"It'll be fine." I don't know why I have the right to reassure Becky. I've never met or spoken to Alison and don't really have a clue how she'll react. "If the worst comes to the worst, she'll sit sulking in silence in the back all the way home and I'll put the radio on loud to ease the tension." As we've stopped at yet another set of traffic lights, I turn and raise an eyebrow at my friend and colleague.

She laughs.

"Fair point. It might come to that though. Anyway, we're not far now."

The satnav is showing it's half a mile down this road to her halls of residence. Irrationally, my heart starts thumping. Why the hell am I anxious? It must be on Becky's behalf. She's infected me with her own worries.

Becky phones her daughter once we enter the grounds. Alison arranges to meet us at the entrance to her block, so when we've parked up, we get out of the car and I follow Becky, who seems to know the way.

There are a few students milling about, mostly carrying bags, suitcases and boxes, but only one person is standing at the entrance to the block Becky points out as her daughter's. The young woman leaning against the brickwork and typing on her phone looks up as we approach. I feel a jolt in the pit of my stomach. It sounds so clichéd, but there's an immediate connection as soon as our eyes meet. I hate how corny that sounds. I try to suppress my reaction to this beautiful young lady. She's nineteen, for goodness sake. And she's the daughter of my business partner, and she's Jewish, and her mum and dad would probably eat me alive if I so much as suggested I fancied her, let alone anything else.

She looks questioningly at me. I hold out my hand to shake hers.

"I'm Will, Joanna's son. I think you've met my mum?" I wait for her to nod, and then continue. "Your mum wanted some company on the journey down. We'll explain more in the car, but I offered to drive her here. To be honest, I've got one of those cars that I love driving, so any excuse." I grin at her, conscious that I'm babbling.

She looks amused, but casts a suspicious glance at her mum. Becky looks faintly guilty, although she has nothing to be guilty for.

"Let's get all your things together, love," she says. "We can discuss details in the car."

It only takes ten minutes to get the car loaded up. Alison's room is immaculate; all her clothes packed into a suitcase; books and electrical items in boxes with lids taped shut. I only know the contents because she's inscribed them neatly on the top of each box. She seems very different from Becky in this respect. My friend has a tendency to untidiness and disorganisation.

Once in the car, Alison barely waits for me to start the engine before asking the question we knew was coming.

"So, why is Will driving? No offence to him, but I don't see why you couldn't have driven down yourself, Mum."

I murmur, "No offence taken," as I navigate my way out of the car park. I hear Becky take a deep breath and look over at her. She's flushed, and anxiety is etched into her face. "Do you want me to explain?" I ask quietly.

I'm focusing on pulling out on to the main road, so I can only assume she nods, but she speaks to Alison.

"I'm going to let Will tell you. It will be easier."

"Fine. Will, what's this all about?"

"Okay, I'm going to give you a quick summary, then you and your mum can discuss the details. A month ago, your mum went down to London for work. She had a bit of a weird incident on the train, with some dodgy bloke pitching up next to her and then hassling her at the end of the journey. Then a week ago, she was out walking with your dad, when she saw him following her – the same bloke. She's also had a bit of an issue with her ex-police-partner, Finn. So, there seem to be a lot of people out to cause trouble for your mum, so we're trying to protect her."

A moment's silence follows this, presumably while Alison digests the information.

"So, Mum's in danger – again." Her tone is deadpan, and I can't quite decipher the thoughts behind it.

While I try to work out how to handle this statement, Becky chips in.

"Come on, love. You've always known there was a certain amount of danger inherent in my job."

"That was when you were in the police. Aren't private detectives supposed to confine their efforts to divorce cases and missing dogs?"

I hear Becky's sharp intake of breath, but refrain from shooting her the sympathetic glance that she deserves. She needs to sort this out with no interference from me. I also have a strange reluctance to antagonise the young woman in the back of the car.

"We're working closely with Wendy on a case at the moment. But actually, the danger seems to be unrelated to that. We've all got baggage, Ali, and sometimes that comes back to bite us. I don't quite know what's going on in the background, but I don't think it's related to our current case."

A sudden thought occurs to me, and this time I don't hesitate to interrupt.

"Becky, aren't you supposed to be going to London on Monday? That doesn't sound very safe."

"I need to do this, Will. I've got to follow a lead on the egg. Roger's put me on to this, so it must be okay." Her face shows her doubt, as I see when a red traffic light gives me the chance to take a good look at her. I have a huge respect for her courage, but this seems highly risky.

"Maybe someone should go with you? I could come?" I suggest.

"I need to do this by myself," she protests. "If I have someone with me for everything, I'll lose every scrap of confidence I ever had."

"You're going to be visiting people who've had contact with the egg in the past. You have no idea whether they're legit."

"For God's sake, Mum. He's got a point. You can't drag Will out to pick me up, and yet wander alone into some lion's den in London two days later. It's bloody ridiculous."

I glance at Alison in the rear-view mirror. She looks exasperated – pretty much how I feel too. This time I send my sympathetic smile in her direction, via the mirror. She must see it, as she smirks. "Listen to Will. He seems to have a few more brain cells than you do."

Ouch. Another glance at the mirror shows she's teasing me, at least, even though her ire is still directed at her mum.

Becky doesn't answer, but digs out her phone and scrolls through the numbers. As we're still wading through Nottingham traffic, I get plenty of chance to glance round at my passengers. A moment later, Becky is speaking on the phone.

"Dan, how are you doing?"

I remember Mum telling me about Dan. He was Becky's best friend at uni and is now married to a lovely American chap and living in London with him and their dog. I remember that last time Becky went to London, while we were working on our last big case, she took some time out to meet up with Dan.

I have to negotiate some busy roundabouts and a confusing lane system, so I miss some of the opening conversation, but when I can listen again, Becky's asking Dan if he's free on Monday.

"Yes, I know you have work, but you're a scientist. Surely you can wangle an extended lunch break?"

I don't hear his answer, but can fill in the gaps when Becky replies, "That's great. And you'll meet me at Euston and drop me off again. Are you sure? It's a bit of detective work. I'm in a bit of trouble, and don't really want to make those visits alone."

I lose track again as it's time to get on to the motorway, so I need to concentrate. By the time we're in the traffic flow, the conversation is over and Becky has disconnected.

"So, what's the verdict?" I ask.

"Weren't you listening?" says Becky.

"Not for all of it. What did he say?"

"He messaged his boss while he was on the call with me and asked if he can take the day off. She said yes. So, as long as you can take me to the station and pick me up again at the other end, and I can stay out of trouble on the train, I'll be fine. I trust Dan completely, so he can come in to all my meetings. I'll sign him in as a member of the White Knight. Your mum knows him. She'll back me up that he's fine."

"She already has. I know about Dan. It sounds as though you've sorted it. Well done."

"I guess that works out, Mum. I would have come down with you, but frankly, I've got loads of revision to do; exams start straight after the holidays, so I need to crack on. Much better for you to meet Dan."

"Do you know Dan, Alison?" I ask.

"Yeah. He used to be Uncle Dan when I was a kid. I

dropped the Uncle when I was about fifteen, but he's a sweetie. We don't get to see him so often since he got married, but he used to come up for a couple of weeks every year, and we'd go down to see him for long weekends in the holidays. He adores Mum. He'll look after her." She speaks with confidence, and I'm happy to trust her testimony on top of what my mum said about Dan.

The rest of the journey back to Manchester passes more harmoniously, with discussions on Alison's course, university life, drinking games and tv shows. She's witty and entertaining, but beneath the dry humour, I can discern a vulnerability. Unless it's my own wishful thinking, because Alison White is bloody amazing. And if she's as strong and confident as she portrays, then I'm screwed.

TWENTY-FIVE

Becky

MONDAY

To be perfectly honest, I'm relieved that I've got cover for the trip to London. Will picks me up at half past seven in the morning, and will collect me later, as long as I call him from the train. If I can't stay safe on a Pendolino between Manchester and London, it's pathetic.

I spent yesterday sorting out Alison's laundry, although there wasn't much of it. She's a lot more domesticated than I was as a student, and makes weekly trips to the on-site launderette in her halls. She surprised me in the afternoon by suggesting we invite Will and Joanna round for a takeaway for dinner. I noticed her and Will got on well, but when she last met Joanna it was under difficult circumstances, and Alison was unfriendly to say the least. The evening went smoothly though, with both parties keen to leave the past behind.

Returning to the present, Will drops me off in the busy short-stay car park.

"Don't forget, if you call me about half an hour before you're due back in to Manchester, I can be here and waiting for you. Or if you prefer, phone me when you get on the train in London. I can track it and make sure I'm here in time."

"Sure. That makes sense. Thanks, Will. I really appreciate the lifts."

The journey to London is uneventful. I read my Kindle, check through my notes ready for the meeting with Wartski's store manager, and take some time to look forward to seeing Dan again. That was a great idea of mine to bring him in on this. The train is fairly quiet. It's due in shortly after 10.30 but is still peak rate fares. Roger's paying, so I didn't mind too much. The meeting with the manager is at 11.45, so I needed to leave plenty of time.

Dan is on the concourse at London Euston, next to the WHSmith bookshop as arranged. He holds out his arms as soon as he sees me and envelops me in a warm hug. I return the hug with interest. It's so good to see my old friend again. It's only been a month this time, but a lot's happened.

"Let's have a look at you, Lovey." He keeps his hands on my shoulders as he surveys me at arm's length. "Yes, too pale, as usual. You're looking tired, honey. What's been going on?"

"How about we get the tube to Green Park and then find a coffee shop? There must be at least one in the area. We can talk there." I resist the urge to hug him again, stepping back instead and smiling up at him.

On the way to the Tube, I spot someone who looks like Chloë's stepdad, Peter. I've only met him once though, so I can't be totally sure. Either way, there's no reason he shouldn't be in London, so I dismiss him from my mind.

At Green Park, we search first for the Wartski shop. I like to know exactly where I'm going if possible, so once we've located it, we find a Pret A Manger a couple of blocks up on the corner of Piccadilly.

"This is good. Not too close to our meeting place, but within easy reach." I scan the menu board behind the baristas. "What do you fancy?"

"Flat white for me, please," Dan says. "I can get them if you want?"

"I'll put them on expenses. Grab us a table – somewhere quiet, if possible."

A few minutes later, we're sitting in a corner with coffee in front of each of us.

"Did you get those notes I sent you?" I ask. I'd spent an hour yesterday writing up a summary of the case and of the weird things that had happened to me recently. I'd figured, correctly, that I wouldn't get enough privacy to speak to him about all these things.

"Of course. I've read them through about three times. They don't seem to add up to anything coherent, but then it wouldn't be like you to be involved in anything straightforward and simple."

"You asked earlier what I'd been up to. I worried that maybe you hadn't read them properly." I throw him a confused glance before taking a sip of cappuccino.

"I just meant that you don't look as if you've been taking care of yourself. Becks, come on, we've known each other too long for this." He lowers his voice and reaches for my hand across the table. "You dropped off the face of the earth for a few months after you left the police force. When we met last month, you didn't tell me about what had happened to make you leave, but I can see that it still affects you. There's a darkness in your eyes somehow. I wish I could make it better."

So do I. Goodness knows why I didn't take him up on his offer of a stay in the flat he shares with Gray. I should have done, then we could have talked properly.

"Maybe one day. How's your sister getting on?" Last time we spoke she was starting a new chemotherapy regime.

"She seems to be responding well at the moment. She's only had two cycles so far, though, so it's early days. We don't know if the cancer's receding, but she's not having too many side effects, so that's a good start."

"And how's the puppy getting on?" I can't remember the pup's name, but hopefully Dan will mention it to save me any embarrassment.

He doesn't let me down and releases my hand so he can wave his arms about as he speaks about his new baby.

"Tilly's great. Neither Gray nor I have an intact pair of slippers between us, but otherwise she's an angel." He continues for at least five minutes to talk about toilet training, crate use and Tilly's favourite toys, but then gives me a hard look. "You're not getting away with it, Becks. I know you're busy right now, but when this case is over, you're coming to stay with me for a weekend, and you're telling me everything. It's what best friends do."

I check my watch – partly to avoid the need to respond. After all, what can I say? I agree with him, and anyway, I'm pretty touched that he's still calling me his best friend after all these years.

"It's eleven-thirty. I think we should go and meet Mr Parker – our Wartski contact. Let's see what he can tell us about the Necessaire egg."

We leave the shop after about twenty-five minutes, fifteen of which were spent goggling at the beautiful treasures inside. We employed the other ten minutes in speaking to Mr Parker, who gave us a very brief history of the egg but denied any current knowledge of its whereabouts. However, he referred us to an ex-colleague of his who he thought could help further. He set up an appointment with this man for half past three this afternoon, and gave us an address in Bloomsbury.

Dan and I kill some time over a leisurely lunch, followed by a walk along Piccadilly, through Covent Garden and Leicester Square and up to the British Library, which we're able to explore for half an hour before heading up the road for our meeting.

The house we've been sent to is an ordinary-looking townhouse. Given its location, it probably costs several times as much as my home, but it doesn't look particularly grand. The street is fairly quiet. There are a few people around, but it's a long way from the bustle that we walked through this afternoon.

"Shall we do this?" I turn to Dan. He chuckles. He's obviously enjoying today's outing.

"Yes, let's go for it. It would be exciting to get some information, but actually I feel like we're being sent on a wild goose chase."

"As long as it's a wild goose that lays golden Fabergé eggs, we'll be okay."

"That's dreadful. Come on." He touches me on the back, gently propelling me towards the door. I take a deep breath and go up the three steps that lead to the entrance. I press the bell.

The man who answers is not someone I would want to meet alone on a dark night. Tall and broad, he's dressed in a white shirt and smart trousers, but looks more like a bouncer in a nightclub than a businessman. His expression is amused.

"Becky and Dan, isn't it? Come along in." His voice is cultured, more in line with his attire than his physique. There's the faintest hint of an Eastern European accent, perhaps Russian or Romanian. He ushers us into a room at the back of the property. It's a rather old-fashioned looking living room, with chintz armchairs and a wooden coffee table. There is nothing here of any interest – no jewels, paintings or ornaments. It doesn't quite fit with this guy's strong-man image. Once we're sitting down, he holds out a photograph. "I believe you're looking for this egg?"

I take the picture from him. It's an old photograph, curled and yellow at the edges, but it looks like the original of the one I've seen online.

"Why have you got this photo?" I glance over at the contact, and hastily add, "If you don't mind me asking."

He laughs. His amusement sends shivers through me. I get a sense that he's making fun of me, but also that he knows something that he doesn't plan on telling. I hate feeling at a disadvantage, but even with Dan here, I can't wait to get out of this house.

"I got it from a friend. There have been many people after this little beauty, and I had to know what I was looking for."

"Have you found it?" asks Dan.

The mood changes subtly, as if that was not an appropriate question. I hadn't particularly given Dan instructions on whether to speak, and although I was a little startled by him asking, it was something I might have asked myself, had I been less wary.

"I'm not entirely sure why my friend sent you here, except perhaps so I would know you in the future. I suggest you cancel this search for the missing egg. You won't find it." His accent is more pronounced now, and filled with menace. I am seventy percent certain that he's Russian – yet another link to that country — and yet, given the egg's history, it would make sense.

"Perhaps we should leave now, but you haven't answered my colleague's question." I refrain from referring to Dan as a friend. I don't want this man to have any hold over either of us. It's safer to let him think we just work together.

The man's face suffuses with red.

"You are leaving now. I answer no further questions. You

will drop this search this minute." He ushers us into the hall and towards the door.

Once we're outside, he slams the door behind us. We make a quick exit from the road, speedwalking to the next street until we're out of sight.

"Bloody hell. What was that all about?" I ask Dan. I shove shaking hands deep into my pockets.

"That was my fault, sorry, Becks. I shouldn't have asked such a direct question."

"I followed it up, so I'm equally to blame. Actually, from the minute I got inside, I wanted to leave. He was seriously terrifying." I worked as a detective in the police force for a long time, and put away a lot of murderers. All the same, I'm not sure how much to share with my old friend.

"Let's get a coffee and then you can tell me what's bothering you. There's clearly something."

"You know me too well." I grimace. "Let's go into that Costa over there." I point over the road, where a conveniently-placed coffee shop is looking relatively quiet from this distance.

We go inside and there are several free tables.

"So, what's up?" Dan sits opposite me after placing the drinks on the table.

"I reckon that man has killed. He felt like a murderer to me."

He looks at me penetratingly. I always suspected he could read my mind, but we've seen less of each other over the last year – perhaps I'd hoped his skill had reduced in this area.

"You've got a lot of experience in this field. I would trust your judgement." He glances down at our still-full mugs. "How about we drink up sharpish and get back to Euston where it's a bit more crowded? I suddenly feel as though we're a bit too close for comfort – only about three streets away."

"I've got a better idea." I pick up our mugs and go to the

counter. "Excuse me, we've decided we need to take these out. Please could you transfer them to takeaway cups?"

The barista is friendly and obliging, so two minutes later, Dan and I are on our way back to Euston, coffee cups in hand.

When we arrive there, I check my watch. It's 4.30. There's a train in ten minutes and another in half an hour. I mention this to Dan.

"I think you should get out of London. I'm going to bolt home too. Get this solved, darling, and come down to see me soon, okay? For social reasons. Come and stay with me and Gray and meet Tilly."

"I will do, I promise. I'll keep you posted about everything."

"Let me know when you get home." He pulls me into a hug and we cling together for a moment, like we used to do thirty years ago as students.

I give him a quick peck on the cheek as the hug ends, and then run for the train. Seven minutes before it leaves, but it's at the other end of the station and I want a seat to myself with no horrible sprawling men next to me.

I make it, with a couple of minutes to spare, sitting in an airline-style seat behind a party of girls who look as though they're on a hen do. They'll probably be loud for the whole journey, but it reduces the chances of me being accosted. I notice quickly that they're not English. It takes me a few minutes to diagnose the language, but I eventually pin it down to Portuguese. Not a language I have much command over, just a recollection of a few words from childhood holidays. I couldn't even guess if it's European or Brazilian Portuguese. I give up wondering, and get out my phone to call Will.

The battery's dead. I get out of my seat and tap the nearest girl on the shoulder.

"Excuse me, do you speak English?"

She stares at me, uncomprehendingly. Her eyes are glazed,

and I suspect her linguistic skills have deteriorated throughout the day. I give up and sit down again. I don't want to draw too much attention to myself, so I'm reluctant to ask around the carriage for a charger and actually there's no charge point near me anyway.

Shit. How did this happen? I think back to when I last looked at my phone and then recall using Google Maps to find the man's house in Bloomsbury. It must have drained my battery, and in all the anxiety that followed, it never occurred to me to check. I'll have to jump in a cab when I get back to Piccadilly and hope that I get home safely. Surely a random black cab can't do any harm.

TWENTY-SIX

Joanna

MONDAY

"Will?" I call upstairs to where my son is working. I've been in the kitchen most of the day, alternating between messaging Glen and searching for clues to Eric Ulyanov's whereabouts. A rumbling stomach has alerted me to the fact that it's now half past seven and Will hasn't yet left to pick up Becky. Dinner was always going to wait until he got back, but time has disappeared and nothing has happened.

"Hi Mum. Everything okay?" He scoots down to the kitchen as he speaks.

"Haven't you heard from Becky yet? Did she say what train she was going to be on?"

He glances at his watch. "I didn't realise it was so late. I've not heard from her. Let me call her." He selects her number on his phone and hits the *Connect* button. He puts it on speakerphone.

"*You have reached voicemail…*"

"Bugger! Either she's in a meeting or on a call with someone." Will looks a little concerned. We both know her well enough to know that she'd have let us know if she was going to be this late.

"I'll send her a WhatsApp. At least if she's busy, she'll see it and get back to us shortly." I type, '*Hi Becks, how's it going?*' into my phone and click *Send*. The first tick appears immediately, showing it's left my phone, but the second one is absent. I wait a moment. "It's not got to her. She must have turned her phone off for some reason."

"Have you got Dan's number?" Will suggests. "Maybe you can check if they're still together. She might not have left London yet."

I have Dan's contact details and give him a quick call. He confirms she left on the 16.40 train and should be home by now. My mouth goes dry as I thank him and promise to let him know when we hear from her.

"Bloody hell. Where is that woman?" I glare at Will as though he might have an answer.

"Shall I drive down to the station and see if I can find her? She might have stopped to get something to eat there."

"That's probably a good start, but why wouldn't she call and let you know what time she wants to be collected?" I swear again – at length.

Will puts his hand on my shoulder.

"It'll be fine. Let me search for her. I'll be on hands-free, so let me know if you hear anything."

I can see he's trying to reassure me, but there's anxiety in his eyes.

Once he's gone, I settle down to wait. At least, I make myself a cup of tea and pace the kitchen. Then I pace the lounge. It doesn't help. I try calling Becky every three minutes, but it continues to go to voicemail. Shit. What is that bloody silly girl up to? I ring Glen and let him know what's going on.

"Dad's sleeping in front of the telly. Let me see if Pat's free to come and look after him, then I can come and at least keep you company while you wait for news. Thanks for the hire car, by the way. It arrived this afternoon."

"Great. Thanks, Glen." I disconnect. A couple of minutes later he messages to say he's on his way.

As soon he arrives, I open the door to him, just as my phone rings. I wave him in, greeting him with a kiss, check the screen, then answer the call.

"Hi Will. Have you found her?"

"No, there's no sign of her. I've searched everywhere. I don't know whether to show anyone photos of her. Is it okay to alert people to the fact that we've lost her?"

"I don't see why not. Go for it and let me know how you get on." I disconnect, and update Glen with the latest.

"I think that's sensible, love. Why don't we get something to eat while we're waiting? You're wilting a bit, if you don't mind me saying so." He's right. I'm feeling washed out. He suggests fish and chips. It's cheap and easy, and I go with him to pick them up, making sure my phone volume is up so I don't miss any calls.

The phone remains silent for the short trip, allowing us to get our food and get back without interruption. I feel nauseous with anxiety by the time we get back, and I'm not sure if I can eat anything.

"Okay if I put the kettle on?"

"Sure. Thanks." Glen's made himself at home over the short time we've been friends, and I'm happy for him to make a cup of tea.

I check my phone again as I sit down at the table and allow him to sort dinner out too. It's probably unfair, but my legs are feeling decidedly wobbly. There's still no message and no missed calls. I send Will a quick WhatsApp. *'Any news yet?'*

There's no reply for a few minutes, but I can see he's read the message. Then he calls – just as Glen has set down the plate of fish and chips and a mug of tea in front of me.

"Well?" I ask, too impatient for preliminaries.

"The lassie who works at Upper Crust noticed someone

who looked like Becky talking to another woman at about 6.45. They went off together in the direction of the tram, but could have been heading to the short stay car park that can be accessed from there."

"It's gone eight now. So she should be home if she got a lift. Did Upper Crust Girl notice what the other woman looked like?"

"Not really. She just said she was taller than Becky and dressed in jeans, a checked shirt and a leather jacket. Not overly helpful. She couldn't even remember the woman's hair colour." Will sounds tired and irritable.

"Is it worth going down to the tram station or the car park and asking around there?"

"Probably not. It's such a fast-moving environment. The best bet is the CCTV. Question is, do I hack it, or ask Wendy if one of her lot can check it for me?"

"I'll ring Wendy and ask her. You may as well come back here. If Wendy's team isn't able to check quickly, you can have a look yourself." I pause. "I don't suppose the station people will let you have a look at the CCTV if you show them your business card, would they?"

"Worth a shot. Let me try that before you call Wendy."

In the twenty minutes before he calls me back, I force down a few chips and finish my drink, but I can't eat any more. Glen is sympathetic.

"I can't eat when I'm stressed either, love. Why don't we sit in the other room and put the TV on for a bit? It might help to distract us."

I agree it's not a bad idea, and we settle down, in an anxious fashion, with a DIY program. It's only really background though. I'm certainly not concentrating on it as we wait impatiently for Will to call me back. Eventually, the phone rings, and Glen mutes the TV while I answer it.

"Any news?" I ask.

"A bit," says Will. "They're letting me look at the CCTV after I get Wendy to message through some sort of authorisation. She's just sorting that out now, but I should get access to it shortly. I just thought I'd better update you. I've tried a few more times to get hold of Becky. Oh, and Wendy said she'd pop round to you as soon as she's sent that email. I guess she'll be with you a bit before I am, but we need to work out the next steps."

My heart sinks as the meaning of this sinks in. Everyone is taking this seriously, which means they're all concerned about her. Shit. I was really hoping that all this worry would be unnecessary. A faint sense of numbness creeps over me as the potential awfulness becomes too dreadful to take in.

"I don't suppose anyone has been in touch with Matt yet?" I ask.

Will hesitates. "Not directly, but Alison and I have been texting a bit. She knows I'm trying to find her mum, so I assume she's told Matt and Cheryl."

I roll my eyes. "I'll phone him in a minute. We need to have a conference once you've seen that CCTV and work out the best way to handle this."

"Sure. Anyway, got to go. Wendy's just sent over that authorisation, so I need to check out those images and see if there are any clues who she's gone with."

Once he's disconnected, I ring Matt.

"Thanks for calling, Joanna. I've been getting second-hand messages from my elder daughter. Why she's suddenly so pally with Will, I don't know, but this is not like Becky to just disappear. Given what's been going on, I think this is serious."

I decide that it's not the right time to go into my suspicions about Will and Alison. He talked about her for over an hour after getting back on Saturday, and he's not talked about anyone like that for a long time.

I arrange for us to go to the Whites' house as soon as

Wendy and Will get here, but promise to message Matt with any new information that comes through in the meantime.

My son rings again about fifteen minutes later to say that there's some footage of Becky in the car park with a woman who fits the description from the girl at the baguette stall. Unfortunately, it's not possible to see if she gets into a car or a taxi with this woman, or even alone.

"I don't suppose it's possible to recognise the woman who's with her?" I ask.

"I asked for the images to be downloaded and sent over to Wendy, but somehow they bloody corrupted the file. Wendy's sent it over to her tech experts to see if they can un-mangle it. Basically, Mum, we're back to square one."

I glance outside. A spring storm is on the way. Rain is coming down in torrents and the wind is picking up. I hope to goodness that wherever Becky is, she's warm and dry.

TWENTY-SEVEN

Becky

MONDAY

I'm lying in a ditch, with my arms bound behind my back and my legs bound tightly together. I'm beyond soaking wet. In the ten minutes that I've been awake, even the sheltered bit of fabric between my thighs has absorbed enough water to make me bloody uncomfortable. The horizontal rain is still battering my face, and I decide to keep my eyes closed for the moment. It was enough to open them to discern that it was pitch dark without keeping them open any longer than necessary.

A migraine-like headache is adding to the general discomfort, but I don't think it's a result of the usual triggers. It seems to stem from a point above and behind my right ear, rather than from above my eyes. I try to recall what was happening before I woke up here.

I had been to London. I remember that. Something to do with the egg heist, and I'd spent a few hours detecting with Dan, my old uni friend. I recall getting on the train. Bugger, it hurts to think, but at least it takes my mind momentarily off the blasted rain. If I'm not rescued soon, I'm going to die here from exposure. The thought chokes me up. I don't want to die.

I want to be back home with Matt and my girls. Nothing is more important than that. What the fucking hell did I do to deserve this?

I force myself to push away the self-pity. Now's really not the time to wallow. I need to make sense of it all. What happened after I left London?

I remember getting off the train. That's it – I'd been unable to phone Will because my phone had died. Shit. Why hadn't I tried harder to borrow a phone? Or a charger? I'm so stupid.

More self-pity. Buck up, Becky. Pull yourself together, woman! Ignore the rain and the cold and this sodding awful headache and the fact that you can't move much. Concentrate.

As I came off the train I bumped into an old colleague. Janice had been a family liaison officer when I was in the police force, and we'd met her briefly during our last case when she'd been supporting Troy. She greeted me from next to the baguette stall opposite the platform exit. I don't know if she'd just got off a train or why she was there, but she offered me a lift when I said I was going to get a cab home. It didn't occur to me not to trust her. We'd been out for drinks on several occasions in the past. I considered her a borderline friend – certainly someone I'd liked and trusted.

My brain is so fuzzy. It's like I don't want to remember. But this is important. Before I can plan an escape, I have to work out what happened. I laugh at myself. How can I possibly escape from this? I just need to pray that someone will come and rescue me before it's too late.

Finally, it comes to me: not how to escape, of course, but the last thing that happened before I lost consciousness. I got into Janice's car in the front seat when a voice behind me said, "Hello, Becky. You've been bloody difficult to get hold of, you know."

I think that's when I must have whacked on the head,

because I remember nothing else until I woke up. That prayer I was talking about just now takes shape.

"Please God, don't let him kill me. He said he protected me last time. Please let him protect me now. Please don't leave me here to die…"

TWENTY-EIGHT

Will

MONDAY NIGHT

As soon as I get home, I grab my laptop. I'm not averse to going to Becky's house to await news and figure out where she is, but I need to check that footage again from the cameras. I can't believe the images they sent over were corrupt.

Mum's jittery as we get into my car. It's good to see Glen supporting her though. He hugs her before she opens the door. He doesn't join us in the car, but comes round to the driver's side. I lower my window.

"Alright, pal," I say. "Thanks for coming round."

"I can't stay much longer. My neighbour's looking after Dad, but she'll be needing to get home. I won't come with you if that's okay, but keep in touch and let me know if there's anything I can do from home."

"Sure. Thanks." I watch him get into his car and turn to Mum. "Are you okay? You look a bit wrecked."

"I'm worried sick about Becky. This is so not like her."

"I know. Come on, let's get round to see Matt and the girls. Wendy's going to meet us there. Then I'm going to have another look at this bloody CCTV footage, if I can unscramble it." I turn the engine on and start driving.

A short while later, we're sitting in Becky's kitchen, supplied with coffee by Alison. I give her a grateful smile as she hands me the mug.

"Thanks." My fingers touch hers as I take the drink from her, and a spark of something like electricity flows through me. I think maybe she feels it too, as she reddens slightly and draws back. Her smile is quick and awkward, but I see it before she turns away.

I open my laptop and start work, leaving the others to chat around me. It's easy to block out the noise though. I've spent years working in busy offices where the only way to get anything done is to focus on the task at hand and ignore everything else.

It doesn't take me long to realise the file is not salvageable.

"Damn! Matt, do you object if a do a bit of hacking? I only ask, because it will go through your server. It shouldn't be easily traceable, but…"

"If it's to find my wife, you can hack into the bloody Kremlin for all I care." Matt rests his hand on my shoulder for a moment. He'd been standing near the kettle but came over when I spoke to him. "Do whatever you need to, lad. Just find my Becky." His voice is slightly hoarse.

"Sure, thanks." I grin up at him. "The Kremlin shouldn't be necessary – only the CCTV at Piccadilly Station."

I get back to work.

Sometime later, I look up. I'm actually alone in the kitchen. I don't recall seeing everyone else leave, but I guess I've been in the zone, totally concentrating on my work.

I take the laptop and go in search of everyone else. I don't have to look far – they're all in the lounge: Matt, Alison, Cheryl, Mum and Wendy. When did she arrive? I really have been in my own little world.

They all look at me as I enter the room.

"Well, folks. First, I have the CCTV of Becky walking to

the car with the strange woman. But also, there was another camera, that they didn't show me. It's got an image of her getting into a car. It's pretty hazy, but with a bit of work, we might get a registration number."

"Wow!" Alison looks at me with something like respect. "Well done. That's impressive. Can we see?"

"Sure." I sit on the sofa and open the lid of the laptop and show them the two files I've downloaded. They all crowd round and I press *Play* on the first file. This is the one I first saw.

"Stop there!" Wendy taps me on the shoulder, and I press *Pause*. "Back two frames," she says. I oblige and then look up at her. There's a look of shock and distress on her face. "I recognise that woman. Unless she's a body-double, that's Janice, one of my liaison officers. What the hell is she doing?"

"Bloody well abducting my wife, by the looks of it," says Matt. I glance over at him. He's almost purple and looks ready to explode. I'm about to say something reassuring when Wendy speaks up.

"Calm down, Matt. This can't be good for you. It won't help Becky if you have another heart attack. We've got a huge clue now to help us find her. Let's get this ball rolling so we can work out exactly where she is, and then we can rescue her."

"You're right. Of course you are. Sure." He manages a weak smile at Wendy, then looks at me. "Thanks Will. This is a huge help. Is there anything else to see?"

"I'm so glad you asked, because…" I minimise the first file and open the other one. This is the one that wasn't shown to me. "Have a look at this." I press *Play*.

We all watch as Becky accompanies the woman we now know as Janice to a car and gets in. The occupants aren't visible, but a fuzzy number plate gets caught on the image.

"Isn't it lucky that they parked in front of one of two

cameras?" Alison remarks. "I mean, could it be a trap, and they're going to transfer Mum to another car when they're further away?"

"It's not impossible, but this was one of four CCTV files that wasn't shown to me. I think the Station Manager was paid by one of the perpetrators to only show one insignificant file on the concourse, and then corrupted it to make sure I didn't get to show it to anyone else. If Janice and her accomplice – because I assume she didn't do this alone – were taking Becky somewhere and covered their tracks to this extent, then surely they wouldn't bother to change cars." I glance at Wendy. "If you give me a bit longer, I can get this blown up and we can see if we can get the details on that reg plate."

With everyone's agreement, I retire again to the kitchen and get to work on enlarging and improving image quality until the registration number is sufficiently visible. I share the image by WhatsApp immediately with Wendy, who comes into the kitchen to join me a moment later.

"The problem we have is that this involves a police officer. I don't know how widespread this is, or what Janice may have been told as a reason she had to entice Becky into that car, but there may be others in the team who are… shall we say, misinformed about Becky." She pauses. "Would you allow me to log into your laptop as a guest? From there, I can use the VPN on my phone to access the ANPR data. Let's keep this search confined to these walls."

I give Wendy access and then wander into the lounge. There's a space on the sofa next to Alison, so I sit down. My mouth goes suddenly dry. I force myself to speak.

"Are you okay?" I ask.

"Obviously not. My mum's missing. Would you be okay?" The sarcasm in her tone cuts through me deeply, but I shouldn't have asked such a stupid question.

"No, of course not. Sorry."

"Me too. You were only trying to be nice. I appreciate it, but my natural bitch comes to the fore when I'm stressed. I don't mean to be horrible, and I'm grateful for all the work you've been doing." She pauses and looks round. I follow her gaze. Mum and Cheryl and Matt are talking softly about something else and aren't paying any attention to us. "Where are you up to now?"

"We've got the registration number. Wendy's logging into her systems to see if that car has been seen on any cameras."

Then two things happen simultaneously. Wendy comes in carrying the laptop, and the doorbell rings. Alison gets up and heads for the door. Wendy follows, after depositing the laptop back on the kitchen table.

"Don't open it without checking who it is," she warns. I go into the hall for extra support.

Alison looks through the glass at the top of the door. "There's someone running away. I can't see much – it's too dark."

"What's that on the floor?" I point to an envelope at Alison's feet.

She bends down and is about to pick it up.

"Wait!" Wendy pulls a pair of latex gloves from her pocket and puts them on. She then picks up the envelope herself. "It might not be connected, but in case it is, let's do this carefully." She opens the envelope and extracts a sheet of typed paper which she peruses, before shaking her head, an expression of disgust on her face.

"What does it say?" Matt has joined us in the hall, followed by everyone else.

"It says, '*You will find what's missing on Winter Hill in a ditch near the mast. Go quickly.*' What's irritating is that I had just pinpointed the car's journey to that area. But this is perhaps a bit more specific."

"Let's go then. We clearly need to get a move on. If my Becky is out there in this…" He points outside to the incessant rain. It doesn't take a genius to realise that time is not on our side.

TWENTY-NINE

Becky

MONDAY NIGHT

Monday night

I don't know how long I've been lying here. It feels like hours, but it could be minutes. The rain has been relentless and continues to sting my face – the most exposed part of me. My hands are slightly shielded from the full force of it as they're tied behind my back. The rope is cutting into my wrists. My shoulders are cramping from this unnatural position. I'm wet through and increasingly chilled to my core.

The terrifying spectre of death is also hovering. The extreme discomfort is almost helpful, as it distracts me a little from the fear, but as time progresses, the worry grows. How on earth will anyone find me up here? Wherever here is.

Darkness is absolute. Keeping my eyes closed against the rain makes no difference to my vision. I open them briefly now and then to see if anything has changed, but no: it's still black as pitch, and only if I concentrate can I even make out my own outline. I try to keep my eyes open for a little longer to see if they adjust to the dark. What's a little stinging rain when I've got this far? It's almost just a minor irritation now compared to everything else. My sense of smell seems to have dulled, or maybe I've become accustomed to the outdoor scent of gorse. It takes a while for my eyes to adjust, during which I'm getting colder, wetter and more afraid, but I try to focus on seeing something. Apart from anything else, it helps to keep panic at bay. Because what would panic achieve? Just a quicker descent into the abyss. I need to keep strong and sane to give myself any chance of survival out here.

A small voice in the back of my head says, '*What's the point of surviving? You're tied up. You can't escape.*'

'*Shut up. If I can stay alive, someone will come. Eventually. They have to. Or maybe I can find a way of cutting these ropes.*' I know the chances of either are virtually nil, but I need something to cling to. I focus again on vision. Perhaps I can see an outline of the terrain. I seem to be in a ditch. Can I move at all?

'*What good will that do you?*' says the irritating pessimist in my mind.

'*I thought I told you to shut up! I need to keep busy. And who knows? Maybe if I sit up, a passer-by can see me.*'

'*It's dark, you stupid woman!*'

'*Well, I need to try.*'

Somehow, I wriggle into a position where I'm half-upright, supported by a wall of mud and grass. I look around again. I think the rain has eased up a fraction, unless it's just that I'm in a better situation – if you can call still being saturated, freezing and in pain a better situation. There still isn't much to see. The outline of the ditch I'm in has lowered relative to my gaze, but not a lot else has changed. I'm just marginally more comfortable sitting than lying on my side with my upper arm trapped beneath me.

More time passes. I have no way of knowing how much, but I'm getting quite shivery. I seem to have stopped delving into how I got here; perhaps because I've worked it out already and I don't need to think about it any more. But maybe it's for a darker reason: I don't want to remember. That voice that spoke to me before I got hit…

'*Stop it. Don't dwell on what you can't change.*' I don't even know which me is saying that. Details are getting fuzzy though. The world is a little fuzzy now too. Transient thoughts and impressions flit in and out – the rain, cold, dark, pain and fear. I can't seem to hold on to any of them for long. My eyes drift shut. I open them a second later, as my brain screams, '*Danger! Don't go to sleep!*'

The many First Aid courses I've attended over the years suddenly become sharp in my mind – at least, sharper than anything else at the moment – there's still a blurred edge to it. Hypothermia kills – and it kills more quickly if the victim falls asleep. If I fall asleep.

My battle now focuses on fighting the drowsiness.

'*I want to go to sleep – please let me sleep.*'

'*No. You'll never wake up. You're behaving like a child. Pull yourself together.*'

I'm shivering uncontrollably now, but no thoughts are staying in my head for long. I'm just trying to stay awake – and alive.

THIRTY

Joanna

MONDAY NIGHT

Monday night

It takes about half an hour to get to Winter Hill. We go in two cars – Wendy takes Matt and the girls in her car, and I go with Will. I've not been there before, but Will has hiked there a couple of times. He finds a road that leads to the mast, and we drive as far as we can to the top.

We arrive at about the same time as Wendy and the others and get out of the car. The rain is torrential – even worse than back at home. We're all dressed for it though, in waterproofs, with warm clothes underneath.

"Poor Becky. If she's really out here, we need to find her quickly," I say to Will. It's a repeat of what we've been saying all the way here. I turn on the torch on my phone, but Will turns on a wind-up lantern he's brought with us. The others are also carrying an assortment of phones and torches. Will, Wendy and Matt each have a rucksack filled with First Aid supplies, foil blankets, chocolate bars and flasks of tea.

"We need to stay in pairs." Wendy takes charge and splits us up. Will with Alison, Matt with Cheryl, and Wendy with me.

She instructs us on how to search and to phone her as soon as we find Becky.

She and I set off up the hill, Will and Ali go down, and Matt and Cheryl take a path off to the right.

"Hey, Matt." Will calls for his attention. "It gets pretty boggy over there. Go carefully, okay? We don't want to have to pull you out."

"Great thanks. We'll be careful."

It's silent for a little while after that. The hill is steep, and the rain is pelting us horizontally. Wendy and I shine our torch and phone lights around as we walk – keeping to the path but focusing the light on the sides. The rain is making it almost impossible to see anything, but neither of us will give up.

"Logically, if someone had to carry Becky, she's not likely to be too far from the path." Wendy justifies our plan, but I don't know if I'm convinced. Becky's about ten stone. A strong guy could carry her some distance. We've been going about twenty minutes in appalling conditions when I stop suddenly and grab Wendy's arm.

"What's that?" I go over to the side of the road, but I'm not sure now what had grabbed my attention. I step off the tarmac for a moment, trying to see better, but my boot sinks up to my ankles. "Shit! Wendy, give me a hand a minute." With her help, I release my foot from the clinging mud and we continue further up the hill, pausing periodically to catch our breath.

"Is that a head?" Wendy pants, several long moments later. We both train our lights in the same place. There's a ditch running alongside the road. Literally a few metres away.

"Becky?" I call out. "Is that you?" The head moves a fraction, turning towards the light. The torch isn't strong enough to see features in such poor visibility, but the stilted movement suggests all is not well. Wendy and I hurry over to the ditch, both being careful of our footing this time. We crouch down. "Becky," I say again. "Are you okay?"

"Don't know."

Wendy stands up and uses her phone to contact the others.

"Station… Phone… Will… Cold… wet." Becky's words are slurred and almost indistinct.

I put my hand against her cheek. She's half-frozen. Her confusion is worrying, as it suggests hypothermia.

"We're going to get you home, Becks. Back into the warm where you're safe. Can you move at all?"

She's propped up against the wall of the ditch, and her arms are behind her. I use the torch and realise her wrists and ankles are bound. About two feet along from Becky is her handbag. I pick it up and glance inside. Purse, phone, Kindle and a few other bits and pieces are inside. Whoever did this, it was clearly not done as part of a robbery.

"Wendy, pass me your rucksack." I notice she's finished phoning. I give her the handbag for safe keeping.

"The others are on their way. What do you need? I know where everything is. Let me fish in there for you."

"Foil blanket and tea, and a sharp knife if you've got one." I lower myself into the ditch next to Becky and wrap my arms around her, trying to give her some body heat while Wendy delves in the backpack. She's totally saturated. I'm mostly dry underneath my waterproofs, but not completely. Apparently 'waterproof' is a relative term, and not much can withstand torrential rain on the Lancashire moors.

Wendy crouches down at the side of the ditch and assesses the situation.

"Foil blanket is a waste of time when she's so wet. Let's get these ropes cut, and then we can get her out of there. Will's on his way, and bringing the car as he'll be passing it en route." She hands me the knife.

"Becks, can you sit forward so I can cut the rope off you?" The Swiss army knife that Wendy's handed me is reasonably sharp, and I don't want to risk cutting into Becky's wrists by mistake.

"Cold." She moves forward a fraction, just enough for me to move her hands towards me so I can access the rope.

"Wendy, can you shine that light here please? I can't hold the torch and cut the rope at the same time." She obliges and I get to work. Becky's head is drooping, and I'm scared stiff that she's losing consciousness. "Wendy, can you call an ambulance? I think we might need… er… better facilities than we've got in the car."

"Sure. Let me juggle things so you can still see."

A moment later, and Becky's wrists are free. I get to work on her ankle ropes and cut those more easily. Meanwhile, Wendy's on the phone to the ambulance control centre, and giving directions to the top of Winter Hill. Goodness only knows what they think, but it's not really relevant at the moment. The important thing is to get my friend safe and warm.

"Becky, are you awake?" I shake her shoulder as gently as I can, but with some urgency. Her head lifts a bit.

"Sort of," she mumbles.

Then, to my intense relief, my son shows up in the car with Alison in the front seat. Ali is taller than her mum, and although wiry, looks quite strong. I know Will's strength. We're going to need both of them for this rescue, as God alone knows how long it will take the ambulance to get here.

Becky's semi-conscious state hampers our attempts to get her out of the ditch. Even with her hands and legs free now, it takes the combined efforts of the four of us, and eventually, when Matt and Cheryl turn up, all six of us to get Becky into the car. I don't time the activity, but it feels as though it takes for ever, and by the end my arms and back are aching. Once she's in the car, we send the men to collect the other car, and Wendy and I strip off Becky's sodden clothes (with difficulty) and replace them with dry things we brought with us – clean knickers and socks and a sweatshirt and jogging bottoms. We don't bother with the bra. Given her state, it's not worth the effort. The aim is to get her warmed up as quickly as possible. Cheryl and Alison are standing outside, shielding the car from unwanted observers. We've just got our patient dressed when the ambulance shows up. Wendy goes to welcome the paramedics, and a few minutes later they're at the car door with a stretcher and a couple of blankets.

"Come on, let's get her to our vehicle, where we can assess her safely." A tall, ginger-haired chap in his forties smiles at me. "Do you want to come with your friend?"

"I'd like to, but these are her daughters. They have priority." I indicate Alison and Cheryl who are looking on anxiously.

He selects Ali as being obviously older, and sends Cheryl to wait with me in the car. Wendy also gets in after whispering something to Ali. I wait until they're in the ambulance before asking her what she said.

"I told her to reveal as little as possible about any of us got here. We need to sort this out as a team. It appears the force has a mole. It's vital that the wrong people don't hear that Becky is safe."

"Is Mum safe?" asks Cheryl, sitting next to me on the back seat. I put my arm around her. We've been good friends ever since I arrived on her doorstep.

"She's in the best place to check that out. Let's all hope and pray." We sit in silence for a while, waiting for the paramedics to come and give us a report. Matt and Will join us and we all sit in the one car. I'm sure I'm not the only one willing Becky's recovery with all my heart.

THIRTY-ONE

Will

TUESDAY - EARLY HOURS

I watch anxiously as they take Becky off in the ambulance with Alison in attendance. The rest of us head back to their house to decide the next steps.

"Perhaps I should pick up Ali from the hospital. Surely they won't let her stay." I've made tea and coffee for the other occupants of the kitchen and they're all drinking in silence, anxiety written on everyone's face.

"That's a good plan, Will. You can let us all know how Becky's doing. I'm going to drop Joanna home as soon as we've finished our drinks. I don't think any of us are quite dry yet." Wendy looks directly at Cheryl. "In fact, love, go up and change into your PJs. We'll let you know as soon as there's news, but there won't be any need for you to go out again tonight. I'm sure your dad will phone school in the morning and report you as off sick."

Matt nods.

"Yeah, of course. I need to phone in and let them know I'm off work too." He looks at the clock on the kitchen wall. My gaze follows his. It's nearly 2am.

"Cheryl," I smile at the tired but brave girl who's about to head upstairs. "When you're changed, please can you bring me some dry things for your sister to change into? We don't want her to get a cold either."

Ten minutes later, armed with a gym bag which Cheryl claims is full of clothes and other things that Alison might need, I'm about to leave.

"What are the 'other things' in the bag?"

"Girlie stuff. We don't know if she'll be allowed to stay with Mum. I threw in some toiletries and a book."

"Cool. Sounds good. Thanks." We're all trying to keep it light to ward off the huge dread in our hearts. Becky was unconscious when we last saw her. Hypothermia had set in. It's up to the hospital staff now to bring her back to us.

With no one to talk to on the journey, my mind spends far too long thinking. I've let Becky into my heart – purely in a platonic sense. She's somewhere between older sister and aunt. Her parity with Mum in terms of age should dictate the latter, but she treats me more like a younger brother and a close friend. I just know she's family, and my love for her is very much in line with that relationship. The thought of losing her is unbearable, and I try to shift away from it.

It doesn't take a huge effort, though, for thoughts to turn to her elder daughter. Ali knows I'm on my way because I sent her a WhatsApp. She replied with a 'Thanks' and a smiley face. I can never quite guess what's going through her head, but I imagine that right now all her focus is on her mum. A picture of Becky lying senseless in a hospital bed springs unbidden to mind. I push it away again. This is ridiculous. I turn on the radio. It's gone 2.30, so the music is pretty low-key – easy-listening stuff – and none of the inane chatter you get on daytime radio.

I focus on the song lyrics: all pop music I've grown up with. It tides me over until I draw up outside the hospital.

I call Ali before I get out of the car.

"I'm here. How do I find you?"

"Head for the main entrance. It's well signposted. I'll meet you there and take you up to Mum."

I agree, and fish the gym bag out from the front passenger footwell before getting out. My car is next to the pay-and-display machine. I grab some coins from a small hideaway near the dashboard and put in enough for a full day. I might only be here for twenty minutes, but I'd rather not be restricted. If Ali lets me wait with her, that's what I'll do. While I was waiting for Cheryl, Matt lent me some of his clothes – we're not too dissimilar in size, and I'm now dressed in dry jeans and a long-sleeved polo. Not quite my style, but warm and dry.

Alison and I arrive at the main entrance at the same time, but from opposite directions. She looks pale and less self-assured than I've seen her so far – even while we were searching Winter Hill, keeping anxiety at bay with the need for action. Now, the stress of waiting seems to have got to her. I greet her with a hug, which she accepts and returns warmly. We may have only known each other for three days, but it feels like a lifetime.

"How's your mum?" I ask as we move apart.

"Still unconscious. They've put her on the High Dependency Unit, HDU, and they're monitoring her closely." Her lip trembles slightly, but she swallows and straightens up.

"Do you want to get some dry clothes on?" I hand her the bag. "You still look damp at the edges."

"Let me take you to Mum, and then I'll leave you with her while I get changed. Thanks for bringing these." She slings the bag over her shoulder and propels me towards the corridor leading through the hospital.

She doesn't say much on the way to the ward, but points out a few useful landmarks – a restaurant (which, in my experience of hospitals, is a posh word for the reality of a canteen), coffee shop, pharmacy, and public loos. Just past the loos is the entrance for HDU. There's a buzzer at the side of the door, and Alison presses this when we arrive and gives her name when there's a response on the intercom. The door clicks and we go inside.

We're welcomed at the nurses' station, and Alison introduces me as a close friend of herself and her mum.

"It should only be family visiting." The nurse manning the desk looks concerned and unsure of herself.

"Will's virtually part of the family." Ali's laying it on a bit thick, but I go along with it. I want to see Becky and relieve the pressure from her daughter. "Mum would want him to sit with her and to keep me company. He's going to be her son-in-law one day. We were supposed to be getting the ring today, but obviously with Mum so unwell." She slips her hand into mine and gives such a soppy smile, I know she's play-acting. I return the smile, gazing into her eyes for a fraction longer than strictly necessary. Beneath the soppiness is a mixture of fear and determination. I'll investigate further later, but for now, it sways the nurse.

"Go on then, both of you. Congratulations. Does your mum know yet?" she asks Alison.

"Not yet, no. We'll break it to her when she's awake and back at home. I know enough to realise it's important we keep her calm for now." Her voice breaks slightly as she adds, "We just need her to wake up."

I squeeze her hand and get a slight pressure in acknowledgement. Meanwhile, the nurse points through to the ward area indicating we've permission to go through. Alison lets go of my hand but takes my arm instead, and ushers me towards the bed where her mum is still unconscious. There's a quiet but efficient atmosphere on the ward, with nurses moving between the beds and checking monitoring equipment.

"Sit next to her. I'll get changed and grab another chair on my way back."

I do as I'm told. Most of the time, I'm good at that. I suspect Alison doesn't have that characteristic. She strikes me as a young lady who likes to get her own way. I brush the thought aside – I seem to spend a lot of time thinking about her just now. It's unnerving. I sit and watch Becky for a while, but nothing much is happening. I fish out my phone and type a message to Mum, Wendy, Matt and Cheryl to let them know I'm here and that Becky is being well cared for. It's only when I finish the message that I see I've had many missed calls and several messages from my ex. I had my phone on silent – it must have changed settings by accident. It's very temperamental. I check the latest WhatsApp – it was from less than half an hour ago.

'*Where the fuck are you? Answer your bloody phone for once. Peter's not come home. He went to London today. He should have been back hours ago.*'

I type back, '*Sorry. Just picked this up. Not really able to talk at the moment, but I'll call you shortly. I assume he's not answering his phone?*'

Bloody hell. Another missing person on the same day. Is this a coincidence? It seems unlikely, but then who knows? Peter has been involved with some dodgy people. There's no way he's had nothing to do with Tania's kidnapping. That went wrong for the kidnappers – we rescued Tania, and the Blackstones avoided having to pay out to get her back. So maybe someone has a grudge.

Alternatively, he could just be a cheating slimeball.

I wait until Alison returns, dressed in clean dry clothes and looking brighter.

"Thanks, Will. I feel better for that. I hadn't realised how uncomfortable I was. It's not cool being soggy around the edges." She rests her hand on my shoulder for a moment. "I'll go grab another chair from somewhere."

"Don't worry about it for the minute. I've got to nip out and make a quick call. I'll get a chair on my way back."

She nods, and I head out to the foyer near Reception. There's an empty corner that looks like a reasonable place, so I lean against the wall and phone my ex-wife.

"Debs, it's Will. Any news?"

"Not yet." She sounds panicky. "I don't know whether to phone the police. What if he's on a job somewhere and I get the police involved? He'll go fucking ballistic."

That, at least, answers one of my longstanding questions. Clearly Debbie does know her husband has criminal tendencies. Probably a conversation for another time, though. I take a deep breath.

"The police probably suspect him anyway. His car was used in a kidnapping, Deb. You live in Preston; the kidnapping was in North Manchester. It's a suspiciously long way to go just to nick a car at random. Go to bed. Keep Chloë safe. I'll call you in the morning. I'm working myself right now, and can't get away."

"How the fuck am I supposed to sleep?"

"Your language has deteriorated since we split up. I hope you don't speak like that in front of Chloë."

"Don't be daft. Of course not. Usually I talk like a bloody BBC presenter. I'm just fucking stressed right now. What if Peter's been killed or something? Or he might have had an accident and need rescuing?"

"I'm not on rescue duty right now. If you think he needs help, you'll need to contact the police. If anything worse has happened, I expect they'll contact you." I say it with no expectation, but her reply freaks me out a little.

"Shit. That's the door. I'd better get it."

I can't see her, but I can hear the terror in her voice. The sound of the latch and the door being opened is followed by a small cry and a thud. A strange voice speaks into the phone – a Welshman.

"I'm Detective Sergeant Williams. Who am I speaking to?" he asks.

"I'm Debbie's ex-husband. Will MacLeod." I'm changing my name to Mum's adopted surname of Knight, but as it's not been finalised yet, it seems more appropriate to give my current one.

"I think your ex-wife might need some support. She's fainted just from seeing us – my colleague is in uniform. It seems to have upset her, and our news will make it worse. How soon can you get here?"

I look at my watch. It's 3.15. I'm torn. Ali needs my support with watching Becky, but my daughter might need a responsible adult around if Deb goes to pieces. It sounds as though there's bad news. Chloë wins, of course. She would always take priority, but there's still a pull in the other direction.

"About half an hour. What's happened?"

"I can't talk right now, because your ex-wife has come round and needs to be the first to hear the news, but come here as soon as you can. You'll be needed."

As soon as I've disconnected, I return to Alison. I crouch down next to her and start speaking in a low tone. I don't know if unconscious people can hear, but this news won't help Becky just now.

"Something's happened to Peter, my daughter's stepfather. I don't know what yet, but the police have turned up and my ex-wife has gone to pieces. I need to get to Preston to make sure Chloë is all right. Are you okay to stay here by yourself for a while longer? Wendy could come out and support you if you like? I'm so sorry. I wanted to stay with you until your mum wakes up. My daughter is the only one who could drag me away."

"Don't be stupid. Of course you've got to go. Chloë's only a little girl, isn't she? Mum told me your background, so this isn't a shock from that perspective. I'll be fine alone. If I message Dad, I'm sure he and Cheryl will be here soon."

I wonder why they sent me here rather than coming themselves, but Alison seems to read my mind.

"I phoned Dad when I got here and told him to get a couple of hours' sleep before coming here. He had a heart attack a couple of months ago, and I don't want to add extra strain. He said he and Cheryl would come along about five-ish. I'll be fine until then." She smiles at me to reassure. I'm not totally convinced, but there's nothing I can do.

"Let me know if there are any developments with your mum. I don't know if I'm imagining it, but she seems to be sleeping a bit more naturally now." I nod towards Becky, and Alison turns and gazes critically at her.

"Maybe she's a shade less white. Hopefully, you're right. Anyway, of course I'll let you know." She lowers her voice. "And let me know what's happened to Peter. It doesn't sound good if the police are there."

I agree, and then say goodbye, squeezing her shoulder before I leave. A hug seems inappropriate this time. I got away with it on greeting her, but she seems to have closed off since then. Perhaps the stress of announcing our 'engagement' put a barrier between us. It's so hard to tell what a woman is thinking.

Half an hour later, I've drawn up outside Debbie's house, just behind the police car. I take a deep breath before knocking on the front door.

It's answered by a middle-aged chap with a ginger moustache and glasses. He stares at me inquiringly.

"I'm Will. Not sure if it's you I spoke to earlier. I'm Debbie's ex-husband and Chloë's dad."

"Oh yes, I remember. I told you to come along. You'd better come in so we can explain." He holds the door open for me and then follows me into the lounge. Debbie's lying on the couch with her knees curled up in front of her protectively. Her face is white and I can see she's been crying. When she sees me, though, she gets up and puts her arms out to me. I go to her and envelop her in a hug. I need the contact too – it's been a tough night and I don't think it's going to get any easier.

For a long moment, I just hold her, then look at the policeman over the top of her head. I mouth the question, "Is Peter dead?" and he nods. I glance down at my ex. In her distress, my old affection has resurfaced. "Shall we sit down?"

She agrees, and I sit next to her on the sofa, my arm wrapped around her shoulders for comfort and support. She leans into me, and briefly it seems like old times when we were together. It can't last, though. Reality will set in.

The sergeant has taken possession of an armchair, and a uniformed constable is standing with her back to the window. There's another chair free.

"Won't you sit down, Officer?" I want someone to tell me what the hell has happened, but I'm unsure how to start. I don't want to send Debbie into hysteria, but I can't help if I don't know the situation.

"I've got a better idea." The constable smiles gently at Deb. "Why don't you come with me into the kitchen and help me make everyone a hot drink?" Tactful lady. I'm impressed, and flash her a grateful look.

The Welsh sergeant waits until the door closes behind them.

"I don't think I introduced DC Jarvis. She's a good girl though. Anyway, let's keep this brief. Peter Donaldson's body was retrieved from the tracks of the Northern Line at 15.05 on Monday afternoon." He looks up from his notes. "That's this afternoon, or yesterday, if that's how you like to look it. Either way, it was a little over twelve hours ago. He'd been hit by an underground train at Charing Cross Station. Eyewitness accounts suggest he was pushed, and his assailant made away with a bag that Mr Donaldson was holding prior to the incident."

"Did anyone give a description of the assailant?"

"The consensus is that it happened too quickly for most people to realise what was going on, and no one had the presence of mind to stop him from getting away. The only detail we have is that it appeared to be a tall white male dressed in a fawn overcoat."

"Well, that eliminates slightly over half the population then." I roll my eyes. Chances of us finding the guy are pretty slim.

"Quite. It would, of course, also be helpful to locate the missing bag. One keen-eyed youth described the bag. He had no idea what the man looked like, but he said the bag was the sort you'd take to a gym – black leather with a Nike logo on the side. He thought it looked odd with the tall man's general appearance, and felt a briefcase would have been more in keeping."

"I suppose Peter died from being hit by the train rather than from the fall?"

"The timing of the incident appears to have been deliberate. He was pushed directly as the train was approaching. The driver tried to stop but had nothing like enough time." He gives me a direct stare. "How much do you know about any activities that might provoke such an act?"

"Do you know Detective Chief Inspector Wendy Lucas from the Manchester force?" I ask.

"I've heard that name. Erm, yes. She contacted us recently in connection with a bank robbery." He frowns. "What's that got to do with Mr Donaldson?"

"Quite a lot, actually. I think you need to speak to Wendy

in the morning, though. The situation is complex and sensitive, and it's not for me to explain." I fish in my pocket and remove my wallet. Inside are several business cards with my name and the White Knight Detective Agency branding. I hand the sergeant a card, and he peruses it with interest.

"You've been working on a case that potentially involves the husband of your ex-wife. Isn't that a conflict of interest?"

"It hasn't been so far, but I could see there's the potential for it. Speak to Wendy. We work closely with her and her team, and she's fully aware of every angle."

"Have you got a direct contact number for her?"

"If you give me back that card, I'll write her number down for you." I scribble her mobile number on the back of the card he returns to me, after checking it on my mobile. I tend to memorise the last few digits of a number so I can easily recognise it, but don't usually bother with the whole thing. "You've got my number there too, so call me when you've spoken to Wendy, and I can fill in any gaps."

"Did you like Peter Donaldson?" He appears to be asking out of curiosity, but I'm sure it's deliberate.

"He wasn't quite my cup of tea, but I might have disliked anyone who was going to be replacing me in my daughter's eyes. He didn't particularly like me either, but I wouldn't say we were sworn enemies."

The sergeant nods and scribbles in his notebook. I was clearly right about the curiosity. It's just his style to draw honest answers from victims of his questioning. Well, I gave an honest answer. Truth and nothing but the truth, but perhaps not the whole truth. I don't feel it's relevant to tell him that Peter was about to drag my name through mud in the courts – particularly as I already had a fairly effective way of stopping him. Murder's not my style.

THIRTY-TWO

Joanna

TUESDAY

When I got back last night, I forced myself to go to bed. It won't help anyone if I'm half-dead through lack of sleep. I manage about five hours, then at about 8.30 I'm woken by the front door opening. I panic for a moment and get out of bed, but I'm greeted by the sight of Will coming upstairs.

"Sorry, Mum. Did I wake you?" He throws me that charming, apologetic smile that has always allowed him to get away with far too much.

"It's fine. I needed to get up, anyway." My heart rate has returned to normal, or at least close to it. "Any news of Becky?"

"No change really. I popped back to the hospital on my way back from Preston."

"What the hell were you doing in Preston?" I stare at him in some confusion. Obviously, I know he has his daughter there, but it wasn't exactly typical visiting time.

"Why don't you come down for a coffee while I tell you everything? Then I'm going to get a couple of hours' kip. I'm knackered."

Half an hour later, I'm sitting in the kitchen sipping my

second coffee of the morning. Will's gone to bed and I'm trying to get my head around all that's happened. *'Becky, wake up, lovey. I need to discuss this lot with you and work out what the hell's going on. You choose your moments to be unconscious, don't you?'*

Thinking of my friend directs me to my phone. There are over twenty WhatsApp messages. Someone has set up a group with all of us who went searching for Becky last night. I scroll through. Alison had been at her mum's bedside all night until Will ran her home on his way here so she could get some sleep. Matt and Cheryl are there now, and Wendy was going to head over later – but has been advised it's family only. The next message has me gasping. It was from Alison at about 5.30 this morning.

'We had to tell the nurses that Will and I were engaged, so that they'd let him in. It was the only way. Obvs I said Mum didn't know yet, and we'd wait until she got home so there wouldn't be any awkward questions or comments from the staff.'

It begs the question of 'Why didn't Ali just send Will away?' but maybe she needed some support in the middle of the night. It's not ideal for a nineteen-year-old girl to be keeping watch over her mum all night, but I guess Matt had to look after Cheryl. In my humble opinion, Cheryl's quite old enough and sensible enough to have been at the hospital too, but it seems they got a couple of hours of sleep and headed over there at about six. Their reaction to Alison's message was remarkably muted – a simple *'Okay'* - and I wonder whether they'd had a private rant on another chat or waited until they got to the hospital.

This also means that I wouldn't be allowed in. I'm sure 'future mother-in-law of the patient's eldest daughter' isn't a qualifying relative – particularly given it's untrue. I content myself with a message to the group chat – the first in a couple of hours.

'*How's Becky? Any news? How are you all doing? I assume they wouldn't let me in if I turned up?*'

Cheryl replies – she's such a sweet girl. '*Sorry, Joanna. It seems to be family only. Ali had to tell all sorts of lies to get Will in! Mum's still the same, but the nurses say her vital signs are improving, so we hope she's going to wake up soon.*'

'*Thanks. Yes, I saw the message trail (laughing emoji). Glad your mum seems to be getting better. Looking forward to having her back with us.*'

A minute later, Cheryl calls me properly.

"I thought I'd get some air and give you a ring. It's stuffy on the ward and nothing's happening for the moment." She pauses. "How's Will? He's been a trouper through the night. Did you hear about Peter?"

"Yes, he told me before he went to bed. He's sleeping just now. He looked exhausted when he got home."

"I gathered he didn't like Peter very much?"

"It was mutual. Peter was involved in some stuff that was not good." I refrain from explaining too much. I honestly don't know how much Cheryl's been told.

"Like kidnapping that little girl? It must be weird for Will though. To be involved in a case where his daughter's stepdad is a suspect. Then to find out he's been murdered. It's pretty crazy."

"It is. Whereabouts are you, pet? I trust you can't be overheard? This is confidential stuff."

"Of course. I've been brought up by Mum and Dad. They both deal with a lot of sensitive information. I always make sure there's no one around if I'm talking about stuff like this."

"So where are you?" I ask as another fear asserts itself.

"In the car park of the hospital. It's kind of busy with people arriving for work and appointments, but I'm at the edge."

"Can you do me a favour and go back inside, pet? I don't

want to scare you, but your mum was abducted. You might be in some danger. Stay with your dad."

"Okay. Heading back inside now. Will you come to the hospital? I know you can't come into the ward, but we can go for a coffee and chat."

"Sure. I'll get myself ready and be with you in about an hour, if that's okay."

"Great. I'm at the main entrance now. Call me when you get here."

I agree, then disconnect.

<hr>

Fifty-five minutes later, I'm at the hospital main entrance, having left Will asleep in bed. I sent him a WhatsApp to let him know where I was going, so he won't worry when he wakes and finds the house empty.

I give Cheryl a call.

"Guess what!" She sounds excited.

"I don't know. Go on." I think I might know what she's going to say, but let her share the news.

"Mum's awake. They're moving her to a normal ward in a few minutes, so I'll come and have a coffee with you as soon as they tell us where they're going. There's a coffee shop on the right as you come in to the hospital. Can you see it?"

"Yes. I'm standing right next to it."

"Great. Can you grab yourself a drink? I'll be there shortly. Hopefully, they'll be a bit more flexi about visitors on the ward." She sounds happy, and I'm reluctant to disillusion her. More than likely, no visitors will be allowed until about two o'clock, but we'll see.

I offer to get her a drink and ask if her dad wants to join us. She requests a hot chocolate for herself, but tells me her dad will stay with her mum while they're moving her.

"He might join us when she's settled, but he can get his own drink. Otherwise, it'll be cold by the time he arrives. See you soon."

Coffee and a chat with Cheryl seem a pleasant way to pass some time until Matt comes down with some news. He comes straight to our table and rests his hand on his daughter's shoulder, but he addresses his comments to me.

"Becky's awake and keen to see you. The doctor's been and examined her. She's got a hint of a chest infection, so they're going to keep her in and start her on IV antibiotics depending on the results of the X-ray that they've just taken her for. But obviously, no one's had time to discuss how this all happened. I guess that will have to wait. The ward they've put her on is quite relaxed about opening hours, though, as she's in a private room."

"How did you wangle that?" I ask.

"I occasionally work here as a locum pharmacist. I know quite a few staff and pulled some strings." He grins. "Actually, the consultant said he wanted her in a private room anyway, but appreciated the sensitivity of her situation as well when I explained that there might be some people who would prefer her not to make a full recovery."

"So, shall we head up there now?" I prepare to swig the rest of my coffee, but Matt shakes his head.

"Take your time. She probably won't be back from radiology for half an hour. I charged up her phone. It was in her bag that you found next to her. I had to dry it out a bit, but it was okay. Anyway, she said she'll message me when she's back. I'm going to grab a coffee myself – do you want another?"

I accept. It's been a long couple of days, and I need all the caffeine I can get.

THIRTY-THREE

Becky

TUESDAY

My first awareness is of a soreness in my left hand and a sharp pain in my chest on breathing in. I open my eyes. There's a needle in my hand, attached to a line, and to a bag of clear fluid. A screen by my side emits gentle beeps every second or so.

Waking up surrounded by drips and monitors is always daunting, and now is no exception. It is, however, a damn sight better than being cold and wet on a moor, which is the last thing I remember before waking. I must have lost consciousness, despite my best attempts. I've no idea how I got here, but Matt and Cheryl are at my bedside talking quietly. They don't notice I'm awake until I speak.

"Hello." I'm not unhappy with the reaction.

"Oh my God. Mum, you're awake. Dad, message Ali and let her know."

"Sure. But first things first. How are you feeling?" Matt gets up and kisses me on the forehead. I suspect he'd have liked to get closer to my mouth, but I've got an oxygen mask covering mouth and nose.

"I've been better, but I've been a hell of a lot worse too. Where's Ali?"

"She was here with you most of the night. She's gone home to get some sleep. Cheryl, you message her. I'm going to tell the medical staff that Mum's woken up."

The next half hour seems to be very busy, with lots of medical staff bustling around. A doctor checks me over and suggests I might have a chest infection, so arranges an X-ray. As I'm now awake, I'm to be sent to a less intense medical ward. There's a notable omission though. So far, no one has asked what led me to be out on the moors in the pouring rain – the obvious cause of hypothermia and suspected pleurisy. One nurse noted bruising around my wrists and ankles, but if she has mentioned it to a doctor, none of them has said anything about it to me. My family is also being reticent about my recent adventures, but I'm assuming they feel it is more appropriate to wait for a quiet moment before asking me about them.

I'm feeling quite fuzzy-headed, and, with everything else going on, don't feel inclined to dwell on the events that brought me here. Cheryl disappears after a while, apparently to greet Joanna and keep her company for a while. I make her promise to bring her to me when she can. Then they come for me to take me for the X-ray. Getting me out of bed is messy, because of the drip and the oxygen, but a nurse unhooks the drip for the moment, although she leaves the needle in. I hate needles in the back of my hand. It's really uncomfortable, and I'm scared to move in case it dislodges it.

Finally, I'm X-rayed and lying in bed on my new ward in a side room. Matt gave me my handbag before I went to X-ray, and has even charged my phone, so I drop him a message to say I'm here, and then allow myself to relax. I must doze a little, because I'm woken by voices. Friendly, anxious voices.

"She's in here. Come along in." Matt's first words are loud, then he becomes quieter, presumably when he sees my eyes shut.

"Is she okay? Is this a bad time? I think she's sleeping. Perhaps I should go." Joanna's keeping her voice low, but in the quiet of the side room, it's clearly audible.

I open my eyes.

"It's okay. I'm awake." I cough and then shiver. To be honest, I'm feeling grotty; feverish, and my chest feels worse. But I'm pleased to see them.

"Let me get the nurse. She might sort you out with oxygen and paracetamol – and antibiotics if needed." My lovely pharmacist husband dwells naturally on therapeutics. I just want a couple of extra blankets. I don't feel as though I've warmed up yet.

There's some more bustle and my guests disappear again. Nurses come and hook things up – the drip and oxygen and another monitor. They're all very pleasant and efficient, but I just want to go to sleep now. Eventually, they leave me and I'm able to doze – except that I can't really, because my chest hurts a lot now, and it's painful to take more than a very shallow breath. The oxygen only helps a bit, but then finally, something seems to click, and my breathing is easier. I fall into an uneasy sleep.

When I wake, I'm feeling better. I look out of the window. I've not got much of a view – a brick building, with a sliver of grey sky to one side. Rain is hammering on the window. I shiver. I've gone right off rain. My phone is next to me and now fully charged. I check the screen. It's nearly five in the afternoon. Hard to believe that just over twenty-four hours ago I was still in London. So much has happened.

WhatsApp has over ten messages. They have added me to a group comprising my family, Wendy, Joanna and Will. Half the messages are asking me to let them know when I'm awake. Apparently, they're all sitting in the hospital restaurant waiting for me to show signs of life. I quickly type, '*Hi, I'm back in the land of the living. See you soon.*' Then I rest back against my pillows and take stock.

The room is off the main ward, facing the nurses' station. There's no one there at the moment, which I assume is why no one's been in to see me. And it's probably why, after two minutes, an unauthorised visitor walks in. A few months ago I would have been thrilled to bits to see him, but now my heart rate rises for a totally different reason.

"Why are you trying to kill me, Finn?" I look at him cautiously. If he pulls out a gun or a knife here, I'm in big trouble.

"You're like a cat with nine lives, love. Why would I want to kill you? I just need to make it look as though I'm trying. I sent your family a note – a big clue so that they'd find you before it was too late."

"But you tied me up and left me in a ditch. By the time they found me, I was barely conscious." I glare at him. I can't believe he's doing this, but also that he's got the temerity to show up here.

Neither of us gets a chance to say anything further though, because at that moment my family and friends turn up en masse. First through the door is Wendy.

"How the hell you have the cheek to walk in here is beyond me. How did you find Becky anyway?"

"Asked for her at the front desk of the hospital. They directed me here." Finn shrugs. "What does it matter anyway? Why are you so fussed? I came to apologise and to check if Becks is okay."

"We identified the car as yours, even though it was Janice who met up with Becky in the station. We know you got Becky into this mess. I assume you've got a new car now, otherwise I'm sure she would have recognised it. What have you got to say for yourself?"

My family huddle around the right side of my bed, ready to protect me if needed. Will and Joanna move to the left of the bed, and Wendy stands in front of Finn, waiting to counter any adverse moves.

Finn looks around the sea of angry faces in the room. His expression is defiant, but I think there's fear there too.

"I did my best to make sure you found Becky. I sent you that note sending you to Winter Hill. You might never have found her if it hadn't been for me."

"You're wrong. We'd identified your car, and used ANPR to track where you'd taken her. We had a pretty good idea where to find her. Your note arrived just as we were setting off." Wendy shakes her head. "How did you and Janice know she was coming off that train?"

"I got a message from my contact, who'd been following her, that she'd got on a train to London that morning. I don't know how they knew which train she was coming back on. Maybe they've got spies in London who were looking for her at Euston, but I got a message late afternoon telling me what time she was coming in. By then, I'd had all day to set things up." His sullen expression changes to one of agitation. "I collected Janice and we went to the station to wait. But all the time I was thinking about how to get Becks rescued. You have to believe me."

"I'm so disappointed in you, Finn. I don't understand why you've done this. You'd better go home now. I'm suspending you from duty as of this very moment. There'll be a full investigation into this. Be grateful you're not under immediate arrest, but I advise you not to leave the country, or even the area, without consulting with me. And if you come anywhere near Becky again, you will be under arrest."

Finn's expression turns mulish.

"I have to explain. I had no choice. You don't understand. They said it was them or me, and if I'd left it to them, she would be dead by now. They'd have left no trail, and would probably have killed her before throwing her in a ditch. The only way I could protect her was to do it myself. And I left her tied up, so she didn't wander off and get lost on the moors trying to get home."

"Thanks Finn. That was really thoughtful of you." I can't quite keep the sarcasm from my voice. I recall he used a similar excuse about the warehouse. He only set that up to protect me too – or so he claimed. "Who are 'they'?"

"I don't know, but they scare the shit out of me. I get printed letters from them telling me what to do."

"Have you kept the letters?" I cared for him once. If there's evidence to save his neck, I'll be happy to believe that someone coerced him into this.

"I was supposed to burn them, but they're hidden under a floorboard in my flat." He looks stricken for a moment, almost as though he regrets telling us.

I have a brief flashback – from twenty-five years ago, before I met Matt. Finn and I were having a brief fling, having succumbed to the blatant chemistry between us. We'd made love on the floor in pretty much every part of that flat. It seems strangely appropriate that he's hidden evidence under there.

"I think I should come with you and retrieve those letters. We can have a little chat when we get there. I've got my car. I'll follow you down." Wendy puts her hand on Finn's shoulder and turns him towards the door. He nods, but looks at me.

"I'm sorry, Becks. I didn't mean for you to be out there so long, but got stuck in traffic delivering the note. You'd have been out of there sooner if I'd been able to deliver the note faster. I'm sorry for everything. Please try to forgive me."

"One quick question before you go. How did you get Janice involved?" I look at him with curiosity. I'd liked Janice, and didn't hesitate to trust her at the station when I was in a predicament.

Finn looks at the floor before looking back at the bed, but he doesn't meet my eyes.

"We've been sleeping together. I threatened to tell her husband if she didn't help me trick you into the car. She thought it was a prank. I'd told her I'd been dared to abduct you and would get some money if I could do it. I said you would be completely safe. After delivering you to my car, Jan went back to her own and went home. She had nothing to do with getting you to Winter Hill."

"Oh well, that's okay then." I glare at him. "You prick! Do you honestly think I'd have got into your car if I'd recognised it – or if it had been you standing on the platform? You used her to fool me into thinking I'd be safe. I think you'd better tell her where her activities led. Otherwise, she might be a bit shocked when she gets arrested as an accessory to abduction and GBH."

Matt touches my shoulder.

"Calm down, love. Finn's leaving now." It's his turn to glare at Finn, who then nods at Wendy and she leads him from the room.

Matt follows her to the door. "Wendy, on your way out, tell Reception they're not to reveal Becky's whereabouts to anyone else."

THIRTY-FOUR

Will

THURSDAY

After Finn left the ward, Becky slumped back on her pillows. She looked exhausted, so we said we would leave her to sleep, but she wouldn't let us go until she'd told us all that had happened the previous day, from getting to London, meeting with the Wartski shopkeeper and then the other big guy, then her phone issues, and meeting Janice, to her awaking in the ditch in the freezing cold and rain. We were there a good hour while she told her story.

I think back on it now. She seemed better for having got it off her chest, so maybe it was the right thing to do, but she clearly needed to rest. I left with Mum almost as soon as she'd finished, but Matt, Ali and Cheryl stayed. Ali gave me a half-smile and a wave as I left. It shouldn't have mattered, but it did.

It's now Thursday morning. Becky's made good progress and is due to be sent home today once the doctor has been round. Mum and I stayed away from the hospital yesterday – I figured Becky needed rest and peace and quiet. She wouldn't get that with us there.

Mum and I are meeting with Wendy this morning, then I'm heading up to Preston to help Debbie sort things out and to pick Chloë up from school. Wendy comes to us at about 10.30, bringing doughnuts.

"Those look amazing. Thank you." I glance over at Mum and see her looking longingly at the goodies. For someone who rarely has a sweet tooth – at least, not compared to me and to Becky – Mum's very partial to a glazed doughnut. "Come in and sit down. I'll put the kettle on."

I return a few minutes later with mugs of coffee and some plates and napkins. Once everyone's settled and Mum and I are eating, Wendy starts talking.

"First, I've got some good news about Xanthe." She turns to Mum. "I know you were worried about her, Joanna. Well, she's out of danger, and looks set to make a full recovery physically." Wendy frowns. "Of course, she'll need some serious counselling. The mental trauma of being attacked in the line of duty isn't something anyone can bounce back from easily."

"At least she's going to survive. I guess we all have scars – physical and mental – that we carry through our lives. I'm sure she'll get the support she needs." Mum glances at me as she finishes, and I suspect it's more wishful thinking than a real belief in that support. She carries enough scars to fill a battlefield. Her healing has only just begun.

"So, just to update you about Finn…" Wendy's been busy following up on Finn's activities, and trying to find out who's been sending him those letters. I can't quite believe he's been following instructions like that without even knowing where they came from. "It's pretty obvious that someone has a serious hold over him. Those letters will certainly help towards Finn's defence if it comes to court. He was surprisingly cagey about handing them over. I'm not sure I got them all, but probably enough to support him if needed."

"Do you think it will?" I ask.

"I don't know. It will depend on his level of co-operation. I don't think he'll be able to continue with the police any longer; I think he understands that. He's abused his position too many times, and this was the final straw. I mentioned that to him and he looked almost relieved, although he did ask me to reconsider whether he could keep his job."

Mum looks thoughtful. "I suppose that if he's being blackmailed about his position – and being told he'll lose his job if he doesn't do such-and-such – then having it out in the open that he's lost his job would be a weight off his shoulders."

"Possibly. He suggested he continue to work and pretend everything was fine so he can go undercover and try to find out who's behind it. He says he's got nothing to lose, but his eyes… I'm not sure. I still don't trust him." Wendy's expression is grim. "I need to have a think about it, because the idea does have some merit. If Finn's out of action, whoever's behind the attacks on Becky could find someone else to do the dirty work; someone who doesn't have Becky's best interests at heart. I now have my own hold over Finn. All his work will go through me. I suspended him, but can reinstate him with a move to my team. Because of Xanthe, I'm a sergeant short, and although Finn's an inspector, it's not unreasonable to borrow him for cover. I think that might be the best solution."

"I agree. A random stranger being responsible for attacks on Becky would be much harder to identify and keep tabs on." I gaze out of the window for a moment. It's an apparently ordinary day outside – in contrast with the turmoil within. I turn my attention back to Wendy. "Finn would need to promise that if he puts Becky in any danger, he makes her as comfortable as possible and alerts us immediately."

"I believe he understands that. He mentioned something similar when he was bargaining with me to get his job back. I said I would think about it."

We leave the discussion there, and move on to Becky's adventures in London. Wendy has done a routine check of the address in Bloomsbury and discovered it belongs to a man named Viktor Kazakov.

"Interesting that it's another Russian. Becky said she detected a faint Eastern European accent."

Something is niggling me, though. I open my phone. "That name rings a bell from somewhere. Let me have a look." I scroll through my contacts, but there's nothing there. Facebook and Twitter also refrain from giving me any clues. I open OneNote on my phone. All my scribbled notes get transcribed in there.

The room is silent as I review all my notes. I have quite a lot and it takes several minutes. Then, as I get to the meeting with the Blackstones where they tell their story, I see what triggered that memory. "Viktor Kazakov is Eric Ulyanov's cousin."

My bombshell is received with wide eyes and open mouths.

Wendy recovers first.

"I'll get my team on to it. They can do background checks on this chap. We're still trying to locate Eric Ulyanov, so maybe his cousin might know something about his whereabouts. I'll liaise with my counterpart in the Met."

"Great. I need to get up to Preston now. Debbie wants me to help her go through Peter's papers. I think she's scared about what she's going to find."

An hour later, I'm sitting on Peter's leather swivel chair in the room that he used as an office. Deb's on the armchair that he apparently used to read long documents when he'd had enough of sitting at his desk. The room is tidy and free of exposed paper. Desk drawers are locked.

"Do you know where the key might be?" I ask. Lock-picking is something I can manage if needed, but I'm slow and awkward and messy. A key would be better.

"I think there might be a spare in his bedside drawer. I'll get it."

As soon as she's gone, I turn on the computer. The login screen appears. I try a couple of password options, but don't manage a lucky guess. Before I have time to use my skills, I hear footsteps. I hurriedly turn off the screen before Deb appears with a key.

"This should open the drawers." She hands it over to me and returns to her seat. I insert the key into the lock. It fits, and gives a satisfying click as I turn it to the left.

Inside the drawer, there are no loose papers, just a black A5-size book. I pick it up and open it at the first page. Bingo. A list of passwords. That's going to save me a lot of time.

I look through the book. There are lists of activities with file locations on the computer. Some of these are harmless, such as fuel bills, others are more intriguing. '*Necessaire*' catches my eye about halfway through the book, as does '*Blackstone*'. Conveniently, there's also an area for '*Life insurance*' and '*Will*'. I show these to my ex-wife, holding up the book for her to see.

"I think I'm going to have to find everything on the computer." I glance at her. She looks exhausted. Her eyes are red-rimmed and there are dark shadows underneath. "Why don't you have a lie down? I can print off all the documents that you might need and sort them out for you."

"Okay. I guess it would be good to rest before Chloë comes home. I've not slept." She lowers her voice and glances out of the window. "I'm scared, Will. What if the guy who shoved Peter in front of that train comes here to look for something? What if he's got it in for me and Chloë?"

"I'm here now. You'll be safe for the moment. If it's okay with you, I'm going to look at his computer to see if there are any clues to his murderer." As I say it, I wonder why the police didn't collect his hard-drive to check these things, but I wasn't overly impressed with the officers who were here in the early hours of Tuesday.

"Okay, thanks. I could do with a nap." She lays a hand on my shoulder on her way out. "You're very kind, Will. I didn't appreciate how important that was when we were together. I was young and stupid."

"Was Peter unkind to you?" I ask.

"Not usually, but he had a temper. When he lost it, it was best to be out of his way. I learnt quickly. He only hit me a couple of times, and never hit Chloë." She drops her hand to her side and looks out of the window, but I don't think she sees anything. "As soon as I saw the signs, I would take Chloë, and we'd go out. If I've put on weight lately, it's because we spent a lot of time at McDonalds." She gives a rueful grin.

"Why did you stay with him?"

"He was very sweet most of the time, and very apologetic when he calmed down after an incident." She lowers her gaze to the floor. "I loved him, you know. He charmed my socks off at the beginning, and could still do it whenever he felt like it. He had a lot of charisma – it was difficult to resist him."

I stand up and put my arms round her. "Your feelings must be pretty confused just now. Don't beat yourself up for falling for him. I imagine it was a heady sensation, someone good-looking and charismatic sweeping you off your feet."

She leans into me for a moment, returning the hug. "Thanks, Will. It's kind of you to be so understanding. I should have recognised what I had instead of treating you like shit. I expect it's too late now."

"I'm afraid so, Debs. Maybe we can be friends, though, instead of bickering and sniping at each other all the time."

"I'd like us to be friends." She reaches up and gives me a soft kiss on the mouth. For a split second, I'm tempted to deepen it into something more. My feelings for her clearly haven't completely died, but an unbidden image of Alison pops into my head. I gently pull away.

"Get that nap. I'll see what I can find out for you from his computer."

"Thanks. I hoped you would. The police were going to take it, but I distracted them and got them thinking about something else. I wanted you to look first."

"Okay. I will. See you soon."

She finally leaves the room and goes upstairs, and with a mental sigh of relief I turn to my task.

With the help of the passwords and the guidance in the book, I'm easily able to navigate Peter's filing system. The question is, where to start? I decide to help Debbie out first. It won't take much time, but will make a big difference to her. I open and print life insurance documents, bank details and his will (a scanned copy – I don't know where the original might be). Other useful information, like the deeds to the house and the mortgage details, is not on the computer. A closer look at the book reveals their location as the safe. Useful if I knew where it was. I'm about to shelve the information until Debbie comes back, but notice a wooden panel in the office that looks different from the others. I go over to it and investigate, pushing in different places until it swings open. Miraculously, behind it is a safe, and in the book I have the combination. It might be my lucky day. I dial up the numbers from the book and have the contents exposed in no time. A neat pile of documents is on one side, and wads of banknotes on the other. I remove the banknotes first and count them. They're in batches of £1,000 in £50 notes. And there are over thirty batches.

My breath stills. This is evidence of likely involvement in crime, but the money could help to support Deb and Chloë if all goes haywire. If the police don't find out about the cash, they can't confiscate it. I put the notes back in the safe and turn to the documents. The original will is there, and also the deeds to the house. Most of the documents are standard family documents that most homeowners would expect to have, but at the bottom of the pile is a list of items that were once stored in a bank vault in Preston. One of those items is the Necessaire, and alongside the name is a note, '*To go to Wartski for £2M*'.

I photograph the note and send it to Wendy with a quick message saying what it is. I think someone official needs to go to speak to the guy at Wartski. Presumably it's the same one that sent Becky and Dan over to Kazakov in Bloomsbury. I put the documents back in the safe, but only after photographing all of them. Then I return to the computer and start wading through anything to do with Peter's business deals. By the time my phone beeps to let me know it's 3pm and I need to pick up Chloë, I have a pretty fair overview of his activities.

I collect my daughter from school and go back inside with her when I get her home. Debbie's up and in the kitchen making a sandwich. While Chloë's getting changed out of her school uniform, I have a quick chat with my ex.

"Are you feeling better?" I ask.

"I think so." She manages a tired smile, but she looks brighter than before.

"There's a package on the desk. I've put together all the documents you'll need to claim Peter's life insurance and set the will in motion." I check that the room's empty except for us before adding, "There's about thirty grand in banknotes in the safe. The combination is in the black book. I've marked the page with a Post-It note and put the book back in the drawer. Here's the key. Don't lose it!"

"I don't lose things," she says. Her tone is indignant, so I apologise.

"Sorry. I'd forgotten. I spend my time with Mum and Becky these days and have to run round after them a bit, especially Becky."

"Did you find anything else?" She keeps her voice low and casts wary glances around the kitchen, as if suspicious that we can be overheard.

"A few things, yes. I've taken a copy of some key documents so I can check some stuff. Look, if I can keep Peter's name clean, I will do. I don't want you or Chloë to lose out on anything you should be entitled to, but there might be some challenges ahead. I need to find out what extent he was involved in that little girl's kidnapping. He definitely had something to do with that, and also the theft of a priceless Fabergé egg from a bank. Let me see what else comes up. I'm sure you'd rather it was me digging than the police."

"God, yeah! Thanks, Will. I know you'll do what you can to protect us."

"The first thing I think we should do is to move you for a while. When does Chloë break up for Easter?"

"Tomorrow."

"You need to ring in sick for her unless you want to traipse up from Manchester. You two are coming to live with us." It's a sudden decision, but I guess it's been building since seeing the various bits of evidence in the safe and on the computer. Debbie looks strangely pleased, so I call Mum and let her know the good news.

"I'd love to have Chloë, but we've not got space." She's probably right. Bloody hell.

"I can't leave them here, Mum. It doesn't feel safe." I don't give her any details just yet. Time enough for that later.

"Give me five minutes," she says and disconnects. She calls back nearly twenty minutes later. "Sorry, took me a while to get something sorted. They're going to stay with Wendy. She's got a couple of spare rooms, and would love to have some company for a couple of weeks or as long as needed."

"Thanks, Mum. That's brilliant. If they're not safe with her, they wouldn't be safe anywhere."

We collect the black book, the safe – which weighs a ton but comes out of the wall with some help from Peter's toolkit from the garage – and the computer, together with some clothes for both Deb and Chloë and Chloë's favourite toys. It all goes in my car boot out of sight, and after a quick call with Wendy to check her address, I drive to Worsley in North Manchester and deposit my family in a pretty detached house on a pleasant modern estate. Wendy greets them warmly and promises me they'll be safe. Her eyes widen somewhat when I nearly break my back for the second time today, lugging in the safe and then the computer, but she says nothing for now. I have a feeling I'm going to hear all about it later.

They're all settled in Wendy's kitchen with drinks and awaiting pizza delivery when I get another call. It's from Mum.

"I've just had a call from Simon Blackstone. Anastasia's missing."

THIRTY-FIVE

Becky

THURSDAY

They let me out of hospital this morning, but I'm still on antibiotics and under strict instructions to rest, so I'm in bed when I get the call from Joanna. Matt's just brought me up a tea-tray containing chicken soup and a tuna sandwich, but I put it aside when the call comes through.

"What did you just say?" I'm sure I sound as shocked as I feel.

"Anastasia is missing. She went out early this afternoon. Simon got a call at half-past three to collect the kids from school as no one had turned up. She hasn't been seen since."

I check my phone. "It's nearly six-thirty now. They should have heard something." I cough. My chest isn't great yet. "Are there any clues on where she might be?" I have a sip of the now-lukewarm lemon squash that Matt gave me earlier.

"None. Will's on his way home. He's had a busy day. Shall I bring him round for a meeting?"

I glance over at the ageing mirrored wardrobes. My pale face stares back at me, defying me to ignore the atrocious state of my hair (that closely resembles a bird's nest) and the outdated pyjamas. "Not tonight. See Simon and try to get some more information from him. Maybe sort out a search party or something. Have the police been contacted?"

"Wendy knows. She's sorting something out. Okay. You don't sound that great. Will and I can sort it with Wendy and keep you posted. You rest, and we'll speak later." She sounds disappointed.

I am too, but I'm really not up to searching through the shrubs tonight. Just thinking about it makes me cough. We say our goodbyes and I return to my dinner. It might seem callous with Ana missing, but I need to get my strength up so I can help in the search behind the scenes.

I hear nothing more until the next morning, when I get a message that Joanna and Will are on their way and that Ana's still missing. Dragging myself out of bed, I head into the shower. I'm pretty exhausted by the time I've pulled on a pair of jeans and a sweatshirt, but after lying on the bed for a few minutes, I force myself to go downstairs and arrive in the kitchen at the same time as the doorbell rings.

Matt passes me on the way to the door and shakes his head. "You look like shit! What are you doing up?"

"I think I might be needed." I gesture to him to open the door, and he returns a minute later with Joanna and Will. Before anyone's said anything, we're joined by Alison and Cheryl. School holidays started yesterday.

"Bloody hell! What is this? A party?" Matt grumbles as he goes to fill the kettle up.

"We want to find out what's going on too, Dad." Alison goes up behind him and wraps her arms around his waist. She rests her head briefly against his back. "Be nice. We only want to help."

"I think there's a case of 'too many cooks' in here." All the same, Matt turns slightly and hugs our eldest.

"Only one cook, Dad, and that's you. The rest of us are

going to sit down and wait for you to bring the tea and toast." She grins at him and returns to the kitchen table.

After a few more minutes of banter and bickering, during which Alison does help Matt provide drinks and toast to everyone, we're all sitting round the table waiting to discuss the news. I look closely at my friends. They both look exhausted and bedraggled.

"Have you two had any sleep?" I push the pile of toast in their direction. They look as though they need it.

"Not much. We've both been out with the searchers for most of the night, but it's been crazy because we've not really had anything to go on." Will drains his mug and then hands it to Matt for a refill with a grateful smile. "We seem to have spent most of the night driving the streets for any clues. Meanwhile, Wendy's been going through the phone records for Anastasia's number. All we've got to go on is a call from an unknown number that lasted about three minutes yesterday morning."

"Maybe it's worth going at it from another angle." I glance round the table, making sure everyone is listening. I needn't have worried. They're all waiting eagerly for me to provide some pearls of wisdom. My confidence wobbles a fraction. "What are the chances that the caller was Eric? I'd guess pretty high."

Will breaks into my pending monologue. "I didn't have time to fill you in on everything I found yesterday, but one of the key things I picked up was definite evidence that Eric was behind the kidnapping of Tania, and Peter was one of the people tasked with making it happen."

"That validates my theory, then. We know Eric was trying to get Ana back under his thumb. The kidnapping was an attempt to do that, assuming the money was just a blind, and it failed. So it makes sense that he's tried a more direct approach and has abducted her himself."

"What do you think that call was about then?" asks Joanna.

"The unknown number?" I check that I've understood correctly, and Joanna nods. "I reckon that was Eric calling Ana with… I don't know… maybe some supposed information about her relatives; maybe a threat to her parents or the kids; but either way, he demanded that she meet with him. The difficulty is to work out where."

Ideas are thrown around the table, with even the girls getting involved. Cheryl has explored extensively on walks with her boyfriend Joel. She suggests a few parks and areas of woodland around Whitefield, a short distance from here. They also have the merit of being reasonably close to where Anastasia lives, and we know she didn't take her car. After a while, we have a list of around ten areas to search. Will sends a message to Wendy and then fills us in on his findings about Peter.

We're just about up to speed when Wendy phones. Will puts her on speakerphone and lets her know we can all hear her.

"Who's there?" she asks. On receiving details, she continues. "Great. Thanks for that list of locations. We do also have a bit of a lead. Eric Ulyanov's car has been spotted through the ANPR system. It was last seen on Park Lane in Whitefield, heading towards Philips Park. Who's up for joining the search?"

Everyone volunteers except me. Obviously I can't go, although I would if I didn't think I would collapse five minutes after leaving the house. Frankly, I'm pretty shattered just from being out of bed for nearly an hour. Matt looks at me.

"Becky, you're going back upstairs for a sleep. You look knackered." He turns to the other adults in the room. "Will, Joanna, if I stay here, will you look after the girls?" A quick look at our daughters reveals that there's no use trying to persuade them not to go.

I can see he's trying to send them a message with his eyes. I have a feeling I know what he's getting at, but just in case they don't, I tap out a quick WhatsApp on my phone. Far more reliable than trusting to mind-reading. *'If you can prevent the girls from seeing anything untoward, we would appreciate it.'*

Will glances at his phone as soon as it beeps. *'Of course.'*

Ali gives us both a suspicious glance, which we ignore. No doubt she'll follow up with Will later. Meanwhile, I go back to bed while the others prepare to go out searching again. I pray they don't return with bad news, but I don't have a good feeling about this. Ana's now been missing for nearly twenty-four hours.

I lie awake waiting for news. After a while, Matt joins me and sits in the armchair by the window reading a newspaper, but I can tell he's not concentrating either.

"Something's bothering you." I put down my phone that I've been playing with to distract myself.

"Everything's bothering me." Matt stands up and puts his paper on the chair. He starts pacing – always a bad sign. "The girls are out searching while there's a potential madman on the loose. You're still not well and shouldn't be having to deal with this stress. I can't work out if there's something going on between Will and Ali – I'm getting strange vibes off the pair of them. And I'm trying to work out what the heck's going on here. Is it time to give Roger a call?"

"I don't think Roger could help you out with Will and Ali. They have to work it out for themselves. There does seem to be some chemistry there, but they both seem reluctant to pursue it. Let it lie, Matt. They'll sort it out one way or another."

He pauses in his pacing long enough to give me an affectionate tap on the shoulder. "Idiot! Obviously, that's not why I'm thinking about ringing Roger."

"I'm only messing. Just trying to keep a sense of humour in this shambolic case. But being serious now. If you think about it, we've been continuously losing things and people. It started with the theft of an egg, then we lost Tania, Peter, me and now Ana. It's crazy." I look across to where he's now wearing down the carpet on the other side of the room. "Can you sit down? You're making me dizzy."

"Sorry." He returns to the armchair, putting the newspaper on the floor. "How's that?"

"Perfect. So what are you thinking? Do you agree it's been weird?"

"Yes, but I don't think your abduction is linked with the others. I reckon that was a red herring."

I stare at him. "Why?"

"Because we know Finn was responsible. Even though he's up to his ears in trouble, I can't see him being involved with Eric and Peter. You know him best, though." Matt glances out of the window, not meeting my eyes.

I never told him about my history with Finn. It was still raw when I met Matt – I'd just found out that Finn saw our relationship as no more than a bit of fun. I'd ended it immediately and tried to pretend I didn't care, but the next day, when Matt showed up in my life, I was too confused to deal with anything and it was several weeks before I agreed to a date. Matt never questioned the delay, because once we started going out, it became clear quickly that we were meant for each other. That knowledge of being with the person who loves and accepts you for who you are was pretty intoxicating, and it came with a solid foundation of kindness, compassion and laughter. I fell in love with Matt and never questioned if we were supposed to be together. It felt right. I shoved my feelings for Finn into the background and demoted him to the role of friend and partner, as we were still working closely in the same team and were usually paired together on assignments. But every now and again the feelings would resurface, and I would have to battle with myself to remember how things had to be.

I push the thoughts away again. Finn's betrayal hurts even more now than it did a couple of months ago, when I first discovered he was involved with the warehouse shooting.

I suddenly realise it's gone quiet. Matt is looking at me now, waiting for an answer. I take a few seconds to remember what he said last. "I expect you're right, even though I have no idea why Finn is doing this. Somehow, it feels different from what's happening with Ana. I don't understand why she could be involved with the egg, though."

"From what Will said, Peter had his fingers in several pies. I think the egg was separate from his work with Eric. According to the computer files, there was a link with Joanna's ex-husband regarding the bank robbery."

"When did you find that out? I don't remember that being said." I stare at him.

"After the others went, while you came upstairs I went to look at my computer. Will gave me copies of his USB sticks with Peter's files on. He wanted me to have a copy as some sort of insurance. That was one of the first things I came across." Matt runs his hand through his hair. "Lou had a hold over Peter, apparently. One of Lou's convict pals had done some work with Peter in the past, and had recommended him to Lou as a bent accountant. They did some work together, and somehow Peter got introduced to Debbie. Peter fell for her really hard, and when Lou found that out, he used it to blackmail Peter into doing whatever he wanted. I don't know how. Maybe he threatened to tell Deb that her new lover was a crook. I couldn't work out how they got to do the bank robbery, or even find out about the egg, but it appears Eric wasn't involved until later."

"How come Eric got involved at all?" I ask.

"According to the files, Lou failed to turn up with the money and Peter had to look elsewhere for the means to get rid of the egg. It's not really clear quite what happened, other than evidence from To-Do lists stored in OneNote, but looking at what we know…"

I interrupt. "Oh God. I've just realised. Lou couldn't turn up because he nearly killed Xanthe and then got arrested. He's back in prison and unable to pay anyone anything. So I wonder where he's got the money stashed. There must be a hell of a lot of it."

"Peter's notes suggest he was expecting five million from Lou. We'll have to let Wendy interrogate Lou to find out where he got that money from and where it is now." Matt rests back in his chair. "The notes also back up what you told me about the bank manager. I know you suspected him of being involved."

I think back to my outing with Joanna to survey the back of the bank. "It looked like it had to be an inside job, but we didn't really have any evidence."

"You have now! Peter's notes provide all the detail you could want about the heist. I guess he figured his computer was a pretty safe place to store everything."

I think for a moment. "From what Will said about all the steps he had to take to access everything, I'd assume Peter thought he'd never get found out. He wasn't planning on getting bumped off."

"Obviously." Matt looks at his watch. "I wonder how they're getting on with the search. Do you reckon Anastasia will be okay?"

"I hope so." I wish I could sound a bit more optimistic.

THIRTY-SIX

Joanna

FRIDAY

Although we now have a focus for our search, it's raining again. I can't believe we're doing this. I called Glen on the way to the park, and he's going to join us as soon as his neighbour pops in to look after his dad.

Wendy insists on keeping the girls with her at the co-ordination post. "I'm not risking letting Becky's girls out of my sight. They'll be safe here with me and my team, and I don't want them to stumble on anything." Her whisper to me makes sense, and I'll admit privately to a sense of relief that I don't have the responsibility.

Philips Park is huge, and extends, via woodland, through to several similar parks surrounding Manchester. Will parks the car along with several others – those of regular park-goers, police and other searchers – and we get out and await instructions. Wendy appears to be co-ordinating the search, and sends me and Will to pursue a path along a stream. Glen arrives with his dog just as we're about to set off. The dog is a red setter – a breed well-renowned for its ability to follow scents. There are a few police dogs in the search party, and they have directed each to smell one of Ana's scarves. Glen approaches Wendy.

"Hi. I'll go with Joanna and Will. My lovely Blue here is a fair hand at following scents. Can she have a whiff of that scarf?" He points to the brightly-coloured square of silk that's being held by one of the dog handlers.

"Of course." Wendy reaches down to pat Blue and gets a licked hand in return. "Terry, can you introduce Blue to Anastasia's scent please?"

Will and I follow Glen and Blue over to where the handler is standing with a gorgeous German Shepherd.

"We've already had a scout round with the dogs. They picked up her trail in the car park and followed it to the edge of the field down there." Terry points down the hill. I've been here before and know there's a large grassy area down there. "Then it just disappears. If you head to the stream that Wendy suggested, maybe your dog can pick up the scent there. I think that's our best chance. She must have been picked up in the field."

"She's only a slim lady, probably easy to carry, but surely she'd have struggled." I look towards the field where her scent was last traced, and frown. "I don't suppose…"

"Forensics are down there assessing the area. We'll soon know if anything happened there." Terry reaches into a bag at his hip and extracts some blue plastic overshoes which he hands round to each of us. "Put these on. If this turns out to be a crime scene, we don't want to have destroyed any evidence by tramping around in it."

A few minutes later, we're on the trail suggested by Wendy. I feel reassured by having Will and Glen at my side, then I pause. "Glen, are you up to a trek like this?" I ask quietly.

"I'm getting stronger. I guess as long as we're not out for hours, I should be okay. Let's hope it doesn't come to that and we find this lady safe and well." He doesn't sound confident.

Neither am I. If she's still in the park, she's going to be injured and suffering from exposure, at the very least. I try not to dwell on the alternative.

We tramp through mud as we follow the trail. Blue is sniffing around but not showing any signs of excitement… and then we reach a pylon and she acts strangely; sniffing round in circles between the metal feet. There's nothing to see except perhaps a patch of flattened greenery.

"Maybe he put her down here for a few minutes to get his breath back or something?" suggests Will.

I frown. "She must have been unconscious then. Otherwise, surely she'd have run."

"Probably." Glen looks at Will. "Have you got Wendy's number? Can you let her know what we've found? It might be an idea to have some more searchers focusing on this patch."

As Will makes the call, I examine my sense of growing unease. I've got a terrible feeling about this. Whoever took her, and it would seem likely that it was Eric, must have rendered her unconscious somehow. She's been missing for nearly twenty-four hours now.

As the other handlers and search teams descend on the area, we focus our efforts on the stream. We're walking for maybe another ten minutes when Blue lifts her muzzle and barks. She follows a path for a moment and then stops at the water's edge and howls. There, half in the water, is the body of a woman. She's naked from the waist down, and there are marks on her neck. As a quick assessment, I would say she'd been raped and strangled. Sudden dizziness hits me and I turn away. Poor Ana. I hope she was unconscious and didn't know what that bastard was doing to her. I move as far away as I can before allowing myself to throw up on the ground.

Glen's at my side in a second. "Are you okay, love? That's a grim spectacle for anyone. Feel a bit sick myself."

"It's not just the sight of it. I just thought, oh bloody hell, Glen – those poor kids – they've lost their mum!"

A couple of hours later, we're showered, changed and fed, and back at Becky's house. Wendy and her team had the unenviable job of breaking the news to Simon and the children. We're all now seated around the table in Becky's kitchen, trying to make sense of everything. Will and Matt are wading through the files from Peter's computer. The girls are shaken by the news, but I'm more relieved than ever that they weren't with us when we found Ana's body. No one should have to see that, but certainly not young women who've not yet left their teens. Even Alison is still only 19. Glen had to go home and see to his dad, but will join us again shortly, and Wendy's left her team sorting out the details as she comes to consult with us all.

"I should talk this through with them really, but they've got enough to be getting on with. I need to get things clear in my head about how all this happened." She looks at me. "I need to speak to Lou again. After seeing what Peter had to say in his files, I think your ex-husband had more to do with this that we first thought."

"Surely the priority is to find Eric? I assume he was responsible for what happened to Ana." I keep my gaze steadily on Wendy. I don't want to see what Becky and the others are thinking just now.

"We're searching for Eric. Before I came here, I spoke with my counterpart in London. They've got a warrant to search that house in Bloomsbury, where his cousin lives. I'm hoping to get news shortly."

As we bat ideas around, desperately trying to make sense of what's happened, time passes slowly. Glen arrives and joins in the discussion, but we make no real progress. It's mid-afternoon by the time Wendy's phone rings.

"Hello? Yes? What? Oh my goodness. Well, thank you. That egg is worth millions. It's a shame Ulyanov wasn't there." She pauses for a moment.

Will stares at her. "If the egg is there, he must have killed Peter."

Wendy nods slowly and speaks into the phone. "The man who owns that house, was he there? Yes? Go back and arrest him?" She sits still, then her jaw drops wide open. "Well, that's good that you've got him. We'll speak again shortly, but there'll be a murder charge added to that list." She thanks her London colleague and disconnects. "They found many things in that house that shouldn't have been there. Obviously, as you gathered, the Necessaire egg was there, but also a large stash of weapons and some bomb-making equipment. They've arrested Kazakov on the back of that, so I'm going to need to get the evidence of the murder sorted so they can add that to the charges."

Will offers to collate the evidence from Peter and send it over imminently. Wendy thanks him and then leaves. I guess she's going to be busy for a while.

Meanwhile, Eric Ulyanov is still missing.

THIRTY-SEVEN

Becky

SUNDAY

We've all spent the last day or two going through all the evidence and wondering where on earth Eric has got to. All signs point to him having killed Ana, but he seems to have disappeared off the face of the earth. We're still waiting for any DNA details from forensics. Joanna said Ana had been raped, so that's a key lead, but it takes at least a couple of days to isolate any DNA from a victim and get it analysed.

I'm feeling better now that the antibiotics are really taking effect, and this morning is the first since my ordeal that I'm up, showered properly and dressed. That's a good thing, because just after 11am, my phone rings. As always, I check Caller ID.

"Simon, how are you doing?" I inject into my voice the carefully-calibrated sympathy appropriate for a man whose wife was murdered a couple of days ago.

"Eric's just pulled up outside my house. If I let him in, how soon can you and your team be here? I'll leave the front door ajar." His tone is urgent, and – not to put too fine a point on it – he sounds absolutely terrified.

I reassure him we'll be there imminently and call Joanna as soon as I've disconnected from Simon. As soon as I've had her promise of immediate attention, I follow up with a call to Wendy. She has to know. She'll need to be there to make the arrest. That's assuming we can stop Simon from doing anything stupid. It's only after I finish talking to Wendy that I realise Simon didn't ask us to contact the police. But I expect he's just stressed out by his wife's suspected killer turning up on his doorstep, and worried about his kids.

Within fifteen minutes of Simon's call, Joanna, Will and I are entering the Blackstones' house. I had to argue fast to get Matt's agreement for me to leave the house, but I'm pleased I did. As we arrive, Tania is looking over the bannister.

"Daddy told us not to come downstairs, but I wanted to see who it was."

"That's fine, sweetheart. You just go back up now and play with your brother." I glance at Joanna, then back at Tania. "Do you want one of us to come up and keep you company?"

"I don't know. Maybe if it gets scary." Tania's such a brave little girl, but I think she'd be better off with an adult upstairs to protect her and Zach.

Joanna obviously agrees with me, because she goes up and takes Tania by the hand. "Come on. I'm going to stay with you and keep you safe." They disappear at the top of the stairs, presumably into a bedroom.

I take a deep breath, look at Will, and follow the sound of raised voices.

We find ourselves in the kitchen, where Simon is threatening Eric with a kitchen knife. Eric has his back against a wall, and has the point of a meat cleaver just inches away from his chest.

"Is that necessary, Simon?" I walk casually towards them and wrap a hand around Eric's arm. "He's not going anywhere. I've got him. Put down the knife, there's a good chap."

Simon moves away a fraction and is disarmed by Will, who returns the cleaver to a knife block on the kitchen worktop.

I tighten my grip around Eric's arm, as I don't want him to run now that he's not being threatened. "Why don't we all sit down, nice and civilised, and talk?"

"Tie him up then. I don't want him causing trouble." Simon throws me a silk scarf from a drawer. I recognise it as one of Ana's – the one she wore the first time I met her.

"I'm just a fucking accountant, mate. I don't know what I'm supposed to have done." Eric doesn't attempt to escape from my grip.

"There are a few things that you're suspected of. Perhaps we should tie you to the chair, but for now, we'll settle for you to sit between myself and Will. I promise, we have quick reactions, so don't try anything." Actually, at the moment, my reactions are probably about as fast as a snail's, but I'm not going to let him know that.

By the time anyone says anything else, we're all seated around the expensive-looking kitchen table – Eric wedged between me and Will on either side, and with the table in front and the wall behind him. He'd really struggle to go anywhere. Simon is on the opposite side of the table, facing us. I can sense Will ready to move if Simon shows any further signs of aggression.

No one seems inclined to start off the conversation, so I kick off. "Why did you come here, Eric?" It seems as good a place as any to start.

"He asked me to." He jabs a finger angrily at Simon.

I flick a quick glance at Will. He looks as surprised as I feel.

"I need to find out why he killed my wife." Simon does some angry pointing of his own.

"I didn't fucking kill your wife. I'm not a killer. Look elsewhere."

"So why did you disappear for such a long time? You kidnapped my daughter, you bastard. At least admit to that."

"Why the fuck would I kidnap your daughter? I was happy enough screwing Anastasia. I didn't need to complicate things."

"Hang on a minute!" I interject quickly, as Simon is looking murderous himself. "I thought Ana didn't want you and you were coercing her."

"She'd cooled it off a bit. Said he was getting suspicious." Eric glares at Simon as if it's unreasonable behaviour.

"She said you were blackmailing her about family in Russia." I frown. The stories are not quite matching up.

"It was a fucking joke. Yeah, I have found out a few things about her relatives. Bloody revolutionaries. They hate Putin and would do anything to bring him down. Mind you, he's not as keen on Jews as he makes out. Neither am I, but I pretend to be one so they'll trust me with their money."

Simon glares at him in disgust.

"Did you actively threaten her in order to get her to have sex with you?" I ask, desperate to sort this out.

"Not at first. She couldn't fucking wait to get inside my pants to start with. Then she cooled off a bit – started pretending she wanted to end it – even though I could tell she still liked it. Then she said she wouldn't be coming round any more, so I told her a few home truths about what'd happen to her precious family if she stopped." Eric smirks at Simon, and we can all see that the volcano is about to erupt.

"He's deliberately winding you up." I reach across the table and lay a calming hand briefly on Simon's clenched fist. "Eric, why don't you tell us about why you took Tania?"

"I don't mess with kids. Oh, I knew about it, but I wasn't getting involved."

"So, who was it?" I focus my attention on Eric. I can see Will preparing to restrain Simon if needed – not obviously, but there's a tensing of the jaw and a slight inclination of his body in that direction.

"Peter wanted more money. Things weren't moving fast enough for him with the e… with other things that were going on. He knew about this family and that they're rolling in it – partly because Simon agreed to work with me after I gave him a bit of incentive." Eric laughs – a wicked sound that annoys me almost as much as I can see it gets to its intended victim. "Peter asked me for a bit of info and I gave it to him, but said I wouldn't help him take the kid. He'd have to sort that. I gave him some keys to a warehouse that I'd been working with recently, just to help him out."

"Were you getting a cut?" asks Will.

"What's it got to do with you?" Eric looks at his inquisitor as if something smelly had appeared under his nose. He gets a raised eyebrow in return, and shakes his head. "I was s'posed to, but it never fucking turned up. They bungled it anyway. Bloody kid got rescued." He looks suspiciously at me and Will. "Was that you? You lot fucking screwed me over."

Will and I remain silent. It's not worth engaging. Meanwhile, Simon is clenching and unclenching his fists in the rhythm of a Belisha beacon.

"So, you blackmailed me. You screwed my wife, helped to kidnap my little girl, and then you killed my wife. Why?"

"I never killed Ana. I liked her. Actually, had a bit of fucking respect for her, even when she backed out of our little arrangement."

I deem it time to get involved again before Simon explodes. "So, if you didn't kill her, do you know who did?"

"Not a fucking clue. It couldn't have been Peter, because he was already dead by then."

"How do you know that?" I ask.

Eric looks alarmed for a moment. "Dunno. I must have heard it somewhere."

"From your cousin, perhaps?" I see him look puzzled, so add some detail. "Viktor Kazakov, resident of Bloomsbury in London, and suspected murderer of Peter Donaldson? Does that name mean anything to you?"

"Never heard of him." He looks guilty as hell.

"What other things was Peter involved with? Are you talking about the theft of a Fabergé egg?"

"No idea what you're talking about." Sweat beads on Eric's forehead.

It's obvious he's lying. Which begs the question: If he's so obviously lying about this, why did he look as though he was telling the truth about Ana's murder?

"We've checked him out, and there's evidence showing that you're in regular contact. Are you due to get a cut from the egg too?" I should probably leave some of these questions for Wendy, but I want to trick this bastard into giving something away.

"I told you. I don't know about any fucking egg!"

"Okay, let's get back to Ana's murder." Will takes the reins for a moment. "What were you doing on Tuesday?"

"I was in London on business. Not that it's got any fucking thing to do with you."

"Did that business involve a meeting in Bloomsbury?" Will stares at Eric, who is clearly uncomfortable with this line of questioning. "You've got a chance of an alibi here, if you admit what you were doing in London. I'm sure your cousin would be happy to back you up."

"He'll do nothing to save anyone's fucking neck but his own."

"So you do know him, then." I manage to keep a note of triumph from my voice, but it's a close-run thing.

"Fuck off, bitch."

"Be nice, Mr Ulyanov. We can still tie you to the chair until the police arrive." Will flourishes the scarf.

We're still no nearer knowing what happened to Ana, but a sudden suspicion comes into my mind. Who has a motive? Other than Eric, there is only one other person I can see who would have any cause to kill her.

The anger and jealousy are clear to see. So is the volatility. If I'm not careful, we could have a crisis on our hands. We've currently got the situation under a fragile control.

Eric is a vicious, nasty piece of work, but I no longer think he killed Ana. His involvement in Peter's murder is, at most, peripheral. That's not to say we can't throw the book at him. Blackmail, sexual abuse, accessory to kidnap, and aiding and abetting a murderer – all enough to send him to prison for a fair while – not to mention the large-scale fraud that we've been uncovering.

I'm frantically thinking about how to proceed when there's a voice from outside. We left the door on the latch for Wendy and her team to get in. It sounds like her now.

"Hello, is anyone here?"

I call out to her. "In the kitchen." The timing couldn't have been better. I wait until Wendy and three uniformed officers walk in, then announce, "That's Eric. You'll be throwing the book at him for several crimes, starting with blackmail and fraud. However, I know you're looking to arrest Ana's murderer. You might want to be arresting her husband for that. Simon had motive and opportunity."

THIRTY-EIGHT

Will

SUNDAY

For a moment, Becky's announcement leaves the others in the room looking like stranded codfish. Then, simultaneously, they all spring into action. Simon is on his feet and looking round for the knife that he had earlier. I'd moved it well out of reach, but before he has time to do more than look, Wendy's officers are either side of him, and one of them is putting on handcuffs. The third officer handcuffs Eric for good measure. He's not exactly Mr Nice Guy.

I turn to Becky, a sudden thought making me feel sick. "What about the kids?"

"You can't arrest me. Who's going to look after my children?" Simon's current position hasn't stopped his aggression, and his shouts suggest anger rather than concern.

"Have they got grandparents who could look after them until something longer-term could be arranged?" I ask.

He looks as though he's about to refuse, but one of the officers pokes him in the ribs and Simon turns sullen. "I s'pose. My mum lives in London, but Ana's parents are round the corner. You can give them a ring." Simon turns to the policeman who put the cuffs on, not the one who poked him.

"If you fish in my right-hand trouser pocket, my phone's in there." He directs the officer to unlock the phone and then to access his in-laws' phone number.

Wendy makes the call and shows her sensitivity to their situation. She was the one who went round to inform them of their daughter's murder, so she's already got a connection to them. Explaining, on top of this, that their son-in-law is suspected of the crime is not something to be done on the phone, so she asks if they could come round and look after their grandkids for a while. "I'll explain more when you get here," she says before disconnecting.

With everything under control in the kitchen, I mutter my excuses and head upstairs to see how Mum's getting on with the kids. All the doors are shut on the landing, so I call out to her.

"In here!" She opens the door furthest from the stairs and welcomes me inside a kind of TV den. The kids are watching *Monsters Inc* at high volume, and I nod approvingly at Mum.

"Is everything all right?" Tania speaks up from her place on the sofa. She's got an arm round her brother and they look very cute together. It's a loaded question, though, and I don't know how to answer. They already know their mum's never coming back to them, although I'm not sure if the little boy understands. How can I tell them their dad's been arrested?

"Your grandparents are coming round. I think you're going to stay with them for a while." It's a bit of a cop-out, but it's the best I can manage.

Mum gives me a sharp look. God knows what she suspects, but she'll know there's more going on than I've admitted to. I glance at the kids again. They're either side of Chloë in age, maybe four and seven. I'm not sure if I've guessed that or if I've been told at some point, but either way they're far too young to go through this mess.

"That's good," says Tania. "Daddy's so angry at the

moment. He's not really taking any notice of us." Her voice breaks a little. "We miss Mummy too."

"Of course you do, darling." Mum sits back down next to Tania and puts an arm around her. I can see from Mum's eyes that this is breaking her heart. She was ever a softie.

No one says anything for a moment, and we allow focus to turn to the movie until the doorbell rings.

"I'll go." I hurry downstairs, blinking a few times, surprised to find my vision blurring with unshed tears. It appears I'm a softie too.

Wendy joins me at the door as we greet an older couple, perhaps in their sixties. They're smartly-dressed, and return our greetings in an accent that sounds Eastern European. I assume from the history that they're Russian, but it's not really important. The critical point is that they have kind eyes and smiles, even though they're clearly grieving for their daughter.

Wendy fills them in quietly, letting them know that we're arresting their son-in-law on suspicion of murder. They seem sad and angry rather than shocked.

"You don't seem surprised." I can't contain my curiosity. "Did you think it was him?"

It's Ana's mother who replies. "He was a lovely man when we first met him, and devoted to our daughter. But he had a temper; every so often he would lash out. He is a very jealous man and could not bear Ana having lots of friends. He hit her a few times, but she refused to leave him because of the children." Her gaze strays to the top of the stairs, where the sound of the TV is protecting those kids from hearing too many painful truths. "She always said he was good with them — that he would never harm them. But we feared for her. As time went on, he became more unpredictable." She stops, her voice cracking as the pain of losing her offspring overcomes her.

Her husband takes up the tale. "He is a miserable, selfish, bastard! The sooner they lock him up for his crime, the better

it will be for those children. They should throw away the key."
He turns to his wife. "Come. Let us tell Tania to help us pack.
She will know what to bring for herself and Zach. She is a
good girl."

"I will go." Ana's mother straightens her shoulders and
heads upstairs. I hear her go into the room where the kids are
and greet them.

"Kateryna will sort everything out. My wife is a good
woman. Come. Let us see this bastard who has lost his temper
once too often and has destroyed the happiness of all."

THIRTY-NINE

Becky

TUESDAY

I still haven't quite recovered from the shock of realising that Simon killed his wife. We'd all been so sure it was Eric, but Simon had a far bigger motive. Will told us what Ana's parents had revealed about Simon. Looking back on our dealings with him, it all made sense, but it didn't answer all of our questions.

I've arranged a meeting this morning with all who've been involved with the case. I want to get everything worked out so we know who did what, and why. Matt's been out for bagels, fish balls, smoked salmon, cream cheese and cake. Everyone is so much more communicative when fed, and I'm after lots of discussion today. It's about half an hour before everyone's due, and I'm finishing the cleaning of the kitchen (with a bit of help from Cheryl – I'm still weak after my stay in hospital) when the doorbell rings. I shove the cleaning spray and cloth into the cupboard under the sink and go to answer the door. To my surprise, Roger is standing there. He's carrying champagne and chocolates, so of course I invite him in.

At my suggestion, he takes a seat in the lounge and waits for Matt to join us. He declines tea or coffee, but is remarkably smiley for one normally so serious. He removes a notepad from his briefcase.

"I want to thank you both for your hard work and success in this case. With your help, we now have the Necessaire egg in our possession."

"You're welcome." I try to keep any sarcasm from my tones. It's been quite a challenge, and two people have died, so I'm not quite feeling his celebration. "We couldn't have done it without Joanna and Will." At least I can share out the credit.

"I know. I'll be visiting them afterwards. You've all done a fantastic job." He pauses and frowns for a moment. "I'm sure you'd like to know that the murderer of Peter Donaldson and the possessor of the egg were the same person. I believe you'd surmised that much?" He glances at me, and I nod.

"Viktor, I assume? The big guy from Bloomsbury? He gave me and Dan the chills. Seriously scary."

"Correct. He's been apprehended and charged with murder, and also with possession of a known stolen object." Roger's grin is a little self-satisfied. "As we found the egg in his house, he'd have a little trouble sliding out of that one. The murder may be a little harder to pin on him, but my team will find a way."

"I don't know how relevant it is," I say, "but we all discussed how the theft from the bank could have occurred, and concluded that Peter bribed the bank manager to leave the back door unlocked before he left for the night. The bribe must have been a hefty one, as the manager also had to tamper with the CCTV to hide the ease with which the burglars entered the bank."

"Yes, we appreciated the difference between the recordings. I'll be thanking Will personally for that excellent piece of work. We did however do some background checks of the bank manager, Iain Trelawney, and I can confirm they did not bribe him. He had some issues in his past that we believe he would have preferred kept concealed. If Peter Donaldson discovered those, and he was usually a clever young man, he would have used that information to get Trelawney to agree to his demands."

I take out my phone and check OneNote before grinning at Roger. "That makes sense actually. It would explain why we couldn't find any transactions on Peter's laptop from him to Iain, and also an obscure entry we found." I scroll through WhatsApp. Will had sent several screenshots of Peter's laptop. "Here we go." I show it to Roger.

'IT owes me. Saved from thugs 6 w ago. Lol.'

"Do you reckon that could have been a set-up?" I put my phone down on the arm of the chair as Roger returns it to me.

"Almost certainly. Easy to get a few heavies to set on someone, then conveniently be available to 'rescue' the victim, who's then in your debt."

The doorbell rings at this point, and Matt goes to answer it. He returns a moment later with a broad smile on his face.

"Looks like you'll be saved a trip, Roger." He stands aside and ushers in Joanna, followed by Will.

"Excellent. So pleased you're here. Well done, you two. I have thank-you gifts for you in my car, and of course a cheque will be on the way in due course." He repeats the news about Viktor's capture, and we follow on with our suppositions about Peter's influence over Iain.

"That would make sense. I don't like speaking ill of the dead, but I'll make an exception in Peter's case." Will shakes his head. "He was a slimy bastard, only out for himself. I could see from his laptop that he did genuinely care about Debs and Chloë, but that was his only redeeming feature." He pauses for a moment. "It's great that you can pin his murder on Viktor, though. I had a feeling the Preston police were looking at me as a suspect."

I give him a quick look. "You may have had a motive, but

you were nowhere near London that day, and the description of the man who did it doesn't match with you."

"Maybe, but that idiot of an inspector was eyeing me up. I reckon he had thoughts of paid assassins going round his head."

"There's no need for you to worry, Will. My team is going through Mr Kazakov's possessions as we speak." Roger consults his notes. "They have examined his computer already, and have found links to Peter Donaldson and to Eric Ulyanov. They're members of a gang that gain and dispose of valuable objects, but they have dealings in a number of different fields. Ulyanov's speciality is fraud. Peter seems to have dabbled in several areas. The kidnapping of Tania Blackstone would appear to have been instigated by Viktor. He had concerns about the activities of Anastasia's cousins and wanted them stopped."

"How did you find this out?" I ask.

"Kazakov, like his sidekick and subsequent victim, kept everything neatly in files on his computer. Some files are in Russian, and we will look to you, Becky, to help us with those, although I have another associate who is fairly fluent who has made a start on translation. Hence our knowledge so far."

"Why do you need me to translate if you already have someone on the team who can do it?" I've spent bloody hours slogging with that language, and the only use it's been to date was to help find Tania. I'm not knocking that. It was important and saved valuable time, but Roger couldn't have predicted that need.

Roger bristles, but deigns to explain. "First, it's important that we have additional resources. If our current expert was incapacitated, we would need to call on you with some urgency. Second, you've already showed your skills and you have considerable talent in that area. Finally, we have enough translation work to keep you both busy. The other associate has kindly stepped in to make a start, but I don't want to overload him with this. You can provide the fine detail later."

Will cuts in. "Becky's not exactly fit at the moment. Do you know what's been going on?"

"I do, yes. I'm not sending Becky running around the country. This is straightforward work that she can do on her laptop in bed if she prefers. The other associate has some more physical tasks to engage in just now."

"So what else do you know about Viktor and his contact with Ana's cousins?" My frustration subsides. Roger's reasons are all valid. Time to get back to the point in hand.

"I gather there was no direct contact between them. Viktor has a field agent in Moscow who has been keeping a close eye on these cousins. They are working against Putin, and strive to overthrow his government if they can. Viktor's plan was to use the kidnapped child to get Anastasia to reach out to her relatives and stop them from any further action."

"It seems bloody far-fetched and unrealistic. Why the hell would they protect a child they've never met? Even if she is some sort of cousin." Joanna makes a valid point. It doesn't really make sense.

"That is exactly what we need Becky to find out for us. I believe the answer will be on that computer." Roger turns to face Will. "There are areas on that computer that we haven't been able to access yet. I want the two of you to work together to access and translate all the outstanding information on that hard drive."

Will frowns. "Did you say the computer is still in London? I'm not sure my skills are up to accessing encrypted files on a distant device."

"The files have been copied electronically to a safe drive. I can send them to you from there. You'll have them by the end of the day. See what you can find out, you two." Roger returns his notes to his case and stands up. "Well, that's all I can tell you for now. I believe the next information will come from you, and will ensure we get Kazakov and Ulyanov put away for a long time. I confess to a sense of shock that Mr Blackstone killed his own wife, but they say jealousy is a powerful emotion." His tone is dry, and I cast him a curious look. I know nothing of his private life, but it would be surprising for someone to have reached his sixties or thereabouts without having experienced jealousy.

Joanna

TUESDAY

After leaving Becky and Matt, collecting our thank-you gifts from Roger on the way out, Will heads to Wendy's to see Chloë and Deb. He drops me off at home, but the sun is shining and the temperature has increased dramatically since Sunday. I don't bother unlocking the front door but instead walk down to Glen's house. I call him as I walk, making sure it's a good time.

"Hi love. Yes, come over. Dad's sitting in a chair in the back garden and there's a very nice bench out there for us to sit on, as long as you don't mind looking at a few weeds."

I suppress a shudder. I will have to wage war on those, even if Glen doesn't know it yet. For now, though, I make myself sound happy to sit in an untidy garden and pick up my pace a little. I am looking forward to seeing Glen.

It only takes a short while to get there, but on the way, I get a call from Becky who wants to chat about the recent visit from Roger.

It's very interesting, and the conversation takes me all the way to Glen's. He greets me at the door with a hug and a kiss on the cheek. "Come through, love. The kettle's on."

It's the first time I've met his dad, and I'm touched when

Glen introduces me as his close friend, particularly as he immediately says in a quiet voice, "I'd have liked to have said 'girlfriend' but wasn't sure if you'd be happy with that. It feels funny at our ages."

"It's been a long time since I had a boyfriend, but I'd like that very much." I blush a little – so ridiculous in anyone over the age of thirty, but I really like Glen, and the thought of what we might indulge in with a more confirmed relationship increases my temperature more than a bit.

With that settled, I chat to his dad about the weather and the garden, but he's really not with it. He seems to think we're in Brighton and can go for a walk on the beach later. I humour him and get him to tell me a bit about his past, but I have no idea how much of it is reality or fantasy. It saves me looking at those weeds though.

Glen brings out drinks and a newspaper. "Here you go, Dad. You have a look at this. See if you can do today's crossword." He whispers to me, "Sometimes he can give it a good go. Other days, he can barely write a word or even seem to know what to do."

I smile sympathetically. "It might keep him occupied for a bit while we talk, though. I wanted to tell you about Lou, my ex."

He raises his eyebrows. "You don't have to, you know. I saw what he was like, remember?"

"It's not that. None of us who were there that day will ever forget, I shouldn't think. Bloody hell. I still have nightmares about it. We probably all do." I look questioningly at him, and he nods. "No, I wanted to update you. Even though Xanthe is doing well, the trauma that she suffered that day in the line of duty, as they say, is enough to put Lou away for the rest of his life. Without parole. Attempted murder of a police officer and GBH with… I can't remember the term, but it means that there are certain factors that complicate a GBH charge. The victim being a police officer is one; psychological trauma or PTSD is another. Basically, they can throw the book at him. He's never coming out."

"Did they ever discover what he was doing down here? Was he just here to plague you?"

"Will found something on Peter's computer. Lou and Peter had apparently met through prison. Peter was an accountant to some of the guys who were in for fraud, and got introduced to Lou some time back. I gather my ex was shocked to find out that this git was knocking off our son's wife on the side, but decided he'd be able to have a hold over him on the strength of it."

"Let me get this straight. Will was married at that point?"

"Yes. And Debbie was screwing this creep behind his back. Lou figured he could use the information to get Peter to do what he wanted. It sounds as though Lou wanted that Fabergé egg as his means of escape from the country. He somehow found out that Peter was involved in the theft, and tried to get him to sell the egg to a contact of his and split the proceeds. Unfortunately for all of them, Lou lost his temper whilst trying to abduct me, and ended up back in the nick for attempted murder, etc."

Glen grins. "That's obviously handy for us, but I guess not for them. So, I suppose Peter didn't meet the contact before Lou got arrested?"

"No. Quite! That's why Peter went down to London. He didn't want the egg. He was just after the money, to fund his expensive lifestyle and potentially a court case to prevent Will from seeing his daughter again."

"My sympathy for Peter is fast disappearing. I bet Will's relieved that can't happen now."

"Obviously." I smile. Will and I were both conflicted when we heard about Peter's death. It's not a nice way to go, but it made a big difference to us. "Anyway, to get back to the story,

Peter had to find another way to sell the egg. He reverted to Plan A. He was never supposed to get involved with Lou, but my delightful ex had threatened Peter that information would make its way to Deb if Peter refused to help him."

"Nice. So what was Plan A? And why did Peter end up dead?"

"Peter had to make his way to London and go to a dealer – the original seller of the egg back in the 1950s – at a shop called Wartski. But this dealer was in the pay of a guy called Viktor Kazakov. The dealer refused to buy the egg and told Peter to go home. As I understand it, the dealer then called Kazakov and told him where Peter would be. Kazakov followed Peter, grabbed the bag containing the egg, and threw Peter in front of the train. This is only speculation, but I would guess that someone had discovered that Peter had been about to betray them, and they weren't having it. Bunch of bastards, the lot of them. I can't say I've got any sympathy for any of them. They all deserve everything they get."

Becky

For the third day running, Will and I are sitting in his kitchen with our laptops and my Russian dictionary working our way through the files from Viktor's computer. It's quite painful going, as my Russian is by no means fluent, and some phrases are being run through Google Translate and I'm then doing a sense check on them. I'm sure it's not quite what Roger intended, but before the case goes to court, we can get a specialist translator to review it. For now, I'm getting a sufficient gist of what Viktor was doing to have him and his gang put away for a long time.

There were eight members of the gang, including Viktor, Eric and Peter. The chap from the Wartski shop was another, as was Boris, the Russian involved with Tania's kidnapping. There are another three names I've never heard of.

The biggest shock, though, is an entry we come across that mentions Simon Blackstone. His name is written in English, which is what attracts my attention. All the rest is Russian, though, and I wade through the translation twice myself, before putting it through the translation tool.

I look at Will when it comes up on the screen. "Do you

think this is right? Would Simon have got involved with Viktor to work against his own wife and her family, potentially betraying his own religious and cultural background?"

"Let me read it again." Will reads out loud from the screen. "*'I pay Simon Blackstone £50,000 for his work against Boris and Mikhail Ivanov. He has not been of high value but will now do as asked. If Anastasia will co-operate no more, Simon will sort this out.'* What the hell? Does this mean Viktor got Simon to kill Ana because of stuff going on in Russia, and this had nothing to do with jealousy?"

"It looks like it." I gaze at the screen. The meaning hasn't changed significantly between my translation and Google's. "Let me ring Roger and get his take on it." I find the number on my phone, hit *Connect* and turn on the speaker. I tell him what I've found and await his thoughts.

"Very interesting, Becky. We already knew that Simon was furious with his wife for the situation with Ulyanov, and there were clearly aspects they didn't tell you, such as Anastasia was hiding the fact that she'd initially been less than reluctant to engage in a relationship with him."

"We don't know that for certain. Eric might say that to save face. It's not as if we can verify it with Ana now." I glance at Will, and he nods. He clearly agrees with me.

"Regardless of whether she was telling the truth, in the background, Ulyanov and Kazakov were obviously working on halting her family's activities in Russia. Ulyanov initially had a strong hold on Simon Blackstone because of the accountancy fraud. I would assume he was brought into the gang in a peripheral capacity and thus introduced to Kazakov."

"So Viktor then used Simon to find out more about Ana's family?" I pause. "We could ask Ana's parents if there'd been any questions."

"Good plan, Becky. I'll leave that to you. Let's see what we can find out through innocent sources." Roger disconnects.

I focus on Will. "Do you want to call her parents, or should I?"

"You do it. You're great at that sort of thing. I'm still learning." Will grins.

I make the call, again putting the phone on speaker. Ana's dad answers.

"Andrei Ivanov here. Who is speaking?"

"Hello, Mr Ivanov. This is Becky White here. We met at your daughter's house a few days ago when Simon was arrested. I have Will McLeod, my associate, with me. We'd like to ask a few questions if it wouldn't be too much trouble."

"My wife is with the children. To be frank, they are a great help to distract from the intensity of grief that would tear us into tiny fragments. If I can be of any help to assist with putting our daughter's killer in prison for a long time, then please ask anything you would like to know."

"Thank you. Did Ana or Simon ask you anything recently about your family in Russia?" I quickly made the connection when he gave his name that it's his family, rather than his wife's, that's involved with all this.

"It was strange. Simon came to me about two months ago, asking about my sister and her twin offspring. They live just outside Moscow and dedicate their lives to ensuring Jews can continue to be Jews in Russia. Am I right in thinking you are Jewish, Becky?"

"Yes, you are. Also, I am married to a Jewish man, and my own kids attended Jewish school. My youngest is still at King David now." I'm not sure why I feel the need to add the extra detail, but it seems to please Andrei. I can almost sense him smile down the phone.

"Then you will understand the importance of protecting one's own people."

"Of course." I give Will a quick glance to make sure he's not feeling awkward, but he's looking sympathetic. His own past has made him sensitive to the needs of anyone in trouble. I return my attention to the phone call.

"I believe I told Simon proudly of their activities," Andrei continues. "I speak to my sister every week, and am kept abreast of all their affairs. Then, when our granddaughter was kidnapped, Ana called me and asked if I could speak to her Aunt Olga and request that they pause in their current mission so that Tania could be rescued. She said she had received word that it was part of the ransom for her daughter."

Will and I exchange glances. That wasn't on the ransom note she showed us.

"I tried to contact Olga, but it was not our day to speak, and by the time I could talk to her, Ana had informed me that Tania was safe at home and no action was needed. I warned Olga that there was someone working against her. She confirmed this, and said they had many enemies as they were working against the Russian government." He hesitates before continuing. "You understand, we did not speak of these things directly in English or Russian, but spoke in Yiddish as we always have, ever since being young children; it has been our code language. Since that time, I have been worried about my sister and niece and nephew. They do dangerous work and put themselves at risk for their beliefs."

"They sound like amazing people. You can be very proud of them. Did Ana or Simon ask anything further about them after that?"

"Ana called me about two days before she disappeared. She said to me that Simon had been asking her to speak to me again about my family. He apparently said it was putting all of them at risk while Russian relatives did 'ridiculous underground rubbish', as he called it. He was always dismissive of any kind of protest or standing up for one's beliefs. As you gathered on Sunday, my son-in-law is not a nice man."

"Did Ana say anything else about it?" I'm getting tingles on my back. It feels as though I'm right on the edge of something here.

"My lovely Ana, having told me what that bastard had said, then informed me she fully supported Olga's work and was proud to have them as her family. She then heard voices and had to disconnect. That was the last time we ever spoke." His voice cracks on the last word.

"I'm so sorry. But you can be proud of her. She clung to her own beliefs and her sense of right and wrong, despite being warned of the danger." I pause, and raise my eyebrows at Will. He nods. "We believe Simon was working with a Russian criminal who was seeking to stop Olga and her children from continuing their work. We don't think Simon killed Ana because he was jealous, but because he'd been paid or blackmailed into doing so."

Andrei thanks us for the information, then disconnects. I let him go, resolving to call him the next day to check they're okay. It's a lot to take in.

Joanna comes in as the call is finishing, and Will updates her on the new information we have just received.

"So, Viktor forced Simon to kill Ana because she wouldn't stop her aunt and cousins from working against the Russian government? Bloody hell! That's not the motive we expected." Joanna looks shocked, and leans back in her chair. "Does the theft of the egg fit in with all this, or is it just randomly tangled up with the same criminals? If it is random, it's one hell of a coincidence that we've been working on both cases at once."

"Good question. What do we know?" I look at my business partners. Pride fills me, knowing I've got such a brilliant team to work with. Not to mention gratitude – they saved my life. But I force myself to return to the question in hand. "Viktor got Peter to steal the Fabergé egg from the bank in Preston. Peter played silly buggers and was going to sell it to Lou's contact, presumably because they'd have gone halves on the proceeds, whereas I imagine Peter's cut from Viktor would be relatively small."

Will interrupts. "We found that bit in Viktor's notes yesterday, suggesting they would award Peter ten percent of the profits."

"Of course. Thanks. I'd forgotten that, considering today's revelations." I grin at Will. "Okay, so because Lou got arrested, Peter has to return to Viktor's sales plan, and consequently gets pushed in front of a train whilst Viktor grabs the bag containing the egg. Meanwhile, Simon is operating on instructions from Viktor, which require him to get Ana's relatives in Russia to stop being revolutionary or whatever. He overhears Ana telling her dad she refused to do as he, Simon, asked. So then what?"

"I reckon Simon would have made a call to Viktor to ask for further instructions. Maybe Viktor thought killing Ana would act as a warning to Olga and her kids. Either way, he gives Simon some money for his efforts so far, and then tells him he has to kill his wife." Will frowns. "There's still a piece of the puzzle missing, though. Give Wendy a call, Becks, and see if she's interviewed Simon yet. Maybe she'll have some more information."

The call to Wendy yields confirmation of what we've been discussing. Simon has been pushing the blame for the murder onto Viktor and Eric, although he's claiming that Eric did the deed. But he has admitted to having got tangled up in the web of intrigue and politics as dictated by Viktor.

"That's very interesting, Wendy, but do you think there's a link between Ana's murder and the theft of the Fabergé egg?"

"Funny you should ask that. Simon mentioned everything had 'kicked off' when some Russian jewelled egg had been stolen. He said the money from selling the egg was to go towards funding the eradication of his wife's Russian family, as they'd been indulging in anti-government activities. But the sale of the egg had been taking too long, so Viktor had been pressurising Simon to get Ana to stop her family from doing whatever they were doing."

I let my brain soak this up for a moment, putting things together. Then it clicks. "Viktor got the egg himself, just a few days before Ana admits that she won't stop her aunt and cousins from their efforts to support Russian Jews. Simon calls Viktor to inform him he's heard Ana saying this, and Viktor decides he doesn't need Ana any more. In fact, she's potentially detrimental to his cause. He tells Simon to kill her. I expect he's already got enough of a hold over Simon from criminal activities so far, and he probably doesn't need to apply much more pressure on him. A 'fee' of fifty grand would ease any misgivings Simon might have. I've begun to suspect that their marriage was not a strong one, and that love had long since gone from it."

"Why did Simon rape his own wife?" Joanna asks, edging closer to the phone.

"Although he's still denying the rape or murder, his attempt to blame everything on Eric suggests a possible motive for raping her." Wendy hesitates. "I think if she'd just been murdered, Simon would have been a suspect much earlier. The rape threw me off the scent, I admit."

There's a moment's silence while we all digest this. Then, at Will's request, I hand over the phone to him, and he checks in with Wendy about his daughter and ex-wife. He provides Wendy with the identity of the other members of the gang in exchange for the news that Deb and Chloë are safe and well. Wendy can reassure us all that the gang will all be safely behind bars soon, and that her guests will be able to return home.

Wendy then asks to speak to me. Will hands over the phone, knocking off the speaker first.

"What's the matter?" I ask.

"I just wanted to let you know Finn is back on the team, but working under my supervision now. He's promised to keep me informed of any further activities against you. He mentioned that he's expecting more action soon. We're checking CCTV to see if we can identify your stalker, Becky, but you need to be on your guard. It seems that someone wants to kill you."

TO BE CONTINUED

Also by Jo Fenton

THE BECKY WHITE THRILLERS

Revelation

Paparazzi

THE ABBEY SERIES

The Brotherhood

The Refuge

Acknowledgements

A huge thank you to everyone who has made this book possible.

Firstly, I'd like to thank my fabulous friend and editor, Sue Barnard. Her support throughout this journey has been incredible, and it's been a massive pleasure working with her on my 5th novel, and third Becky White thriller.

Thanks also to all the Manchester Scribes, including Sue, but also Pauline Barnett, Louise Jones, Karen Moore, Claire Tansey, Awen Thornber, Helen Sea and Grant Silk. The regular honest critiques have helped to keep me grounded and to shape my books in the direction they were meant to go.

My awesome beta readers, Sue Barnard, Ray Fenton, Rachael Webb and Karen Moore, have also been invaluable in providing the feedback that was needed to eliminate plot holes and tighten up the wobbly bits.

My lovely other writing group, Writers United, as usual provided the moral support and meet-ups (between lockdowns), that kept me motivated to continue writing, despite the chaos going on around me. Thanks WU - Helen Lane, Lucy Goacher, Gareth Hewitt, Libby Carpenter, Sue Burrows, Carol Lucas, Anya Stojanovic Chand, Bean Sawyer, Paul Stephenson, Laura Sillett, Joan Bullion El Faghloumi, Susan King, Suzanne Harbour, Lee Sloan and Caroline Harris. Particular thanks to Libby for kindly reading and providing the wonderful endorsement for the front cover.

Thank you to Celebrity Cruises for providing the

fascinating Baltic cruise, including the talk on missing Fabergé eggs which inspired the premise for this novel.

As always, my family are essential in supporting me through writing my novels. I could not do without my wonderful husband, Ray, for all his help and advice, reading, sharing ideas, and continuing to do far more than his share of housework so I could have valuable writing time. My amazing sons, Michael and Andrew also listened to me bounce ideas around and were very honest with their feedback. My lovely mum was also a great help in listening to me waffle on; whether about plot, character or just the challenges of juggling writing with a full time job.

A massive thank you to my first publisher, Darkstroke, and particularly to Laurence Patterson and Steph Patterson for believing in me, assisting with cover art and marketing advice, and for everything they've done to launch this novel and my four preceding ones.

And finally, huge thank you to my new publisher, Bloodhound Books, for republishing Faberge, and for all the help and support on bringing it back out into the world.

About the Author

Jo Fenton grew up in Hertfordshire. She devoured books from an early age and, at eleven, discovered Agatha Christie and Georgette Heyer. She now has an eclectic and much loved book collection cluttering her home office.

Jo combines an exciting career in Clinical Research with an equally exciting but very different career as a writer of psychological thrillers.

When not working, she runs (very slowly), and chats to lots of people. She lives in Manchester with her family and is an active and enthusiastic member of two writing groups and three reading groups.

A note from the publisher

Thank you for reading this book. If you enjoyed it please do consider leaving a review on Amazon to help others find it too.

We hate typos. All of our books have been rigorously edited and proofread, but sometimes mistakes do slip through. If you have spotted a typo, please do let us know and we can get it amended within hours.

info@bloodhoundbooks.com